The Devil's Own Duke

As a girl on the brink of womanhood, Hetty had spent far too much time imagining what it would be like to be kissed. Wondering if there were rules to follow, and whether it would be awkward, or if she would magically know what to do.

Seventeen-year-old Hetty had heard rumors of *tongues*.

Twenty-four-year-old Hetty could confirm that rumor.

He tasted of vanilla and citrus, from her wine, and his tongue . . . well, she was becoming intimately acquainted with it.

He explored her mouth gently, with light kisses and teasing strokes, while his large hands framed her waist, holding her captive against his solid frame.

Her hands spread against his chest, not to push him away, but to be closer, to feel his muscles bunching and the warmth of him permeating her body.

Kissing was most definitely dangerous.

It gave her a restless feeling, a desire to have more than just a little taste.

A bell sounded in the distance, a rhythmic chiming to match the pounding of her heart. Nine. Ten. Eleven . . .

Midnight!

She pushed him away, her breathing ragged. "It's midnight. I must go."

The Devil's Own Duke

 A Wallflowers vs. Rogues Novel

LENORA BELL

AVON BOOKS

An Imprint of HarperCollinsPublishers

THE DEVIL'S OWN DUKE. Copyright © 2021 by Lenora Bell. All rights reserved. Printed in the United States of America. No part of this book may be used or reproduced in any manner whatsoever without written permission except in the case of brief quotations embodied in critical articles and reviews. For information, address HarperCollins Publishers, 195 Broadway, New York, NY 10007.

First Avon Books mass market printing: October 2021

Print Edition ISBN: 978-0-06-299346-5
Digital Edition ISBN: 978-0-06-299336-6

Cover design by Guido Caroti
Cover illustration by Paul Stinson
Cover photography by Shirley Green Photography
Back cover images © Shutterstock

Avon, Avon & logo, and Avon Books & logo are registered trademarks of HarperCollins Publishers in the United States of America and other countries.

HarperCollins is a registered trademark of HarperCollins Publishers in the United States of America and other countries.

FIRST EDITION

21 22 23 24 25   CWM   10 9 8 7 6 5 4 3 2 1

For Rachel, friend and beta reader extraordinaire.
You've saved me more times than you know.

The Devil's Own Duke

Chapter One

❧ 🌹 ❧

"Iᴛ's ᴛɪᴍᴇ ғᴏʀ your grand entrance, Papa," said Lady Henrietta Prince.

Her father crossed his arms. "I don't wish to make any kind of entrance, Hetty, much less a grand one."

"Nonsense. There are a dozen lovely and accomplished duchess candidates waiting to fawn over a handsome lion of a duke." She fussed with his cravat. "You're the belle of this ball, please remember."

An elderly belle with a decidedly mulish expression on his heavily lined face.

"Duchess candidates. Bah! You make it sound like a borough election. Are they going to stand on chairs and make speeches? Am I to cast a ballot to choose a wife?"

Hetty suppressed a smile. "I'll grant you that the situation is unconventional, to say the least, but we've no other choice and you know it. If I'd been born Henry, not Henrietta, the title and lands would be mine. As it is, you must do your duty, remarry, and sire a new heir or we'll lose everything to the Crown."

She'd seen what happened when peerages reverted to the Crown. She'd lose Rosehill Park. The monarchy would own her vineyards and plant them over with timber. Their tenants would be subject to indifferent treatment from a land steward with only profit on his mind.

She'd lose her independence, her freedom, and everything she'd worked so very hard for—all because she'd been born female.

The duke frowned. "What right did my brother Walter and his son have to go and get themselves drowned?"

"I don't suppose they had a choice. Their ship sank and they along with it."

Her Uncle Walter had been a quiet man, fond of flannel nightcaps and sweet-meal biscuits. He and his son had drowned in a shipwreck off the Channel Islands less than a year ago, leaving the dukedom without an heir.

Hetty shuddered to think of their cold and lonely demise. She'd grieved for them, but she'd also been mourning the loss of certainty and security, the loss of her future.

"Bloody inconvenient, leaving us with no heir to speak of," grumbled the duke, "not even a sixth cousin twice removed, or some such."

"Language, Papa. You promised to behave tonight. No drinking whisky and no swearing in front of the ladies."

"They might want to meet the real me before they decide to become leg-shackled."

Heaven help them if the ladies saw the real duke. She quite despaired of him most days.

He wasn't a mean-spirited drunk, only an extremely naughty and highly unpredictable one.

There was the time he'd bellowed a bawdy song during the vicar's sermon about the sufferings of Job.

Which had been vastly preferable to the time he'd propositioned the poor vicar's wife. At a funeral.

"You don't have a flask in your waistcoat pocket right now, do you?"

At his sheepish expression she held out her palm.

"It's only a few swallows."

She raised her eyebrows. He handed over the small silver flask.

"We should be hosting balls for you," he muttered, "not for me. It's high time you found a husband. Your mother wanted you to marry."

A memory washed through her mind in a soft, hazy palette of cream-colored satin and pink rosebuds. Sitting at the vanity in this same London townhouse, preparing for her very first ball. Her mother, brown eyes sparkling, tucking a diamond clip into Hetty's upswept curls.

Her own brown eyes, so like her mother's, shining back at her from the glass, so hopeful and romantic. The smell of melting beeswax candles interchangeable in her memory with her mother's scent—warm, sweet, and comforting.

My darling, you're so beautiful. You're a woman now. You'll have your pick of gentlemen. You'll start your own life away from Rosehill Park. Away from me.

A teardrop falling from her mother's eyes and landing on Hetty's shoulder. She could still feel the small spot of damp, the harbinger of tears to come.

She'd never had the chance to begin that new life. Her mother had taken ill with a fever and died within the week.

And her father had started drowning his sorrows at the bottom of a whisky glass.

No time to dwell in the past. There's work to be done.

"I'm four and twenty and far too busy for marriage. We have the grape harvest next month and then there will be wine to press and bottle, and food to put by for winter, cottage roofs to repair, and—"

"Don't we employ someone to worry about those things?"

"You've sacked two stewards already, don't you remember? And I never hired a third."

She'd made do as best she could, learning to manage the estate and attempting to restore her father's spirits. She'd even continued the work her mother had begun, nurturing their ancestral vineyards into a promising venture, producing sparkling white wine to rival the finest French champagne.

He sighed heavily. "I'm afraid I haven't been much of a father to you, m'dear. I've let you down. Left you too much to your own devices."

"I like my freedom, thank you very much. And no moping, now." She needed him to be merry and charming tonight. She threaded her arm through his and gave him a bright smile. "This is a happy occasion. Your duchess candidates await."

"What do I want with romancing widows?"

"This has nothing to do with romance. This is about saving our family fortune."

He pulled his arm away, the expression in his eyes turning to near panic. "I can't do it. I can't remarry."

"I know you still miss her terribly," Hetty said softly. "I miss her too. But she would have wanted us to thrive. She loved Rosehill Park and the vineyards more than anyone. Do this for her, Papa, if not for me."

"You're so like her, you know." He touched her cheek. "Brimming with life, beauty, and ambition."

"Enough." Her voice sounded husky and there was a lump in her throat. She wasn't accustomed to tenderness from her father. "Here, have a sip of wine and then we'll go down together."

She poured a small glass of sparkling wine from Rosehill for her father, and one for herself.

Bubbles tickled her nose and the tart-sweet flavors of citrus and vanilla burst on her tongue with just the right amount of full moon brightness.

It was very good wine, if she did say so herself.

"The ladies are clamoring for a waltz with a legendary rake. Will you disappoint them?"

"I did cut quite the swathe in my day." Her father squared his shoulders. "Very well, my dear. Deliver me to the bloodthirsty horde."

When they arrived at the top of the stairs, he gave a nod to the waiting footman below.

"His Grace, the Duke of Granville, and Lady Henrietta Prince," the footman announced in ringing tones.

Ladies in pastel-hued silk gowns, glittering jewels, and feathered headdresses craned their necks. Excitement was running high. Her father hadn't hosted any entertainments since the death of his wife. Well, not respectable entertainments, at least.

"Smile, Papa," she whispered as they descended the stairs. "What about Mrs. Dudley?" she asked, gesturing toward a comely brunette, who responded with a gracious dip of her head that set the pastel-dyed ostrich feathers atop her head waving. "She's a widow with a considerable income and most amiable."

"She's half my age."

"Most gentlemen would consider that an incentive."

"She'd be too much for me. In the bedchamber."

Not a conversation Hetty wished to have with her father, though the ultimate goal of this evening was to install an infant heir in the nursery at Rosehill Park.

The widow Dudley would make a wonderful duchess. She had young children from her previous marriage and was still of childbearing age. It would be so delightful to hear the pitter-patter of little feet running through the halls of Rosehill.

There'd been a time when Hetty had longed to start a family of her own, to be a blushing bride, and a proud mother.

But she was content with the busy and useful life she'd built. And she'd be able to go back to that life if her father could produce a new heir.

"Don't you see any pleasing prospects, Papa?"

"The only prospect that pleases me is a bottle of good old Scotch whisky and a box of the mildest Havana cigars."

"You promised to conduct yourself with propriety,

remember? When the clock strikes midnight, I'll expect you to have made your decision," she said firmly. "And now I'll leave you to become better acquainted with your adoring public."

She steered him toward Mrs. Dudley. When she'd safely deposited him into the vivacious widow's care, Hetty made her way across the room to her friend Miss Viola Beaton, whom she'd invited for moral support. Viola would stay overnight and the two of them could have a lovely long chat. Hetty didn't often visit London, being so occupied at their estate in Surrey.

She clasped her friend's hands. "Viola, I'm so glad you could come."

"I wouldn't miss it," Viola replied with a warm smile that displayed her deep dimples. "How is the heir-begetting scheme progressing?"

"Precariously. Papa is most reluctant."

"He does look rather peevish."

"I'll have to watch over him like an eagle-eyed chaperone. It would be just like him to escape down the balcony stairs and run straight for a tavern."

"Everyone else appears to be enjoying themselves."

The room was lit by beeswax candles casting a warm glow over the polished parquet floors and shining jewels worn by the ladies. Everyone was smiling, talking, and drinking wine from crystal goblets.

"I instructed the footmen to keep the guests' glasses filled with my sparkling wine. Perhaps I'll win some customers for my future wine cellar."

"How are your plans progressing?"

"I'm concentrating on producing the best wine possible, and earning an endorsement from a wine expert, before opening the cellar. No one will buy my wine unless it has a reputation for excellence. This vintage promises to be the best yet. The grapes are already bursting with flavor. We had too much rain last month, but August makes the wine, my mother always said."

Hetty felt her mother's presence here tonight, heard her lilting French accent echoing in her memory. The pain of losing her was still fresh and sharp after all these years.

It had been her mother's goal to restore the ancestral vineyards into a profitable wine venture. The grape vines were all she had left of her mother.

"Wine does help ladies feel disposed toward romance," said Viola. "I seem to remember your wine playing a role in the courtship of our friend Lady Beatrice."

Several of their friends were happily married, but not Viola. She, like Hetty, was too busy for marriage, though for different reasons. Her father was a famous composer, but he was going deaf and their income had shriveled to practically nothing, while their debts kept mounting.

Viola had been forced to take employment as music instructor to the Duke of Westbury's sisters.

"I'm very sorry, Viola."

"Whatever for?"

"I should have invited some eligible bachelors for your sake. I don't know why I didn't think of it."

"Never mind bachelors." Viola plucked at the skirt of her plain white muslin gown. "If there were prospects here, I'd be dreadfully conscious that this gown is four seasons old."

"The gown is charming and so are you." Viola had an irrepressible good humor, despite her reduced circumstances.

"You're the one who's glowing tonight, Hetty."

"Do you think so? I've been living in the countryside too long, wearing serviceable cotton gowns to prune the grapevines. I'm not accustomed to whalebone corsets and tissue-thin silk. This gown was created for my debut seven years ago and I seem to have changed considerably in the intervening years."

Hetty glanced down. The bodice of the ballgown was proving unequal to the task of containing her much-more-ample bosom. And she was no longer the blushing, naive young girl with a head full of fairy tales who had swirled in front of the glass, dreaming of handsome suitors and stolen moonlit kisses.

Viola leaned closer. "Don't look now, but there's a broodingly handsome gentleman standing across from us and he's been staring at you the entire time we've been speaking with rather a hungry look in his eyes. Gives me the shivers, really."

"Maybe he's staring at you."

"No, he can't take his eyes off of you."

"Do you recognize him?"

"Never seen him before, though that hardly signifies since I rarely go out in society. Oh, Hetty." Her eyes widened. "He's striding this way with the most predatory expression on his face. I do believe he means to speak with you." She shivered. "Or possibly swallow you whole."

"No doubt he's a brother, or nephew, of one of the ladies, thinking to ingratiate himself with the duke's daughter. I'll soon put an end to any such notion. Tonight is about my father, not me. The decision will be his alone."

She swiveled to face the man, ready to fix him with a forbidding stare to halt his forward progress.

Her breath caught in her throat.

He was just as Viola had described. Brooding and predatory, with piercing gray eyes that caught and held her gaze. His hair was overlong, wavy and brown, streaked with gold where candlelight fell.

He was tall, broad-shouldered, and so handsome that she glanced behind her to see if perhaps he meant to bestow all of that smoldering appeal on some other lady.

The way he prowled wasn't suited to a society ballroom. There was something almost brutish about him, nearly uncivilized. It was the way he held his ungloved hands, half-curled into fists.

Something about the slight crookedness of his nose, the blunt edges of his stubborn jaw.

Capturing her hand, he bowed his head and brushed his lips against her knuckles as if they were intimately acquainted.

There was a faint shadowing of whiskers along his angular jaw. His evening attire was ill-fitting, the coat straining at the seams, as though the man beneath was too much to be restrained by a tailor's art.

He wore a scarlet embroidered waistcoat, a gaudy gold watch on a fob, and his black dress shoes were scuffed.

Straight from Savile Row, he was not.

"Lady Henrietta." His lips quirked into an audacious half smile that said he had a secret he would reveal to her alone. "May I say that you are the loveliest sight I've ever beheld?"

"I'd prefer that you didn't."

"Too late. I'm going to extol your beauty and there's nothing you can do about it. You are a goddess, Lady Henrietta, created from starlight and roses, sent to this earth to—"

"That's quite enough, Mr. . . . er." Hetty stopped, realizing she had no idea with whom she was speaking. "You have me at a disadvantage, sir. I don't recall your name."

An unruly lock of hair flopped over one of his eyes. "Ellis. Ash Ellis."

She mentally searched through the guest list, attempting to match him with one of the ladies she'd invited, but no connection came to mind.

He slid the tip of his finger over her palm. Good gracious. He was still holding her hand.

She snatched her hand away, her cheeks flaming as though she'd swallowed an entire glass of wine in two gulps.

Somewhere far away the orchestra began to play, a violin bow dragging across the taut string of her nerves.

"Waltz with me, Lady Henrietta." It was more an order than a request.

She hadn't planned to dance this evening, but before she could object, he grasped her hand and led her onto the floor. She glanced back at Viola, who gave a little shrug of her shoulders with an amused expression dancing in her green eyes.

Hetty could refuse to dance with him, but her father was being surprisingly well-behaved at the moment, dancing and talking with the ladies, and she didn't want to be the one to cause a scene.

As her hand came into contact with Mr. Ellis's solid shoulder, and he placed a hand against the small of her back, a quiver traced the curve of her spine. She hadn't danced with a man since her first—and only—ball, in this very room seven years past.

He smelled of vanilla-laced cigar smoke and a heavy-handed eau de cologne. Her friend, Miss Ardella Finchley, a chemist and perfumer, would have been able to pinpoint the scent immediately.

All Hetty knew was that he wore far too much of it, and it had too much musk and cedar to it.

When they were halfway across the room, and her feet had remembered the familiar pattern, Hetty finally collected her thoughts enough to fix him with that forbidding stare she'd been meaning to employ. "I didn't wish to dance with you, Mr. Ellis. I was having a conversation with my friend."

He smiled lazily. "Ah but waltzing with me is so much better than decorating the wall."

Hetty bristled. The man was insufferable. And he hadn't seemed the least bit discouraged by her quelling stare. "Not all wallflowers are longing to be plucked from the wall, Mr. Ellis."

"Dancing with a skillful partner is one of life's great pleasures."

It was, rather, though Hetty wouldn't admit it to the domineering man who'd given her no choice but to stand up with him.

She'd forgotten how much she liked dancing. She was tall for a woman, but he was taller, and that was a pleasure, too. She remembered towering over one disastrously diminutive duke at her debut.

"I'm not supposed to be dancing," she said sternly. "Tonight isn't about me, it's about my father."

"That doesn't mean you can't have a little fun." The wicked gleam in his eyes made her neck and bosom feel heated, as though it were a hot day, and she was working in the vineyards.

She couldn't even blame it on the wine. She'd only had half a glass. "When the clock strikes midnight, my father will choose a bride and my life can resume its customary schedule."

"Rather a role reversal, isn't it? A daughter compelling her father to choose a bride."

"It's his duty to our family. If I were forced to marry to save our family fortune, I would make the sacrifice."

"Do you know what I think, Lady Henrietta?"

"No, and I'd rather not become acquainted with the workings of your mind, Mr. Ellis. I'd rather we finished this waltz in silence."

The sound of his low laughter did something suspiciously fluttery to the pit of her stomach.

Control yourself, Hetty. You don't do fluttery.

"I think that you like to manage everything, Lady

Henrietta. For example, you've been attempting to take the lead and guide my steps since we began waltzing." The pressure of his hand on her back increased and he tugged her closer. "Try to relax," he murmured. "Allow me to do all of the work."

The way he said those words so seductively, in that deep, rumbling voice, made her heart hammer in her chest.

"There. That's better, isn't it? I know what I'm doing." He stroked the small of her back. "Sometimes it's best to let the expert lead."

Did he know what he was doing to her?

Gazing into his eyes, she had the fanciful thought that they were the only couple on the dance floor, and everyone else had faded away into colorful blurs, like swirling autumn leaves.

Time tilted backward, until she was seventeen again, with butterflies waltzing giddily in her belly, and a song bubbling in her heart.

She closed her eyes and allowed herself to melt into the lilting sway of the music. Just for a moment.

Just for a few more steps.

After all, they might take one more step and float effortlessly into the air, dancing between the chandeliers, leaving the real world far below them.

"Very good," he whispered into her ear, his breath fanning her cheek.

Her eyes flew open. She'd allowed herself to melt a little too much. They were dancing far too close.

A proper distance must be maintained.

She didn't do giddy, either.

She straightened her spine and angled as far from

him as possible. "I wasn't trying to please you with my compliance to your whispered instructions, Mr. Ellis."

Another lazy smile lifted his sensually curved lips. "Of course you weren't."

"I was lost in a memory from my first ball."

It had been the memory, not the man. The man was much too cocksure and controlling.

Though he did dance like a dream.

"You have many pleasant memories from many balls, do you not, Lady Henrietta?"

"Not really. I've only attended one ball in my lifetime before this evening."

His brow furrowed. "How can that be? You're young and beautiful. Doesn't your social set dance every evening?"

"I'm four-and-twenty, Mr. Ellis. And this will most likely be my very last waltz." She had no time for frivolous pursuits. She had a schedule to maintain. The vines wouldn't harvest themselves.

"What a terrible shame to deprive the ballrooms of London of your radiant presence."

There he went again, slathering on the compliments like butter on a breakfast roll. He probably thought he was an expert in seduction, as well as waltzing.

Well, this was one female who wouldn't fall under his spell. Thankfully, the waltz was nearly finished.

"Why is your waistcoat embroidered with playing cards?" she asked.

"Not just any playing cards. The Ace of Spades. The highest card in the deck. To bring me luck."

"Are you a gambler?"

"Always."

"I don't approve. My friend is music instructor to the Duke of Westbury, and he's gambled away his entire fortune at the low gaming hells in St. James's."

"Poor blighter. Shouldn't play cards if you don't know how to win." He held her gaze with an intense focus that made the rest of the room fade and blur.

"You must be related to one of the duchess candidates I invited."

"Must I?" he asked.

"Tell me your connection."

"It amuses me to leave it a mystery for now." His slate-gray eyes glinted with devilish humor. "Haven't you always wanted to waltz with a mysterious and devastatingly handsome stranger?"

"You must have me confused with a lady who thinks you're handsome." *Lie.* He was sinfully attractive. And well he knew it.

"They told me you were a bluestocking with a tart tongue. You don't disappoint."

"It's probably best if you keep such impolite observations to yourself."

"Never expect politesse from me."

"What should I expect?"

"Danger, Lady Henrietta," he said in a low, intimate voice. "Expect danger."

His gaze caught and held her captive.

His fingers slid along the back of her gown, slipping ever so slightly beneath the fabric to stroke her back.

A quiver traced the curve of her spine and raised gooseflesh on her arms.

He wasn't the stuff of her seventeen-year-old dreams. He was rough-mannered and dominant. Unpolished. Nothing pretty, poetic, or respectful about him.

She'd never been touched in such a sensual, commanding way. Never seen desire flare to life in a man's eyes like a warning beacon on a hilltop.

An answering fire lit within her. The heat of it gave her a flush that bloomed across her bosom and spread up her neck and across her cheeks.

Surely he recognized the effect he had on her.

"You're blushing, Lady Henrietta."

"It must be the sparkling wine."

"Or it could be that you like relinquishing control for a few minutes. You like following my lead. Your body betrays you when you sway against me like that."

Couldn't everyone in the room see what he was doing? Seducing her in plain sight. Controlling her movements. Undressing her with his eyes.

But no one was paying them any attention. All eyes were focused on her father and Mrs. Dudley. Everyone was wondering if she would be the lucky new Duchess of Granville.

Once the scandal sheets had reported that the duke was on the hunt for a new bride, the gossip had flown thick and fast. Wagers had been placed in the betting book at White's club.

Young widows and debutantes had formed a

queue, writing letters extolling their accomplishments and virtues, and hinting that they had every expectation of fecundity.

Which one of the ladies she'd invited had brought this wolf to their door?

ASH STARED INTO those big brown eyes of hers. Eyes that held a velvet, near-purple darkness, like the heart of a violet.

The lady hadn't recognized him. Everyone else in the room knew exactly who he was: The Devil's Own Scoundrel. Owner of the notorious gaming hell known as The Devil's Staircase. Because he led people to sin.

To ruin.

He wouldn't mind leading Lady Henrietta to sin.

He'd known Granville had a bluestocking spinster daughter living on his estate in Surrey. He'd pictured a mousy, bespectacled thing. Not a voluptuous goddess with lush curves poured into a tight silk gown the color of clotted cream. Abundant brown hair begging to be freed from its jeweled hairpins.

And more than enough wit and fire to talk circles around him.

Candlelight spilled over the graceful lines of her shoulders and breasts. They were dangerous, those curves. They felt entirely too good in his arms.

He'd never danced with a genteel lady before. Polite society snubbed him when it suited them, deeming him of inferior birth, and resenting him for what they saw as his ill-gotten riches.

Once the lady put two and two together, she'd stare down that straight nose at him disdainfully. Purse her lips with displeasure at being sullied by waltzing with the devil.

He pulled her closer. Only a sliver past propriety . . . but enough to make her blush deepen. She relaxed into him with a dreamy look on her face that made him think about her draped across his bed after being thoroughly pleasured.

Attraction, strong and immediate, spiked through him like the first deep drink from a bottle of strong spirits, quickening his pulse and settling low in his belly.

He was here to speak to the duke, not to seduce the daughter.

The duke had been a difficult man to pin down. He had thick walls around him—solicitors, servants, sycophants—to keep the devil out.

So Ash had taken matters into his own hands, forging an invitation to the ball and presenting it with the combination of confidence and crisp banknotes that always seemed to get him whatever he wanted.

He had to take what he wanted. No one was going to hand him anything on a silver platter. Life was something to be conquered, a game to win, and he was good at winning.

He redistributed ill-gotten wealth. Trimmed the fat from bloated budgets. Skimmed from the top of tainted cream. He ran high-stakes card games that were mostly honest, but he'd selected a small list of targets to lead along the garden path to ruin. Wealthy, rash young bucks who could afford to lose their fathers' money.

Landed gentry, born into privilege and ease, greedy, arrogant, and cruel-minded.

And one of those reckless young bucks had inadvertently given him what he needed to win an even more glittering prize: a dukedom.

The lady in his arms was a symbol of the order he meant to topple.

She'd been born to wealth, coddled and cared for by servants and family. Blinded to the suffering of those less fortunate than she, all wrapped up warm and cozy in her privileged life.

Heedless and ignorant of the source of her father's wealth.

She was French champagne, expensive and sweet; he was back alley gin.

But his day would come.

The music had ended. He released her and bowed.

"Our waltz is over, Mr. Ellis," she remarked, with a slightly dazed expression.

"Perhaps you'd like another?"

"I would not." She gave him a curt, discouraging nod and walked swiftly away, soon swallowed by the crush of people.

Where was Granville? Ash searched the room but couldn't find him. Damnation. He'd been too busy dallying with the daughter to keep track of the duke.

Eyes on the prize, Ash.

Tonight, your fortunes change forever.

Chapter Two

❧ 🌹 ❧

Why are you so flummoxed?

Hetty leaned over the balcony railing and inhaled the scent of roses drifting up from the gardens, attempting to calm her breathing.

She'd had a few glasses of sparkling wine, it was true. But not enough to turn her head, make her giddy, make her have *thoughts*.

Naughty, wanton thoughts.

It had only been a waltz.

It was more than that, though, wasn't it?

It was a reminder of all the things she'd tried so hard to forget, to ruthlessly suppress, to ignore. Girlish longings and dreams. An awareness of her body, of its curves and hollows. Of how it might fit together with a partner.

A strong, confident, experienced partner.

Like Mr. Ellis.

She couldn't go back inside until she'd regained control over her thoughts. Over her body.

There had been a moment while they'd been dancing, several, if she were being honest, when she'd even wondered what it would be like to kiss Mr. Ellis.

Kiss him . . . and more.

She had several married friends, fellow members of a ladies' society she belonged to, and they sometimes divulged interesting details about what happened in the marital bed. Or, according to her friend Beatrice , the marital desk . . . or floor . . . or wherever the mood struck her and her handsome husband.

The mood had struck Hetty on the dance floor. Full force. Stealing away her scruples along with her breath. Entirely uncharacteristic and absolutely unacceptable.

Her life had purpose and passion, vineyards and goals.

Kisses not required.

She needed a few more minutes to compose herself before resuming duty as her father's matchmaker and chaperone.

The sound of footfalls turned her head. She flattened her back against stone.

It was Mr. Ellis. The flummoxer. The awakener of buried desires.

He was looking for someone, searching the dimly lit balcony, holding a crystal wineglass in his hand. Was he searching for her?

He walked closer, peering over the balcony railing. He was nearly to her now. If he didn't turn his head, if he continued gazing over the railing, he wouldn't see . . .

He'd seen her.

Nothing to do but unflatten herself, shake out her skirts, and pretend that meeting him on a moonlit balcony, with no one else in sight, didn't make her heart pound. "Mr. Ellis. I see you're enjoying the libations on offer tonight."

"It's good French champagne."

"I'm glad you think so, but it's not French."

He cocked his head. "It's not?"

"It's the sparkling wine I create from the vineyards at Rosehill Park."

"*You* created it?"

"Don't look so incredulous. Is it so very astonishing that a female could manage such a venture?"

"Er, not particularly. Every lady needs an activity for her leisure time. Your little hobby is more interesting than most. And more delicious, I'd add."

"My little hobby?" The muscles of her jaw clenched. "This is so much more than a leisure pastime. I'm distributing my wine to several cellars in London, and all of my influential friends serve it at their parties."

"Congratulations." He seemed distracted. What had happened to his predatory stare? He wasn't attempting to seduce her anymore. Why should she care?

"Does the subject of enterprising women make you uncomfortable?"

"Not at all. I'm acquainted with numerous enterprising women, and they are astute businesspeople, all."

"We British have been creating wine since Roman times, and yet the reputation of our vinicultural efforts is inglorious, at best. I aim to change all of that."

"Going for the glory, are you?"

"I only want a seat at the table for English sparkling wine. There's absolutely no reason why we must be relegated to a joke, a laughingstock, everyone chortling about pigswill, and such."

"An uphill battle. England's not known for its winemaking."

"I may be an amateur vintner, struggling with the English drizzle and muck, but my family has roots in the Champagne wine region of France. My mother brought seeds, and vines, and a French vigneron with her when she arrived from France to marry my father. Our vines at Rosehill Park have had the strictest care and attention, and the soil composition in our area of Surrey is very like the chalky soils near Épernay."

She was rambling, she knew it, but he made her so flustered. The words kept spilling from her mouth like wine from a bottle.

"Is that so? Think I'll try some, then." He raised his glass and swallowed deeply.

"Wait! Don't drink it like that. Savor it slowly."

This time he took his time about it, the tip of his tongue rimming the edge of the glass, catching a stray drop, before he took a sip.

Hetty had the decidedly inappropriate thought that she wanted to be the glass he held, the wine he drank.

"Well?" she prompted when he'd finished drinking.

"It's good."

"What do you taste?"

"Grapes."

She shook her head sadly. "How unimaginative."

"I'm not a wine expert."

"Wine experts. Charlatans! The bad reputation of

English wine is due in large part to Mr. Clive Ross, author of *A World of Wines*. Besides the usual French, Italian, and Spanish wines, he devoted hundreds, literally *hundreds*, of pages to the lesser-known wines from Germany, Russia, Hungary, and Persia, and relegated the whole of our winemaking efforts to a mere fifteen pages, filled with 'unsuccessful this,' and 'unprofitable that.'"

"The scoundrel." His eyes glinted with humor.

"Are you laughing at me, Mr. Ellis?"

"You're very passionate on the subject of the dastardly Mr. Ross."

"He insulted Rosehill Park." She gripped the balcony railing. "He said our soil wanted fertility. And was deficient in depth."

"Someone should challenge him to a duel."

"Don't think I haven't considered it! I have a pistol, and my friend, the Duchess of Thorndon, has taught me how to use it. I'm not to be trifled with."

"I've always said that a bluestocking with a pistol is an extremely dangerous combination."

"I thought you were the dangerous one, Mr. Ellis."

"I am. The truth of it is that you're far too controlled to truly be a threat to the scoundrels of this world. I'll wager you write out a schedule each morning to govern what you do every second of the day."

She loved making daily to-be-done lists. But it irked her that he'd been right about it. "I can be impulsive."

"I don't think you can. It's not in your nature."

He was right. She was never impulsive. She planned everything out. She'd never broken any rules. She'd lived a blameless, staid, disciplined life.

She'd been so busy developing the vineyards. Taking care of everything, managing the estate and her father, solely responsible for the welfare of the tenants and the servants.

Tomorrow she'd return to that life. The thought should have been calming. Her life wasn't lacking in excitement. Tomorrow everything would go back to normal.

"How do you know what's in my nature?" He was so sure he had her classified. The buttoned-up spinster. The rule follower. "I could do something outrageous. Something . . . wicked."

And that's when the idea took hold. She could have her very first kiss. Her one and only kiss. See what she'd been missing. Just a small, manageable thrill. A test to determine whether kissing was something she'd been missing out on, or something that she could file away in the not-worth-the-ruination category.

"Very wicked, indeed," she whispered. "I could . . . kiss you, Mr. Ellis."

He raised his dark brows. "My dear Lady Henrietta, I'm shocked." The smolder was back in his eyes. He stepped toward her. "What gave you such a scandalous idea?"

Was she really going to do this?

It was like those dreams she had sometimes where everything was so much more vivid than ordinary life and the laws of reality didn't apply. Where she took a few steps on the lawn and then bounced high into the air, soaring up to meet a flock of starlings and looking down at her vineyards from a bird's eye view.

The world spread before her.

Endless possibilities.

"You." She swallowed. "Dancing with you. I feel that I must take this opportunity to prove to myself that my life is not lacking for want of kisses."

"Kisses are against the rules for proper, unmarried ladies like you." He advanced closer, setting his empty wineglass on the balcony floor. "Kisses can be dangerous."

Maybe this wasn't the brightest idea. He was suddenly much larger and less manageable than he'd appeared only a moment ago. Silvery moonlight in his eyes. His lips curved into that mysterious half-smile, hinting at sensual secrets, promising unknown pleasures.

A small sampling of pleasure. Like the first sip of a new wine from an oak barrel. That moment of tension, of anxiety, and then the flavor, tart and new. Something never before tasted.

Before she could talk herself out of it, she lifted onto her toes and brushed her lips against his.

"There," she said, when she was finished. "It's done. My one and only kiss." She'd felt nothing except a fluttering nervous feeling in her belly and then the firmness of his lips against hers. "I can cross it off my list and never wonder about it again."

He backed her against the wall, covering her with his powerful body, cupping her face in his warm, strong hands. He gazed into her eyes. "That, my lady, was only the precursor to a kiss. You can't cross anything off your list yet. *This* is a kiss."

As a girl on the brink of womanhood, Hetty had spent far too much time imagining what it would be like to be kissed. Wondering if there were rules to follow, and whether it would be awkward, or if she would magically know what to do.

Would there be a question of what to do with one's hands? Would the gentleman's breath smell of something objectionable, such as onions, or would his lips taste as sweet as honey from clover fields? Seventeen-year-old Hetty had heard rumors of *tongues*.

Twenty-four-year-old Hetty could confirm that rumor.

Mr. Ellis tasted of citrus and vanilla, from her wine, and his tongue . . . well, she was becoming intimately acquainted with it.

He explored her mouth gently, with light kisses and teasing tongue strokes, while his large hands framed her waist, holding her captive against his solid frame.

Her hands spread against his chest, not to push him away, but to be closer, to feel his muscles bunching and the warmth of him permeating her body.

When he gave her pause to breathe, her good sense came rushing back, telling her that this was more than a small taste of danger, and highly improper.

And then the naughty, reckless part of her that wanted to be spontaneous and wicked returned with a vengeance.

The fizz of the wine still buzzed on his lips. His kiss was headier still, bringing her body to life in a new way.

Giddy and breathless.

He kissed a sensitive place behind her ear, his hands stroking her back. Her breasts felt heavy and swollen against his chest.

Kissing was most definitely dangerous. The thrill chasing up and down her spine, the heat flooding her body, pooling in her belly and between her legs.

A restless feeling, a desire to be closer, to have more, more than just a little taste.

Pleasure bubbling inside her mind, a feeling as though she was about to shatter . . . explode.

A sonorous bell sounded in the distance, a rhythmic chiming to match the pounding of her heart. Nine. Ten. Eleven . . .

Midnight!

She pushed Mr. Ellis away, her breathing ragged. "It's midnight. I must go." But before she could leave him, a large shape pounded across the balcony, hurtling toward them.

Mr. Ellis pushed her behind him, to protect her from view.

Hetty peered around his shoulder to see who was running down the balcony stairs.

"Oh no," she moaned. "It's my father." Had he seen them kissing? This was a disaster. No time to wonder about that. "I have to catch him!"

She sprinted after him, with Mr. Ellis thundering behind. The duke was halfway across the gardens and heading for the archway when Mr. Ellis managed to catch him by the coattails.

"Let me go!" said the duke, attempting to twist free.

"Papa, stop struggling," Hetty scolded. "You have to go back inside. It's midnight and time to choose a bride."

"I only want a little whisky. I must fortify myself for the task."

"Is it whisky you want, Your Grace?" Mr. Ellis released his hold on the duke and pulled a flask from somewhere inside his coat.

"Don't give him—" But it was too late. Her father already had the flask and was drinking thirstily.

"That does take the edge off, I must say," said the duke. "You have an admirable taste in whisky, sir."

"Thank you, Your Grace," Mr. Ellis replied.

"Say." The duke cocked his head. "Don't I know you?"

Mr. Ellis cleared his throat. "I believe we've met on occasion."

"The Devil's Staircase! That's where I've seen you. You're Ash Ellis."

"Guilty as charged."

"Had a capital time there last month. Those barmaids of yours . . ." The duke winked lasciviously. "Prettiest in London."

"Glad you approved."

Hetty's mind was reeling. Mr. Ellis was not some mildly scandalous and rakish cousin attached to one of the guests she'd invited. Mr. Ellis owned a gaming house.

The garden path disappeared from beneath her feet and was replaced by the gaping maw of hell.

"Mr. Ellis. You own The Devil's Staircase. Then you are . . ." This couldn't be happening. Surely she was a better judge of character. She wouldn't have launched herself into the arms of the notorious man the scandal sheets had dubbed . . .

"The Devil's Own Scoundrel," said the duke, returning the empty flask.

The ruthless man who'd ruined the Duke of Westbury, and countless other noblemen.

If anyone had seen them kissing, she was ruined, too. More than ruined.

"Ah, I see now that you're fully aware of who you waltzed with, Lady Henrietta. I told you to expect danger."

More than a waltz. She touched her lips, still swollen and warm from his kisses.

"What are you doing at my ball, Ellis?" asked the duke. His gray whiskers trembled. "And what was that I saw you doing with my daughter?"

Chapter Three

DAMN IT ALL! Ash scrambled for a plausible explanation. If he didn't come up with something quickly he could be facing the duke's pistol at dawn. Not the outcome he'd planned.

He hadn't fought his way up from the cutthroat alleyways of Seven Dials without learning how to think on his feet.

"Oh, that?" he said. "Lady Henrietta was explaining to me the process she uses for creating the excellent sparkling wine I tasted this evening."

"It looked like you were tasting more than the wine, m'boy."

"It's a dark night, Your Grace. There's only a sliver of moon. She was divulging her secret recipe, whispering it in my ear. I have an interest in spirits, you know. My business partner, Jacques Smith, has invented a new gin still that produces a much cleaner and more pure spirit that he infuses with botanical extracts."

"Hetty," said the duke, turning to his daughter. "Is this true?"

Lady Henrietta had been standing, frozen, her

face set in a rictus of horrified shock. The exact expression he'd imagined she'd have when she learned his true identity.

She recovered in swift fashion, turning to her father with a sweet, innocent smile. "Of course, Papa. What else could it have been? I was whispering the measures of sugar I add, or, as the French call it, the *dosage*." She glanced at Ash from under thick, dark lashes. "Mr. Ellis may wish to invest in my wine venture, isn't that right, sir?"

"After a fashion." He cleared his throat. Things were getting complicated. Best to come out with what he had to say. "Your Grace, I've been attempting to speak with you, but you're a difficult man to pin down."

"Here I am, Ellis. I don't suppose you have a second flask?" the duke asked hopefully.

"No, but we could go to 20 Ryder Street and I'd serve you an excellent Glenlivet I'm quite fond of."

The duke perked up. "Then what are we waiting for? Lead the way, good sir. Lead the way."

"Just one moment," Lady Henrietta broke in. "Papa—you have a duty to perform. You're not going anywhere."

"I'm going down The Devil's Staircase," said the duke gleefully. "With Mr. Ellis."

Lady Henrietta placed her fists on her full hips. "It's past midnight. You must select a bride before you go." She wasn't one to deviate from her schedule.

Ash leaned toward the duke. "You don't have to marry, Your Grace," he said in a conspiratorial tone.

"I don't?"

"And just what do you mean by that, Mr. Ellis?" Lady Henrietta asked sharply.

"I mean that he has no need to marry any of the assembled ladies and sire another heir." Ash straightened to his full, considerable height. He spread his hands, pausing for dramatic emphasis. "Because I am the long-lost heir to the dukedom of Granville."

"Hetty, it's a midnight miracle!" her father cried.

"What did you just say, Mr. Ellis?" Hetty asked.

"I said that I'm the long-lost heir to the dukedom." His expression was unreadable in the dark, but Hetty was certain that she heard a predatory, wolfish tone in his voice.

"Are you making a joke, sir?" she asked.

"I'm in earnest."

"Well, you could have made this shocking announcement a little earlier, I must say."

Before he'd tempted her into kissing him.

"We're saved, Hetty!" cried the duke, practically dancing a jig. "I don't have to marry any of those desperate duchess candidates."

Hetty's mind scrabbled for a foothold in the treacherous mire of this disastrous evening.

The man she'd danced with, the man she'd kissed, was making a preposterous claim to her father's title. He must be lying. A gaming hell owner who brazened his way into a private event with no invitation couldn't possibly be a legitimate heir presumptive.

"Papa." Hetty pulled her father away a few steps, whispering urgently. "We don't know Mr. Ellis from

Adam. He may very well be a pretender, a swindler. Why did he come to the ball uninvited? Why not contact your solicitor like an honest claimant would do?"

"Nonsense." Her father brushed away her words and turned back to Mr. Ellis. "Anyone can see the family resemblance. Look at that strong chin and those steely gray eyes. Now, why don't we go inside, and I'll introduce you to everyone. Won't they be disappointed."

Over Hetty's dead body. "We certainly won't be introducing him to anyone, Papa, not unless ironclad proof of his claim is presented."

"Of course, of course," said the duke. "You have evidence of your claim, Mr. Ellis?"

"Ironclad."

"And . . ." The duke squinted at him. "Who are you claiming to be, exactly?"

"A descendant of the Honorable Ashbrook Prince. A branch of the family that split off long ago."

"Of course! The lost baby. The secret marriage to a scullery maid from Spain."

"I arrived at an orphanage at the age of three," Mr. Ellis said. "My mother was dead and my father unknown. I told the matrons that my name was Ash. I have only vague memories of my mother, but I know she used to sing to me in Spanish. And she told me never to forget that I was a prince. I thought she meant that I was a prince among men, but now I know the truth. I am a Prince. I'm your heir, Your Grace, and I'll gladly present further proof at a time of your choosing."

"Splendid, m'boy, simply splendid. My solicitor is Higginbottom, of Pall Mall. He's a good sort. Extricated me from plenty of scrapes, I can assure you."

Mr. Ellis nodded. "I'll contact him right away."

This was all happening too quickly. Hetty didn't approve of Higginbottom. His card should have read Solicitor of Mayhem, for he was a very bad influence on her father.

"You could be a fraud, Mr. Ellis," she said. "An opportunist."

"It's been known to happen."

"You could be engaged in skullduggery of the highest order."

Mr. Ellis made a snorting noise, as if attempting to restrain a laugh.

"Hetty," her father remonstrated. "Don't insult your cousin."

"Seventh cousin, actually," drawled Mr. Ellis, all ease and affability. "Once removed."

"We'll see about that," Hetty muttered.

Mr. Ellis's gaze raked across her bodice, lingering on the swell of her bosom. It was rising and falling rather rapidly, given the mixture of dread and fury coursing through her veins.

"I think you'll agree that we're about as distant as relations could be, Lady Henrietta." His tone said the opposite. There'd been precious little distance between them not more than a quarter hour earlier.

"Good evening, Mr. Ellis," she said sharply, taking her father's arm. "Please show yourself out, since you arrived unannounced and uninvited."

"Good evening, Lady Henrietta." He bowed, his

eyes flashing silver in the gloom. "I look forward to our next meeting."

"As do I," the duke enthused. "Bring some of that Glenlivet, will you?"

"Indeed, Your Grace. A bottle of aged Scotch whisky is one of life's great pleasures."

"A truer word was never spoke, m'boy."

Hetty hauled her father away before he bonded any further with his new best friend.

It had been no accident that Mr. Ellis had repeated his line about life's great pleasures.

He'd been reminding her of their waltz. And of their midnight kiss.

Reminding her who was in control.

And that's when the full enormity of her folly pierced her like arrows raining down from a battlement.

Instead of courting the edges of danger, indulging in a manageable little thrill . . . she'd flung herself from the cliffs of doom.

Why? Why had she done it? This was a nightmare.

It was because she was wearing the gown she'd worn at her debut. She'd become seventeen-year-old Hetty again. Foolish and naive.

So very foolish. She'd deviated from the plan, the schedule, her duties, and her dreams.

She'd kissed The Devil's Own Scoundrel. A ruthless gambler who'd set his sights on her father's title.

And, make no mistake, there'd be hell to pay.

Chapter Four

A FEW HOURS LATER, Hetty and Viola sat together on a heap of cushions and bedding, garbed in cotton nightgowns with their hair loosely braided.

"You kissed *whom*?" Viola asked, her eyes wide with shock.

"The man I waltzed with. Ash Ellis. The Devil's Own Scoundrel." Hetty hugged a pillow to her chest. "I didn't know it was him."

"But what were you doing kissing *anyone*?"

"I don't know." Hetty groaned. "It's difficult to explain. I hadn't been to a ball in seven years—not since my debut—and I was having all of these memories of what it had felt like to be seventeen and to dream of moonlit kisses from handsome rakes. Do you remember what that was like, Viola?"

"I never had a debut. My father couldn't afford one."

"Oh, that's right. I'm sorry, I forgot."

Viola shrugged. "That's all right. I never wanted a debut. I would only be a wallflower with such poor prospects. But tell me more. I wondered why you disappeared for so long. How did it happen?"

"I danced with Mr. Ellis, and he was so confident and commanding, and I forgot myself. Or maybe I was trying to find some lost part of myself? We were on the balcony. There was the scent of roses. He's sinfully handsome, but that's no excuse, is it? I made a mistake. An enormous, irreparable mistake."

Viola clasped Hetty's hand. "He's the devil who ruined Westbury—took his fortune at the gaming tables. Left him with nothing. And now his poor sisters have no prospects."

"I honestly didn't know it was him. I thought he was a nephew or a cousin of one of the guests I invited to the ball."

"He didn't . . . force himself upon you? If he did, I'll strangle him with my bare hands," Viola said fiercely.

Hetty smiled to think of the petite and peace-loving Viola strangling a dangerous beast like Mr. Ellis. "No, he didn't force me to do anything. In fact . . ." She took a deep breath. Viola was one of her best friends. She could reveal the extent of her error. "I kissed *him*."

Viola's mouth dropped open. "Oh, Hetty. You didn't."

"I did. And that's not even the worst of it!"

"There's more?"

"My father saw us kissing, but I think he was misled into believing that we were only talking."

"Your father saw you—oh, Hetty. You could have been ruined. You could have had to marry that . . . that fiend!"

"It gets even worse." She covered her face with the pillow. "It all went wrong."

Viola tugged softly on Hetty's braid. "I can barely hear you through that pillow. What went wrong?"

"After our kiss, Mr. Ellis claimed to me and my father that he was the distant and long-lost heir to the dukedom of Granville."

"He didn't!"

"He did."

"And what did your father have to say about that?"

"He was overjoyed. 'It's a midnight miracle,' he said. 'I'm saved! I don't have to marry.'"

"Your poor father. He really doesn't relish the idea of taking another wife."

"He's dead-set against it, and now Mr. Ellis has given him false hope."

"You believe him to be a pretender?"

"What other explanation could there be? He's a ruthless, fortune-hunting scoundrel. He wants to own Rosehill Park. He wants to own *me*." Hetty clenched her hands into fists. "I'll never let that happen. I'll fight him tooth and nail."

"Who is he claiming to be?"

"A descendent of the Honorable Ashbrook Prince, a distant relation from a junior line of the family. He'd be my seventh cousin. One would have to trace his ancestry back to the sixteenth century to find any connection, and it all hinges on a secret marriage to a scullery maid. It's preposterous."

"Did he present any proof of his claim?"

"He said he'd send it to my father's solicitor tomorrow." Hetty set the pillow aside. "I'm certainly not going to wait around for that crooked Mr. Higginbottom to decide the fate of my family. I'll conduct an investigation of my own."

"We'll call an emergency meeting of the Boadicea Club," said Viola. "The ladies will know what to do."

"He's a common trickster, an obvious imposter. The whole situation is unbelievable. And untenable. And I have to stop him. Wait." She grabbed her friend's hand. "I just had an idea."

"What is it?"

"What does a gambler desire?"

"Why, a fortune, of course."

Hetty leaped off the sofa and ran to her dressing table. She opened a drawer and pulled out her jewelry box. "I have a fortune in jewels, Viola." Hetty began stuffing jewelry into a velvet reticule.

Only a few days ago, she'd been kneeling to examine the grapes, inspecting them for insects and mold, wearing her old gray gown with her hair tied up under an enormous straw bonnet. Now she was contemplating desperate acts of bribery to stop wicked scoundrels from stealing those vineyards away.

She would do whatever it took to make Mr. Ellis disappear from their lives. And then her father would select a new bride and sire an heir. And Hetty could return to the plan, set her life back on course.

"What are you going to do, Hetty?"

"I'm going to bribe him to relinquish his claim."

"You think that will work?"

"It must. I'll visit him tomorrow evening at his gaming hell."

"You can't go there!"

"I have to, it's the only way. I'll wear a cloak, and I'll take a strong footman with me."

"I won't allow you to face that man alone. I'm coming with you."

"I can't allow you to do that."

"He ruined Westbury. I'll help you defeat him," Viola said staunchly.

"All right, we'll go together." Hetty drew a wooden box out from under her bed. "And we'll take this."

"Your pistol?"

"You never know what might happen when we descend The Devil's Staircase."

"Hetty, you don't need the pistol. Your footman will carry one."

"I'll do whatever it takes, Viola. My future, the future of my vineyards, and the livelihood of every tenant at Rosehill Park are at stake. I'm going to make a bargain with the devil. Every scoundrel must have his price."

IT WAS THE day after the ball, and Ash was having regrets. He shouldn't have kissed Lady Henrietta.

An innocent highborn lady might think she wanted a little thrill in the gardens with a handsome devil of a stranger she assumed was connected with her social set.

Until that stranger made a play for her family fortune.

Ash had to admit that it hadn't looked good. Kissing her and then making his claim. The timing had been all wrong.

The duke had been eagerly receptive to his announcement, but Lady Henrietta had gone from amorous to infuriated when she'd learned of his identity and his plans. She was bound to cause trouble.

He grabbed a bottle of gin from behind the bar and headed for his usual table against the back wall of the gaming house, where he could observe the clientele without being observed himself.

It was early yet. They'd only just opened, and their barman, Gus, had the staff lined up for inspection.

The young bloods and working girls of London hadn't yet begun the hedonistic whirl that would bring some of them through his doors, where they would drown in spirits, play games of chance and luck, perhaps make use of the upstairs rooms, and then be swept out again in the small hours of the morning, when the night-world began to lose its luster in the harsh light of the rising sun.

He downed a large quantity of gin, trying to drown out the memory of that kiss.

Soft, tentative response at first, and then . . . soft breasts pressed against his chest, her fingers wound through his hair, pulling him closer, her tongue meeting his stroke for stroke . . .

He drank more gin.

A spoiled, headstrong lady like Henrietta required a steady hand, a clear head, and subtle persuasive tactics.

That kiss had been anything but subtle.

Ash groaned, staring into the bottom of his glass. If he could read gin dregs like tea leaves, the streaks would spell out: *You're a hot-blooded fool.*

Didn't matter if she was the one to initiate the kiss. It had been a mistake. And Ash couldn't afford mistakes.

He'd planned this so carefully. There was too much on the line.

His business partner and best friend, Jacques Smith, known as Jax, joined him at the table. He was impeccably dressed and bright-eyed, while Ash hadn't slept a wink last night, had thrown on the first clothes he'd found, and felt like hell warmed over.

Jax poured himself a stiff drink. "How'd it go last night? Did the swells throw you out on your ear?"

"Far from it. The duke welcomed me with open arms. It's the managing daughter I'll have to persuade."

"Managing daughter, eh? Sounds like trouble."

"She's definitely trouble. Tall, tempting brunette trouble. With lush, kissable lips."

"I thought you told me she was a spinster?"

"No idea why she's a spinster. Those curves of hers should be illegal."

"Ah . . . *that* kind of trouble."

"*All* the kinds of trouble. She's sharp as a knife and has a way of getting what she wants." Ash smacked the heel of his hand against his forehead. "I really bollocked everything up last night, Jax."

"What did you do?"

"We were in the gardens. There was champagne involved . . ."

Jax raised both of his eyebrows. "What the hell did you do?"

"She kissed me."

"*She* kissed *you*?"

"At first. Then I kissed her. Quite thoroughly."

It had been more than just a kiss. Something had happened to him out there on the balcony. The earth had shifted beneath his feet.

She'd made him feel like the king of the world.

"And someone saw you. And the duke called you out, and now it's pistols at dawn. You bloomin' idiot!"

"The duke did see us, but I gave him an excuse, said she was whispering wine recipes in my ear."

"And he believed that rubbish?"

"He's desperate not to remarry. Practically welcomed me into the family. Said to send proof of my claim to his solicitor."

"Then what's the problem?"

"Lady Henrietta. She wasn't too happy about finding out she'd just kissed The Devil's Own Scoundrel. *Furious* would be the word. She's the one who wants to challenge me to a duel. She's a bluestocking with a pistol. I'll have to watch my back. It complicates things . . ."

"You think she'll stand in your way."

"Nothing I can't handle." Ash leaned back in his chair and clasped his hands behind his head. "She likes to be in control. But I have evidence of her pliability. I'll find a way around her."

Or over her. Under? She'd probably want to be on top. She'd want to set the pace.

What in hell was wrong with him? He had to stop thinking about Lady Henrietta Prince as anything other than an obstinate bluestocking obstacle to his plans.

Jax gazed at him steadily. "You're really going through with this?"

"This is the only way, Jax. The only way to create real change. I've been saving as many lads as possible from the factory, but it's not enough. I'm going to be the next Duke of Granville."

"And then what? We'll all have to bow and touch our forelocks every time you pass by?"

"I'll never become one of them, you know that. Heedless and cruel. I'll be a different breed of nobleman. One who never forgets his dark, twisted roots. Who never stops attempting to right life's inequities for those less fortunate, those less privileged."

"You'll be a hero for the ones at the bottom of the heap."

"They've been kicking us down for too long. To change the rules, I have to climb to the top, become one of the ruling class."

"They won't accept you into their hallowed halls."

"They'll have no choice. I'll change the nobility from the inside out. I'll be just as ruthless as they are, but for the benefit of the child laborers."

Jax refilled his glass. "I just don't want to see you swinging from a noose. Blood is everything to the Fancy. As far as I know, you ain't got a drop of the blue."

"That's the glorious thing about this game. It's plausible that I am the heir. There's a lost baby. A secret marriage. A family resemblance. The memory I have of a woman holding me and crooning to me in Spanish. I said my name was Ash when I arrived at the orphanage. It could be short for Ashbrook."

"Or it could be because your father was a chimney sweep and you were cradled in a coal scuttle."

"I'm the heir. I have to believe it, or no one else will. I'll change the world, Jax. I'll settle for nothing less. Times are changing. The nobility with their wealth steeped in blood can't rule the world forever. The children dying in their factories, in their rookeries, don't have a voice. I'm going to be their voice. But they won't listen unless I'm one of them. They won't listen unless I have a title. And I'll have it. It's within my grasp. It's almost mine. One spinster bluestocking isn't going to stand in my way."

"You always did have grand ambitions. But how can you prove it?"

"You didn't think I'd run such a high-stakes game without an ace up my sleeve, did you? I have a fairy godmother."

"A what?"

"Haven't you read any fairy tales? A fairy godmother. But this one didn't magically appear and transform me into a duke. She was recruited."

"I'm confused."

"All will be revealed, Jax. All will be revealed. In the meantime, 20 Ryder Street is yours. Everything we built. The moment I'm acknowledged as the heir, I'm signing it over to you. You deserve it, Jax. The future profits will be yours. I'll never forget my origins and my loyalties. Brothers forever."

"Brothers forever," Jax replied, filling Ash's glass to the brim with gin.

He and Jax had made a pact when they were young lads forced to labor sixteen hours a day in the harsh, unhealthy conditions of a bottling factory that they'd use their wits and charm to rise above their sordid origins.

They'd give as good as they got. Live life by their own rules.

They'd escaped the factory by joining a gang of pickpockets, but that had been exchanging one form of servitude for another. Ash hadn't seen it that way at first. He'd thought that joining John Coakley's motley group of thieves was gaining the family he'd never known. Coakley had taught them the ropes, the tricks of the trade. He'd taught them to gamble.

He'd been like a twisted version of a father. At first. And then the beatings had started. And Coakley's true nature had been revealed. He'd ruled his band of thieves and card sharps with merciless cruelty, demanding all of the profits for himself and thrashing any boy who tried to escape.

He'd taken Ash and Jax with him overseas, to Spain and France, where they'd had no choice but to carry out his crooked schemes.

Don't think about it. The glass in Ash's hand shook, gin sloshing over the edge.

Coakley was dead. Ash had put a bullet through his heart.

"You'll have to be damned careful, Ash. We have dark secrets to hide," Jax said.

"You're the only other person who was there that night. You're the only one who knows what we did."

Memories slammed into his mind before he could fend them off.

A fist smashing into his nose. Blinded by pain. By blood.

Cold steel fused to his fingers. Gunpowder singeing his nostrils.

He gulped the rest of the gin, wiping his lips with his sleeve. "The past is dead and buried." He raised his glass. "Here's to a brighter future!"

They clinked glasses, and Ash drank deeply, the cold fire of the gin burning his throat and settling like liquid fire in his belly.

It was a dangerous game, but then, he lived for danger, for the spice of it, the thrill that kept him coming back for more.

Danger meant he knew that he was alive, that his heart was still pumping.

He wasn't like the law-abiding citizens in their stone houses behind iron gates, their only aspiration a grave plot with a marble headstone. A crypt if they were lucky. Watched over by a stone angel.

Sleep through life and then Rest in Peace.

No thank you.

He lived on the knife's edge of life. Pursuing bigger and better prizes.

His goal when he'd moved back to London had been to open a gaming house and make it profitable. But when fate presented an even bigger opportunity, he'd seized it..

"Really, once Lady Henrietta thinks about it rationally, she'll see that I'm doing them a favor by coming forward," Ash said. "If her father's dukedom reverts to the Crown, she'll be left with nothing. She'll probably have to become a governess or something. There's no guarantee that the duke can produce another heir."

"That's an excellent way to look at it. You're doing them a favor."

"What am I taking from them? Nothing. I'm giving them security. Lady Henrietta is independent-minded and doesn't like to think that a man like me could wield any power over her, but everyone wins in this game. I'll save her estate and she can live there forever if she wants to."

"Did you say the lady was tall?" Jax asked.

"A statuesque goddess."

"Full lips?"

"Like plump, ripe cherries."

"And a generous bosom?"

"Curves for days. Why do you ask?"

"Because I think she just walked through the door."

"She what . . . ?" Ash sputtered, wiping gin from his chin and swiveling in his seat.

Jax was right.

Lady Henrietta stood inside the doorway, flanked by a burly footman and another young lady. She was wrapped in a hooded cloak, but there was no mistaking her height, and the startling beauty of her face.

This was all kinds of wrong.

"What the devil is she doing here?"

Jax chuckled. "From the looks of it, she's out for your blood. Let's hope she didn't bring that pistol."

Chapter Five

❧ ✿ ❧

"*H*E'S SEEN US," said Hetty.

"He doesn't look pleased," Viola whispered.

Mr. Ellis sat at a sheltered table in the back of a large central gaming room with an ornamental plaster ceiling and green-baize-covered tables. It was early yet, and the games hadn't begun.

In order to access 20 Ryder Street, they'd descended a long, winding stone staircase with brick walls. Once they'd gained admission to the perfectly ordinary-looking stone building from a ruffianly doorkeeper, and passed through a second portal, monitored by the use of a spyhole, the interior was fully as decadent and depraved as she'd imagined it to be.

The furniture was covered in crimson and purple velvet, and the walls sported gilt mirrors and bawdy oil paintings. The disreputable chamber was presided over by a bare-knuckle bruiser of a barman with a shock of red hair and ruddy cheeks, wearing a curious green cap, who dispensed gin and other spirits from behind a long mahogany bar stretching the length of the wall.

Rose-tinted lamps cast a sensuous glow over everything. The pretty barmaids the duke had mentioned were garbed to match their surroundings in crimson velvet with gold braiding.

This wasn't one of the exclusive gentleman's clubs, which were by invitation only and banned females. And yet it also wasn't one of the lower hells. It was somewhere in the middle. A gambling purgatory, where rough ne'er-do-wells mingled with noblemen eager to shed the cumbersome burden of family fortunes at the hazard tables.

Viola studied the room with obvious trepidation. "I don't like the way those men at the bar are leering at us as though they're perusing a menu at a chophouse and have decided to order the Young Lady Special."

"I'll make this as brief as possible." Hetty turned to the footman she'd brought for protection. He wore a greatcoat to disguise his livery, so as not to divulge their identity. She must keep a low profile. It wouldn't do for word to get out that she'd visited this wicked establishment. "This way, Leland," she said, leading them across the room.

Mr. Ellis rose and made a bow.

Hetty had forgotten quite how much of him there was. He towered over his companion, a handsome, elegant man with closely cropped curly black hair, fashionably garbed and clean-shaven.

Mr. Ellis's coat was rumpled, his cravat askew, and he hadn't shaved since they'd met last night. He was still handsome as sin. And entirely too self-possessed, standing there with a mocking smile on his face, brawny arms folded across his chest.

He was enjoying this.

Go ahead, try that seductive smile as many times as you like. I'll remain impassive.

Her heart wouldn't pitter-patter any faster, her palms would remain dry, and her temperature low.

"Lady Henrietta," he said smoothly. "May I present my business partner, Mr. Jacques Smith?"

When he spoke, he held her gaze with such heated intensity that Hetty nearly grabbed a tumbler of gin from the table and gulped it down. But that would only add flame to the fire. She must keep her wits about her.

It didn't matter one jot if she found him attractive. He was her opponent now, and a dangerous one, at that.

"Mr. Smith." She nodded. "This is my friend, Miss Viola Beaton."

Mr. Smith bowed. "A pleasure to meet you both, Lady Henrietta. Miss Beaton."

Viola turned to Mr. Ellis. "I know you, sir," she said with a stern expression on her normally placid face.

"I don't think so, Miss Beaton," he replied.

"I'm music instructor to the Duke of Westbury's sisters. I know that you ruined him."

"And how is Westbury? Haven't seen him here lately," Mr. Ellis replied.

"That's because you've stolen all of his money."

"No one forced him to walk through these doors,

dear girl," said Mr. Ellis. "Speaking of which, why are you ladies here?"

Had she thought his eyes held silvery moonlight? They were more like a silty pond. Murky and difficult to read.

He was hard-edged. Cast in bronze. He was danger. She felt it like an icy wind at her back.

He'd seen the underbelly of life. Done wicked things. Stared into the yawning maw of hell. Perhaps he hadn't fallen completely yet, but he had one foot over the edge.

"Is there somewhere private where we could speak?" Hetty asked.

"This is a secluded table. The room is mostly empty."

"Very well." Hetty took a seat and Viola sat next to her. Leland remained standing behind Hetty's chair. He was stalwart, and loyal, and she trusted that he would never repeat a word of this to anyone.

"Mr. Ellis," Hetty said sharply. "I'll be brief. I know you can't possibly be the heir to my father's dukedom. Besides your dreadful reputation, and your reprehensible habit of ruining noblemen, I've done my research and determined that you are a fortune hunter. I'm here to find out the price to be paid for you to withdraw your preposterous claim."

Mr. Smith chuckled, giving Hetty an appreciative stare. "You're everything Ash led me to believe you'd be, Lady Henrietta."

A cold light entered Mr. Ellis's eyes. "Here to buy me off, is that it?"

She nodded at Leland. The footman glanced around

warily before opening the velvet-lined jewelry box he carried to reveal a mound of gleaming diamonds, rubies, and pearls.

Mr. Ellis whistled. "My, my, Lady Henrietta. I don't come cheap, do I." He reached into the jewelry box and hefted a diamond necklace. "Very impressive."

"I was given this necklace by my father on my sixteenth birthday. I wore it to my first ball."

"It's lovely." He held it toward a lamp, and rose light danced through the diamonds. "But it's a forgery."

"I beg your pardon!"

Mr. Ellis turned the necklace to the clasp. "Someone has taken your real jewels and replaced them with diamonds made from paste. See here?" He pointed to the clasp. "The original was crafted by Bailey and Hart, Master Jewelers to the Crown. They always incorporate a distinctive filigree box clasp. This clasp is not nearly so intricately carved, nor does it have their insignia displayed correctly. This is a clever forgery, but a forgery nonetheless."

"How can that be?"

"That I can't answer."

Hetty's heart skipped a beat. She remembered how furtive her father had been lately. The guilty glances she intercepted when he arrived home early in the morning, smelling of whisky and cigars and unsubtle perfume. Was he in financial trouble? She knew he'd been gambling, and making some questionable investments, but she'd been so wrapped up in planning the grape harvest that she hadn't been paying close attention.

"This piece, on the other hand . . ." He touched the

diamond and amethyst bracelet she wore. As if by accident, his fingertips slid across the inside of her wrist. A warmth radiated outward from his touch, spreading through her body. "It's worth a small fortune."

"That one's not on offer." She snatched her hand away. "It was my mother's favorite."

Mr. Ellis caught her eye, his gaze as hard and icy as diamonds. "And I'm not on offer, either."

"I have access to more jewels, and cash reserves. Name your price, Mr. Ellis."

He lifted a gaudy gold timepiece from his waistcoat pocket. "My customers will be arriving soon. I think you should leave, Lady Henrietta."

"Name your price."

Mr. Smith was watching the conversation with obvious amusement, and Viola kept glancing toward the door, as if longing for escape.

"It's inadvisable to display such valuable trinkets," said Mr. Ellis. "You're a pigeon begging to be plucked."

"Is that how you see me?" Hetty tossed her head. "I assure you, I'm no pigeon."

"There are dangers lurking in wait for innocent young ladies who flash expensive jewelry in places like this."

"And you chief among them, Mr. Ellis."

"You wound me." He mimed thrusting a knife through his heart.

"I'm sure you'll recover."

"The last time I checked, there's no law that says

a notorious gaming hell owner can't be proved to be the heir to a dukedom, Lady Henrietta."

"I know what goes on in this room, Mr. Ellis. And Mr. Smith. The good men you've ruined. The families left destitute."

"We run a gaming house, Lady Henrietta," Mr. Smith replied. "There must be winners and losers."

"I've heard rumors of cheating. Rumors that you two are sharps."

Mr. Smith waved his hand through the air. "Vicious gossip."

"Even if those rumors were true, which they're not, my past and my present activities have no relevance to my claim, Lady Henrietta."

"The past always has relevance. It shapes us, Mr. Ellis."

"My past matters only insofar as it proves my lineage. Which I intend to do when I meet with your father and his solicitor tomorrow."

"I will most certainly be present at that meeting. I won't allow my father to be swindled by you. You're trying to manipulate him, prey upon his disinclination to marry. I'm here to tell you that it won't work."

"Look here, girlie," drawled Mr. Ellis. "I'm your best hope to keep your estate, and you know it. Forcing your father to attempt to sire another heir is a desperate gambit, and no sure bet."

"Did you just call me girlie?" Hetty's pulse raced.

Viola laid a hand on her arm. "Perhaps we should leave," she whispered.

Hetty leveled her gaze at Mr. Ellis. "You think that

you can charm and cheat your way into a title. I refuse
to see my family fortune turned over to an audacious
profiteer on evidence that will no doubt prove false."

The man didn't blink an eye. He just sat there and
regarded her with steely composure. "Your precious
estate is nearly bankrupt. Did you know that?"

"I review the books. I know everything there is to
know about Rosehill."

"Maybe not everything. But I'll leave that to your
father to explain."

How, and why, did this man seem to know more
about the state of her family's finances than she did?
It was infuriating.

"You, Mr. Ellis, are a scoundrel. An unprincipled
rogue. And you more than live up to the name the
scandal sheets have given you."

ASH KEPT HIS face blank while Lady Henrietta continued excoriating his character. He'd been called
many bad names in his lifetime.

Most of them well-merited.

Her large brown eyes were accentuated by thick,
dark brows. Brows that were set in a line because she
didn't trust him.

Intelligent woman.

He had to give her credit. She was desperate, yet
unflinching. Her eyes flashed with ire, and her spine
was ramrod straight.

She was every inch the highborn lady, daughter
of a duke, come to throw her wealth around to rid
herself of a pesky pretender.

Her companion, Miss Beaton, was pretty in an

unremarkable way, with dimples and light brown hair. She wore a drab cloak, no jewelry, and kept staring at the door, longing to fly away from this den of iniquity.

". . . and unscrupulous mountebank!" the lady concluded.

"Mountebank, ha!" Jax said. "You've described him to a fault."

Traitor.

He could at least put in a few good words for Ash. In the old days, when they'd been running games in Europe, Jax and Ash had been perfectly attuned. They'd had an arsenal of roles to play, well-practiced characters and excuses to get them out of any hot water.

Lady Henrietta was so hot, she was nearly boiling. Steam was practically rising from her ears.

"If you expect me to believe that a notorious gambler just happened to recently learn that he's the heir to my father's dukedom, after staying silent for his entire life, you must think that I'm gullible. I assure you, I'm not."

He wouldn't use the word *gullible* to describe her. She was clever, sharp-witted, and she was gorgeous.

The most gorgeous thing he'd ever seen.

A lamp with a milky pink shade cast a soft, flattering light across her face. Not that she required flattering. She'd be devastating in any light.

She was the type to make men lose their minds, but there was something underneath, something he sensed . . . What was the word he was searching for?

Unsullied. Untainted by hardship. She might as

well be a portrait hanging in a museum for all the experience she'd had of real life. Real problems.

She hadn't been dragged through the muck and mud of ordinary life. She'd been born into money, and she'd led a protected life.

The protection of inherited money, of being born into a ruling class.

You lived by your fists and your wits when you didn't have daddy's money to smooth life's path.

"Are you listening to me, Mr. Ellis?" she asked with a puff of breath that lifted a brunette curl from her cheek.

"No. I was admiring you."

"You," she sputtered. "You make me want to scream."

"It's not very English of you, Lady Henrietta," he replied with a smile. "All of this public displaying of emotion."

She tossed her head, sending the long dark spiral of hair that fell over one shoulder swaying. "I'm French on my mother's side."

Miss Beaton plucked at her friend's sleeve. "It's time to leave now."

Lady Henrietta nodded her agreement. "I will ask one last time, Mr. Ellis. Will you name your price and withdraw your claim?"

"I won't. Because I'm the rightful heir to the dukedom, and it doesn't matter how many jewels you offer, or what you uncover in my past."

She rose from her chair, and everyone else rose with her. "You'll never be the duke."

"We'll see about that, won't we?"

She really didn't know what kind of man she was dealing with. He wasn't easily intimidated. He'd seen the midnight side of life, he'd been raised in the underbelly of London where only the strong survived.

Show no weakness. Show no fear.

One privileged lady wasn't enough to stop him from getting what he wanted. She was just like everyone in her social class. She saw him as a nuisance to be bought off—she came into his world flashing her diamonds around, thinking that he'd just slink away.

Take the money and run.

He didn't want her jewels. He wanted the title, and the power it gave. The power to change England's labor laws.

"If you think about it, Lady Henrietta, I'm doing you a favor. You should be thanking me for discovering my origins and making my claim to save your family fortune."

"Thanking you?" Her laughter was hollow. "This isn't over, Mr. Ellis."

"It's only just begun, Lady Henrietta."

"Come along, Viola. This is obviously a waste of time." She left in a swish of silk and a swaying of hips. He liked watching her leave as much as he'd enjoyed watching her walk across the bar, eyes flashing, with murder on her mind.

The lady was a formidable opponent, make no mistake.

When she and her companions were gone, Jax laughed so heartily he doubled over, and had to be slapped upon the back to end a coughing fit. "P-pliable, is she?"

"I may have underestimated her just a touch," Ash grumbled. "And thanks for leaping to my defense, by the way. You could have given her a glowing review of my character, at least."

"I was having too much fun watching the fireworks. I do believe if Lady Henrietta had brought that pistol, she'd have shot you right through the heart."

The scorn in her eyes had been piercing enough. "She'll be more of a challenge than I thought, but she'll come round." Ash slapped his palm on the table. "Show's over," he said to the gawking barmaids. "The customers are starting to arrive. Back to business."

Ash knew very well how to run a gaming hell. It would be a more thorny challenge to convince Lady Henrietta to accept his claim.

She'd find out that he'd be a better duke than most.

A better duke than her father. He'd restore her family fortune. He already had investors lined up for his new schemes. He was expanding into breeding Thoroughbred racehorses.

He'd replace her paste diamonds with real ones, soon enough.

She'd be thanking him when this was all said and done.

"WHY DO MEN hold all the power in this world, Viola?" Hetty asked as their carriage traveled back to Mayfair. "Does he think I was born yesterday?"

"Not after that speech," Viola replied. "You were unequivocal in your denunciation. You made your opinions crystal clear."

"As our friend the Duchess of Ravenwood is constantly reminding us, there have always been powerful women throughout history. Matriarchal societies, female rulers, women who were the decision-makers. I'm not going to sit idly by and do needlepoint while Mr. Ellis ruins my life. He's utterly unsuitable to be my father's heir. Anyone can see that."

"I agree. But what can we do about it? He wouldn't accept your bribe. If he's proved to be the heir, by fair means or foul, he'll eventually own Rosehill Park, Granville House, and your father's other holdings. He'll have a vast amount of control over your life."

"He would practically own me. He would decide my fate. The land is entailed, thank goodness, and he can't sell it off piece by piece, but he could make my life miserable. And he could gamble away our other assets."

"I'm beginning to think that Mr. Ellis, blast him, might find a way to win. You may have to accept that."

"I simply won't allow myself to believe that a man like him is anything other than what he appears on the surface. A scoundrel who's trying to steal our fortune."

"Hetty, don't be cross with me for making this suggestion, but I was wondering if perhaps your vehement reaction to Mr. Ellis's claim might have something to do with what happened on the balcony?"

"You mean our kiss?"

"It occurs to me that you feel that you let your guard down, that you acted against character."

"I suppose it plays a role. He knows how attractive he is, and he uses that advantage to manipulate people. I succumbed to his charm once. I shall never do it again."

"Don't be so hard on yourself. We all have our moments of weakness." Her gaze traveled to the dark carriage window. "I more than most."

Hetty suspected, and several of their friends agreed, that Viola nursed a secret and doomed amour for her employer, the dissipated Duke of Westbury.

"How is Westbury?" Hetty asked gently.

"Searching for an American heiress to marry," Viola said brightly. "It's to be the answer to his financial woes. The girls are very excited about it. They can't wait to live in style again. Soon they will have dowries to entice husbands."

"Oh, Viola. I'm so—"

"Don't." Viola held up a hand. "I'm his music instructor, nothing more. I don't know why he still goes gambling when he knows he'll only court further ruin. He's always stumbling home in the early hours of the morning, and his clothing smells of gin and cigar smoke . . . and perfume."

"Just like my father." Her words struck Hetty. "How do you know what Westbury smells like in the early morning?"

A guilty expression crept over Viola's face. "Sometimes I sleep over in one of the spare bedrooms because the girls' governess quit. And the cook is threatening to leave, as well."

"Is he paying you enough for all the duties you're performing in his household?"

"He hasn't paid me in months."

"That's terrible! Leave his employ immediately."

"I couldn't do that. He'll pay me eventually. And I've grown fond of those girls as if they were my own sisters."

That's not all she cared about, Hetty feared. And Westbury was not a worthy recipient of the affections of her dear, sweet friend.

"But we're speaking of your trials, not mine. Don't worry, Hetty. We'll weather this storm together."

"Thank you. It's good to have friends to rely upon."

"What's the next plan?"

"I'll find a way to convince my father that Mr. Ellis is not the solution to his financial problems, if it's true that he's driven the dukedom to near destitution."

"You think your father might overlook a lack of evidence?"

"I wouldn't put anything past my father and that crooked Mr. Higginbottom. I'll need to uncover irrefutable proof that Mr. Ellis is lying. I'm not sure how, but I'll find a way."

"You won't put yourself in harm's way, will you? Promise me you won't do anything foolish or dangerous."

"I must save Rosehill," she said with grim determination. She must find a way to disprove Mr. Ellis's preposterous claim. He would never own the estate.

He would never own her.

Chapter Six

THIS WAS BOTH foolish *and* dangerous, Hetty reflected. But she'd come too far to turn back now.

It hadn't been difficult to bribe Mr. Ellis's landlady to let her into his rooms after he'd gone out for the day. In fact, Hetty probably could have offered her less than a sovereign.

The frowsy matron had snatched the gold coin from Hetty's fingers, bit down on it with what was left of her teeth, and handed a key to Hetty, giving her instructions to find the right door. As easy as that.

Hetty stood outside the door, listening for any sounds from within. She'd been lurking in a doorway across the street when Mr. Ellis had departed the building, but one never knew what one might find in the chambers of a notorious scoundrel.

There could be a mistress inside the rooms, just waking after a long night of debauchery. Hetty was vague on the specific details of said debauchery, but she knew the gist of what occurred in the bedchambers of rogues. Which she would not waste precious time imagining. What Mr. Ellis did with his mistresses was no concern of hers.

She pressed her ear to the keyhole. All was silent.

Her heartbeat quickened as she fit the brass key into the lock and turned it until the door clicked open.

Never having stolen into anyone's chambers before, she was naturally trepidatious, but she must set aside any missishness in pursuit of her urgent goal: to find evidence that Mr. Ellis was knowingly conspiring to dupe her father into acknowledging him as the heir to the dukedom.

And find it she would.

She wasn't going to sit meekly by while Mr. Ellis assumed control over her life and her vineyards.

Squaring her shoulders, she pushed the door open and slipped through, closing it quietly behind her. She'd keep one ear cocked for any noises in the hallway. If he happened to return, she needed an escape route.

She'd learned that much from her friend and fellow member of the Boadicea Club, Mina, Duchess of Thorndon.

When entering any new room, always take note of the location of all doors and windows. Be aware of your situation, and of your potential avenues for escape.

Mina liked to give the ladies of the club instructions in weaponry, both improvised (such as hairpins or knitting needles) and more conventional (she was a crack shot with a modified pistol of her own design).

She regularly regaled the ladies with stories of her espionage activities in service of the Crown, at least the details she was allowed to share.

Hetty took careful note of the windows in the parlor. The curtains were drawn most of the way, so at least she didn't have to worry about being observed by anyone in the buildings across the way.

She unlatched one of the windows and propped it open with one of her hairpins. There was a large ledge directly below. If she must, she could go out the window, land upon the ledge, and then hop down to the ground.

Having established her (hopefully unnecessary) escape route, Hetty set about examining his rooms. The parlor, bedchamber, and study were furnished in the same garish manner as his gaming hell. The curtains were red velvet, and there was an ostentatious amount of gold—on the walls, on frames and mirrors, and painted over the furniture. It was as though Mr. Ellis had hired someone to decorate his rooms and given them instructions to make it look as expensive as possible, with no regard for comfort or harmoniousness.

Despite the opulent furnishings, the rooms were in a state of chaos, as though a storm had blown through, scattering clothing, books, and odds and ends to every corner. How on earth could he find anything?

Hetty's rooms were kept pristine. If even one book was askew on a shelf, she would notice.

She revised her earlier opinion about the potential for mistresses to occupy the premises. No woman, not even a chambermaid, had visited these rooms in days.

Her fingers itched to start folding clothing and restoring books to shelves.

His bed was unmade. She fancied she could still see the imprint of his huge body in the center. He probably slept facedown with his arms flung out to either side. The bedclothes were tangled, as though he'd had a restless sleep. No rest for the wicked, she thought.

And then she thought, *I'll wager he sleeps entirely in the nude.*

An image sprang to mind of his taut, firm buttocks, much like the ones she'd seen on marble statues in the British Museum.

Giving herself a mental shake, she set about making a methodical examination of the room.

The problem with the clothing draped across the chairs and hung over the fire screen was that it could be obscuring evidence.

She did hope there weren't any half-eaten dinner plates underneath any of the piles. That could attract rodents. She'd waged a war at Rosehill Park against the pests by employing the services of a tiger-striped tomcat whom she'd named Bacchus. Rodent hunting to Bacchus was a hedonistic pursuit, and he was bloodthirsty and tireless in his endeavors.

He slept in the barns, but always greeted Hetty with a cheerful brush of his head against her leg when he saw her. Her heart twinged. She should be in Surrey, tending to the vines. If August continued sunny and warm, she'd have a record-setting harvest.

Blast Mr. Ellis for making a mockery of her schedule.

His bed sheets smelled of cigar smoke and cologne. Smoking in bed, what a reprehensible habit.

In the wardrobe she found rows of gaudy crimson waistcoats, all embroidered with playing cards. The Ace of Spades. The highest card in the deck, he'd said. It all made sense to her now. He was a gambling man, and he was playing for the highest stakes of his life.

Her father's dukedom.

She lifted some linens off a chair in front of the fireplace, and the adjacent pile twitched. Leaping backward, she hit her hip on the edge of a table.

Arming herself with a fire iron, she approached the clothing and poked at it.

A fluffy gray head emerged. Not a rat—a cat. A very large, very fluffy gray-and-white cat with sleepy blue eyes and a nose with a white spot that made it look as though it had been dipped in cream.

"Mrrow," said the cat by way of greeting, and then nestled back into the linens.

"Why hullo there, pretty puss." Hetty replaced the poker and bent down next to the cat to scratch between its ears. "What are you doing here? Is that wicked man keeping you trapped in his rooms? You should be running free out-of-doors."

The cat purred her agreement, rolling over onto her back, presenting Hetty with a glorious amount of belly. The light gray fur of her belly was long and matted into peaks.

"Your fur is all tufted, poor thing. You need a good brushing. And where in the world do you relieve yourself?" Hetty sniffed the air, unable to detect any odors that might indicate the cat had used the carpet as a privy.

The cat curled its paws, kneading the air, as Hetty scratched her belly.

"My, my, at least Mr. Ellis appears to feed you well. Your belly is most magnificent." Nothing like Bacchus, who was lean and muscular from chasing mice and birds and climbing trees with his razor-sharp claws.

Strange that Mr. Ellis kept a cat as a pet. It didn't fit with her first impressions of him. He was a cold-hearted scoundrel. Not a father of fluffy cats.

She didn't have time to unravel more than one mystery. The landlady had said he'd be gone at a bareknuckle boxing establishment for two hours.

She consulted her timepiece. She must move swiftly.

She searched through the remaining piles of linens, finding nothing other than a loose brass button and several shillings.

She moved to the bookshelves. A collection of ancient philosophers, books on the subject of gaming, *The General Stud Book: Containing Pedigrees of Race Horses*, and a thick tome on the subject of pugilism, its roots in ancient Greece, and its rise in London as a pastime for gentlemen.

Gambling, racehorses, and pugilism. Mr. Ellis's interests were everything disreputable. She wondered that he didn't own a guide entitled, *How to Steal a Peerage*.

She pictured him stripped to the waist and wearing white trousers, pummeling one of his friends with his huge, bruised knuckles. Pugilism was nothing but fisticuffs with a thin veneer of civility. In Mr. Ellis's case, that veneer was nonexistent. Pugilism was a perfect pastime for an arrogant brute like him. It allowed him to indulge his primal need for dominion in a socially sanctioned manner.

Since everything he did was done with a reckless conviction of mastery, she hoped that he'd left something damning here in his chambers, not even considering that anyone might invade his lair. There could be a letter from him to a friend stating that he was planning to dupe a duke.

That would do nicely.

Or perhaps some legal document proving him not to be the distant relation he was claiming to be. That would clear things up.

She searched through the desk in the office. Some receipts for a shipment of spirits from Portugal, and a stack of documents pertaining to 20 Ryder Street, all signed with the name Ash Ellis.

Here was something—a hastily scrawled note. She moved to the window and held it up to a crack of light streaming between the curtains.

His penmanship was atrociously florid. Oh, it wasn't his penmanship. The letter was to him from a woman. She was describing what she wanted him to do to her in the Violet Room, one of the upstairs bedchambers at the gaming hell.

The writer described the violet and rose silk upon the walls, the purple velvet curtains, and the gilded mirrors hung upon the ceiling. And then she described in lurid detail what those mirrors would reflect. Silk cords tied around wrists . . . ostrich feathers brushed across nipples . . . naked, heaving flesh . . . her lips closing around his thick, hard—Good heavens! Did his mistress have to be quite so explicit in her love notes?

She hastily restored the letter to its shelf. Next, she found a document outlining Mr. Ellis's agreement to pay for the room, board, and education of several children. The gossips said that he'd fathered illegitimate children by several different women.

Damning, but not grounds for denying his claim to the dukedom.

She searched his dresser drawers, blushing as she touched his undergarments.

A rifling through the pockets of the coats hanging in the wardrobe yielded several calling cards for merchants, and a receipt for a daily delivery of fresh kippers, most likely for the cat. He was spoiling her, it seemed.

There was a bawdy illustrated book under his bed pillow of the sort that her friend Lady Beatrice had several copies of in a locked bookshelf at their lady's clubhouse on the Strand, which used to be the premises of a scandalous bookshop.

Frustrated, she glanced around the room. What was she missing?

There was a stack of books piled on the nightstand. She read through the titles: *Debrett's Peerage of England, Scotland, and Ireland*; an etiquette guide to the titles and forms of address of the British aristocracy; and a history of English country estates. One of the pages of the history book was marked with a strip of silk, and she opened it to a description of the gardens at Rosehill Park.

She added it all up. Peerage. Forms of address. Country estates. This wasn't pleasure reading.

He'd been doing research for a hostile takeover.

The Debrett's was to research the branch of their family that he intended to infiltrate, and the history of country estates was to learn about his target: Rosehill Park.

Separately these books meant nothing, but taken together, it was a logical assumption to make that he'd been studying her family history, preparing for the game he'd set into motion at the ball. But she needed more than assumption.

The cat roused itself and picked its way daintily across the floor to rub up against her ankle.

"Where does your owner hide his legal documents?" she asked the cat.

Do you have any kippers? If not, I'd settle for another belly scratch, the cat replied.

Another sweep of the rooms revealed nothing more of interest. Either he had a secret hiding place for his important documents, they were hidden in the general disorder of the room, or he didn't keep them here, but at the gaming hell.

There must be *something* incriminating in his rooms.

And she must find it. Swiftly. He was due to return in less than an hour.

ASH STOPPED BY the boarding house on his way to the boxing club. He liked to visit the children from time to time, to see how they were getting on with their schooling.

The house always gave him a quiet sense of accomplishment—of having done something to balance the scales against his past misdeeds.

The children were all orphans, like Ash and Jax. They were the ones who wouldn't have survived the harsh conditions of the bottling factory. He couldn't rescue them all, but he'd done what he could.

Mrs. Badger, the housekeeper, kept the house neat and shipshape, the brass handle polished, and the steps scrubbed clean.

The children were at their lessons—he could see their heads bowed over schoolbooks through the window—but two of the lads were playing in the garden when he let himself through the gate with his key.

"Mr. Ellis," cried Max, dropping his hoop and stick and running toward him. Young Harvey lagged behind. He walked with a pronounced limp, having mangled his foot in the machinery at the bottling factory.

"Good day, boys. And what sort of trouble have you been getting up to?"

"No trouble, Mr. Ellis," said Max. He was a bright lad with an aptitude for maths. "But I don't like having to memorize poetry. Don't see the point. Too many fluffy clouds and daffodils."

Ash laughed and ruffled his hair. "Girls like poetry. It may seem useless now, but in a few years, you'll be able to dredge up some pretty phrases and impress the fairer sex."

"Ew. Don't want to impress any girls."

"And how are you, Harvey?" Ash asked.

The delicate boy had taken ill after the accident at the factory and nearly died. "I'm doing well, Mr. Ellis. I'm reading a new adventure story."

Ash had been a reader when he was younger. He'd soon learned to hide his bookish ways from the older boys at the factory, for fear of the bullies with bigger fists than his.

He hoped Harvey would be able to read in peace here.

"I brought you more books," he said. "And sweets. But you have to promise to share them with all of the children."

"We will," they said in unison, holding out their hands.

Ash smiled and distributed the presents he'd brought.

"How's Tobias's cough?" he asked.

"He's better. But isn't he at your house, sir?" Max asked, his nose scrunching up.

"Why would he be?"

The boys exchanged worried glances. "He told Mrs. Badger that you asked him to come and train as your valet. He left days ago in a hansom cab with a man that had a gold tooth and wore a beaver hat with a playing card stuck through the band."

Icy fingers trailed along Ash's spine.

John Coakley had had a gold tooth. And he'd worn a card through his hatband. The King of Diamonds.

Coakley is dead. I saw him die.

Ash dropped to one knee, at eye level with the

boys. "I never sent for Toby. I'm afraid that man might have taken him. Did Toby look frightened?"

"No, he was quite proud. He had a new gold watch and was showing it all around," Harvey said.

Dread gripped Ash by the throat. He fingered the gold watch in his pocket.

The trinket Coakley had used to lure him, and Jax, away from the factory. He kept it as a talisman, a reminder of his dark and troubled past. A reminder of the trusting boy he'd been and the cold, jaded man he'd become.

"Boys, listen to me. I'm going to find Toby, don't worry. And if anyone offers you money or trinkets to go with them, you know what I've warned you about. It's a trick. It's best to stay in school, to learn your lessons. Even the poetry, Max. If you see that man again, the one with the gold tooth, I want you to immediately send word to me. Don't talk to him. Run away. Do you understand?"

"Yes, Mr. Ellis."

"Now go inside and share your treats. I'm due at the boxing club."

"I'm going to be a famous pugilist when I grow up!" said Max.

Ash had rather been hoping he might become an accountant's clerk.

He left with a heavy heart. Toby was his favorite, a likely lad with a quick mind and a good heart.

Ash feared the worst. Toby had been recruited. Lured into a life of crime with promises of riches and freedom.

You'll only work six hours a day, lads. Them wealthy

coves won't miss their pocket watches. They have ten more for any you take. You'll feast on roast meat every night. Sleep by a roaring fire. The offer I'm making you, boys, it don't come along more than once.

Ash would search for Toby tonight, under cover of darkness. He'd bring his barman, Gus, and a loaded pistol. He was well aware of the dangers lurking in Seven Dials. He fancied staying alive long enough to make his case to the duke and his solicitor.

Long enough to establish to a suspicious and highly resourceful bluestocking that he was her new lord and master.

HETTY WAS GETTING desperate. She had no desire to be here when the devil returned to his lair. She searched through the rooms one last time. A rolled piece of paper wedged behind the desk caught her eye. She wriggled it out and spread it, fixing the edges with paperweights and an inkwell.

She quickly determined that it was an architectural plan of Rosehill Park. There were notes scrawled in the margins and large X's drawn across certain areas.

She bent closer. That was the area of her vineyards. What did that large, black X signify? And why were the words "Thoroughbred stables" scrawled across her vineyards?

Panic surged in her breast. Mr. Ellis sought not only to own Rosehill Park, but to destroy it!

He was planning to rip up her vineyards and breed racehorses on the grounds of her beloved ancestral estate. It even looked as though he had plans to tear down the Temple of Bacchus her ancestor had built near the vineyards. This was even worse than she'd thought. Much, much worse.

She had to stop him.

Hetty hastily scrolled the plans, stuffed them back behind the desk, and headed toward the door, her heart racing. She hadn't had a chance to speak with her father yet about the fake diamond necklace. Now she would confront him with the knowledge of Mr. Ellis's plans for Rosehill.

"Now, don't go running out the door when I leave," Hetty told the cat. "Though, do you ever run? You appear to be more of a lounging sort of cat." She planted a swift kiss on the cat's silky head. "Goodbye, sweetheart."

She was halfway through the door when a large hand caught and gripped her by the wrist.

"I've got you," a deep voice growled. "Don't try anything foolish."

She shrieked. Mr. Ellis tightened his grip.

And the cat took one look at them and streaked between Hetty's legs, escaping into the hallway.

Chapter Seven

❧ 🌹 ❧

"Deuce take it——you've let the demoness out!" Ash released his grip on Lady Henrietta and raced down the hallway. He'd seen a streak of gray fur disappearing around the corner. At least she'd run in the opposite direction from the stairs.

He cornered the beast at the end of the corridor.

"There's nowhere else to run, succubus. You're trapped. Hold still now . . ." Ash approached cautiously. He'd been the victim of her claws more times than he cared to remember in the first week of their acquaintance.

After a month they'd reached a sort of truce, but it was precarious, at best.

Come to think of it, the infernal cat and Lady Henrietta had much in common. Why had she been skulking around his room?

He'd tend to one problem female first, and then the other.

"I've caught you, she-devil," he growled.

The cat hissed.

"You shouldn't speak to her like that. Cats know

when they're being insulted," said Lady Henrietta from behind him.

The cat rolled over on her back and squirmed voluptuously.

"There's a pretty kitty," Lady Henrietta crooned.

Ash glared at the cat. "It's time to go back now. I've brought you some kippers from the shop. You like kippers." He tiptoed closer.

Nearly there now.

He pounced on the feline, but she immediately exploded into diabolical motion, lashing out with her claws and launching herself back the way she'd come.

"Fuck, that hurts!" Ash cursed, nursing his scratched hand. "Bloody little fiend."

"I've got her," came a high voice from the next landing down. Ash bent over the balustrade to see Lady Henrietta holding the cat in her arms. "There's a good girl," she said, stroking the cat's head. "I know you're frightened by that horrid man who shouts expletives that should never be heard by our delicate ears."

Ash pounded a fist against wood. "Bring her back to my chambers. I'll deal with her, and then I'll deal with you."

"Would you rather come home with me, precious?" the lady asked the cat, her voice dripping with sweetness.

"You're welcome to her. But not before I have a chance to interrogate you. Get up here this instant before I come down and throw you over my shoulder."

"There's no need to growl, Mr. Ellis. I'm the one

who wishes to interrogate *you*." She marched up the stairs with the cat held in her arms like a baby.

Ash opened the door and Lady Henrietta sailed through, head held high. She glared at him as she brushed by and entered his rooms.

Ash could swear the devil cat was glaring at him too.

He shut the door behind them.

Lady Henrietta deposited the cat back on a pile of linens, where she promptly began licking her front paws as if nothing had happened.

"Now then, what were you doing in my—?" Ash began, but the lady turned her back on him and walked into his study. She re-emerged seconds later holding the architectural plans of Rosehill Park.

"What, pray tell, is this?" she asked, brown eyes blazing with fury and chin tilted at an obstinate angle.

If looks could kill, he'd be writhing in agony on the floor, breathing his last, tortured breath.

Damn her! She hadn't been meant to see that. Not until he'd already been declared the heir.

"I'm the one asking the questions here." He folded his arms over his chest and moved to stand over her. "Why are you sneaking around in my apartments, and how the devil did you gain access?"

"A sovereign."

"Is that all? I'll have to have a word to Mrs. Dougherty. She let you in too cheaply."

"I'm very persuasive. And you arrived home early. You never would have known I'd been here."

"I would have known. You'd have left a lingering scent. Eau-de-meddling-bluestocking." He advanced, wanting to intimidate her, make her show a little remorse for invading a man's private chambers.

"And your hair smells flowery—my cravat is still scented like you from our first meeting. When you rested your head upon my chest. And lifted your lips to mine."

A slight twitch of her luscious lower lip was the only indication that he'd shaken her composure.

"And then there's the fact that you rearranged my bookshelf," he concluded.

"I didn't."

"You did. I think you placed the books in alphabetical order, by the looks of it."

Her hand flew to her lips as she studied the bookshelf. "I didn't even know I was doing it."

"Your compulsion for orderliness in all things overrode your ability to be devious. Please don't attempt a career at thievery."

"I wasn't thieving," she said curtly. "I was searching for incriminating evidence."

"Unauthorized entry into a person's private dwelling is a crime."

"I'm not the criminal here."

"What were you hoping to find?"

"No one could find anything in these rooms. How can you stand to live like this? So disorderly and chaotic."

He shrugged. "I don't like strangers in my room. Chambermaids and bluestockings alike."

"Obviously. Though I did manage to find several items of interest during my search, Mr. Ellis. Your choice of reading materials is quite telling. You were studying the peerage, forms of address, and great country houses. You were researching my family with nefarious intent."

"It's not a crime to read research books, Lady Henrietta."

"And these architectural drawings. I'm taking these to my father."

"Be my guest," he replied coolly. She wouldn't find any cracks in his armor.

But he knew exactly how to disarm her. She was a woman. A woman who'd smiled dreamily and relaxed into his arms as they waltzed. She might be brave and bold, but he knew the truth of it: Lady Henrietta Prince was soft and romantic at heart.

She shook the rolled plans at him like a warrior's spear. "You're planning to build stud stables over my vineyards."

"Breeding Thoroughbreds is a profitable business. I've already purchased a prime bit of blood."

"May I remind you, Mr. Ellis, that you haven't been declared my father's heir, as yet. And if I have anything to do with it, you never will be. How could you draw up these plans? Rosehill is a majestic estate designed by the fourth Duke of Granville. The gardens are renowned throughout the world for their beauty."

"I don't want the gardens. I want access to the river, and your vineyards run right alongside it. Making wine may be a delightful hobby, but those grapes of yours aren't profitable."

"Hobby! I'm so tired of men like you, Mr. Ellis.

My winemaking isn't a hobby. It's a well-thought-out venture with potential to reap great financial rewards, as well as establish a foothold for English wines in the world market."

She paced about his rooms, waving the architectural plans around so vehemently that hairpins began popping loose and unleashing her brunette curls. "If I were a man, you wouldn't scoff at my ambitions. 'You shouldn't trouble your pretty little head with such weighty masculine matters.' I've heard it so often that when I die, I'm quite sure some man will engrave it upon a stone: 'Here lies Lady Henrietta Prince, who involved herself in weighty matters, to a tragic end.'"

"While I'd simply love to stand here and be lectured by a burgling bluestocking all afternoon, if you haven't noticed, I'm bleeding, and I should like to attend to it."

Gus had landed a sneaky undercut on his jaw, and Ash had bit down on his lip. He turned his head so she could see the cut on his lip and the trail of dried blood.

"Oh. You're bleeding."

"Please tell me you're not a fainting kind of female. Because I don't keep any smelling salts. I'd have to pour gin down your gullet."

"Of course I'm not the swooning sort."

"Then march back the way you came, Lady Henrietta. Before the servant brings my bathwater." He took a menacing step closer. She quailed but stood her ground.

He was sweaty and grumpy from the beating he'd taken. His reflexes weren't what they once were. And he was worried about Toby.

And he'd been distracted by thoughts of this very same lady, suddenly materialized in his rooms.

A lady who refused to be intimidated by him.

And refused to leave.

"I won't leave," she said. "Not until you present me with more evidence of your birth."

"That's for the lawyers to see."

"I want to judge for myself."

"Now see here, Lady Henrietta, you're the one who stole into my rooms. I don't have to answer to you for anything. You'll be able to judge my evidence at Granville House tomorrow. Where I'll be declared the heir."

"I'll see you in hell first."

They faced each other like opponents in a boxing ring. Circling warily. Seeing who could land the decisive blow.

"I'm seconds away from throwing you over my shoulder and bodily depositing you outside my door," he warned.

She shoved a lock of hair away from her eyes. "I should like to see you try."

He towered over her, crossing his arms and flexing his muscles in a display of strength. "Does your father know that you go around bribing landladies and sneaking into private chambers?"

"I'm doing this for him. The end justifies the means."

His reasoning, precisely.

He wanted to throw her off balance. Keep her on the defensive long enough for him to button up this heir business.

The lady was far too intelligent for her own good.

He swiftly closed the distance between them. To her credit, she didn't back away. "Now that we're speaking in private, are we going to talk about what happened at the ball?"

"What happened?" she asked, with an innocent fluttering of her thick, dark lashes.

"You can't pretend that kiss away. It's burned into my memory, and I'm quite certain you've been thinking of it ever since."

"Don't flatter yourself. It wasn't that memorable."

"Shall I refresh your memory?" He gazed at her full, pink lips.

Her lower lip trembled. "You wouldn't dare."

Damn his reaction to her. He was meant to be asserting his mastery, but his heart was beating suspiciously fast, and his palms had gone damp.

Kissing her again would be grave folly. He should make good on his threat and bodily carry her out the door. Or he could frighten her away and do it so thoroughly that she'd learn a lesson about trifling with scoundrels.

There were other ways of forcing highborn ladies to leave one's rooms.

He loosened his cravat and flung the cloth over a chair, holding her gaze all the while. "I'm injured and in need of a good scrubbing and a soak to ease my aching muscles. Of course, if you want to stay while I have my bath, you're welcome to continue searching my rooms."

He undid the buttons at the top of his shirt.

She swallowed. Hard. And her gaze swept over the exposed triangle of chest with an almost physical weight.

He moved to the washbasin and turned his back on her, shrugging out of his braces and stripping his shirt all the way off.

A startled gasp. Excellent.

"I, er . . ." she mumbled.

"Yes?" He turned around.

"I'm leaving." She backed up and stumbled into a chair.

"Don't forget to return the key to Mrs. Dougherty on your way out, Lady Henrietta."

She escaped out the door.

The lady wouldn't be back, that much he could be certain of. She'd seen quite an eyeful of handsome beast, and it had thoroughly addled that too-sharp mind of hers.

He slapped the washcloth on his chest and wiped his armpits. He stripped out of his trousers and wrapped a towel around his waist.

There was a knock at the door and, assuming it was the landlady's nephew come to pour his bath, he shouted, "Enter."

"Oh. My," pronounced a wobbly female voice.

It was Lady Henrietta. Eyes round, throat working, she clutched the doorknob, her gaze roaming over his chest, over his towel-draped hips, and down his legs.

His cock stirred, as if it wanted to give her an even better show.

"Did you forget something, Lady Henrietta?"

She swallowed. "I, er . . . yes. My reticule. I think the cat is sitting upon it."

SOME SPY SHE'D make, rearranging bookshelves and leaving reticules on chairs.

Was it possible to perish of embarrassment? What a disastrous hash she'd made of this whole business.

Mr. Ellis was nearly naked now, with only a towel wrapped around his narrow hips to protect his modesty.

He had a boxer's frame, heavily muscled with a broad chest and powerful shoulders. The middle of his chest was covered in dark brown hair, and there was a thin line of hair that disappeared underneath the towel.

Only one area was hidden from view. Though the general shape of his . . . maleness . . . was clearly outlined.

He made no attempt to hide more of himself away, standing with one large fist gripping the towel closed at his hip.

Hetty had the indecorous thought that a man so breathtakingly handsome should never hide himself away, but parade around naked all the day long, causing traffic accidents and inspiring the female poets of London to feverish heights.

She snapped her gaze to his face.

Avoid the towel area.

Leave swiftly.

The grin he bestowed upon her was knowing and wolfish. He might as well have bared his teeth. "I'd fetch your purse for you"—he waved his free hand toward the towel—"but I'm not clothed for perambulations."

"I won't be a moment," she squeaked, crossing the room on unstable limbs.

The cat gave a disgruntled squawk when Hetty dislodged her.

She circled her caretaker's feet, meowing and rubbing up against his leg. She looked up at him with big blue eyes, and his lips curved into a smile.

Growl as he might, Mr. Ellis was smitten with the cat. Anyone could see it.

"What is your cat's name?" she asked.

"She arrived with the horrendous moniker of Duchess Froufrou. I renamed her Lucifer. Suits her better."

"You can't name a female cat Lucifer."

"And why not? She's a devil."

"I shall call her Lucy instead. If you dislike her so much, why do you keep her here?"

"She was a parting insult from a former mistress, who ran off to France with some doddering viscount."

"And so, you've been entrusted with Lucy's guardianship?"

"Wholly against my will. There have been quite a few times I've considered turning her over to that questionable butcher shop to be made into a pie."

"Cover your ears, Lucy! He didn't mean it. He's only joking."

Mr. Ellis grunted. "I'm not."

"Where does Lucy . . . do her business?" she asked.

"She's a fussy feline. She'd never soil herself or my carpet. In the morning and the afternoon, when she wants to go out, she meows at the door and I take her to the park, where she chooses a discreet shrubbery to use as a privy. If I'm not here, I hire my landlady's nephew to take her out."

"How interesting. I've never known a cat to be so well-trained."

"Everything has to be on her terms. Like someone else I'm beginning to wish I'd never met."

"She adores you."

"She's only pretending to like me. As soon as I give her the kippers, she'll forget my existence."

He'd be impossible to forget. Not in that towel. He was so . . . potent. So manly and large, all hard muscles and sleek flanks. Barrel-chested and wide-shouldered.

He had interesting scars and bruises scattered about his body. From the bareknuckle boxing, she assumed.

Everywhere she looked was . . . man chest. Small nipples surrounded by a dusting of hair. Ridges of muscles across his abdomen.

She was more than a little flustered by the sight. She grabbed her reticule too quickly and it fell, the clasp opening and items falling over the floor.

"Drat." She bent to retrieve the contents, and he

crossed the room and bent down at the same time. Their fingertips met.

Their gazes locked.

Suddenly all of that manly chest was way, *way* too close.

Awareness sent tendrils through her body, curling like new grapevines through her belly and up to her breasts and into her throat.

She tore her gaze away, stuffing everything back into her reticule haphazardly.

"Was there anything else you left in my chambers, Lady Henrietta?"

Her sanity. "Only this." She clutched her reticule to her chest like a shield and stood up, edging along the wall toward the door.

His knowing smile followed her.

It wasn't as if he'd deliberately attempted to discomfit her or had done anything unseemly. She was the one barging into his rooms. She was the one breaking and entering.

"You're welcome any time, Lady Henrietta. If you'd like to time your visits to coincide with my bathing, I do usually wash myself after pugilistic exertions."

"Good day, Mr. Ellis. My sincere hope is that this is all resolved swiftly, and I may never have to lay eyes on you ever again."

"We'll see about that."

She fairly raced from the room. As a person who prided herself on always remaining on task, on schedule, and on top of life, she'd found the one thing in the world that demolished her control, and his name was Ash Ellis.

Chapter Eight

❧ 🌹 ❧

"Do you have something to tell me about our finances, Papa?" Hetty asked the next morning in the breakfast parlor.

A guilty look flitted across his face. "I don't recall anything. My head aches this morning. I may need to go have a nap."

"You drank too much last night. Have some coffee."

Sunshine sashayed across the breakfast table, choosing a silver coffeepot here, a peach-colored dish there, to bestow its gilded smile upon. This fine weather would be excellent for the grapes, but it didn't suit Hetty's mood. She'd passed a sleepless night, tossing and turning over what she'd uncovered in Mr. Ellis's chambers.

"Is that better?" she asked, when her father had swallowed more coffee.

"Not particularly. I think I'll add a little brandy." He nodded, and a footman appeared. "Brandy, please."

"Yes, Your Grace." The footman bowed and left.

"I'd like to speak with you about a few things I've discovered, Papa."

"Can it wait?"

"It can't. Mr. Higginbottom and Mr. Ellis will be here within the hour." She lowered her voice. "It's come to my attention that certain jewels of mine have been replaced with clever forgeries. Do you know anything about this?"

He flinched. "I was hoping you wouldn't notice."

"Is there something you'd like to tell me?"

His face crumpled, his white whiskers drooping into his coffee cup. "The game's up, then. I ought to have told you before now, but I didn't like to admit it. We're on the brink of ruin, Hetty."

"I don't understand."

"I don't understand, either. I thought I was making good investments. I thought our fortunes would improve. But it all seems to have slipped away." He rested his head in his hands. "I'm sorry, Hetty."

"It can't be as bad as all that. The rents are fair but profitable at Rosehill. And we still have the other properties in England."

"Anything I could sell, I have."

"Oh, Papa. But I've been reviewing the ledgers. Everything adds up. I've seen no indication of insolvency."

"Those were altered ledgers. I thought you'd never need to know. And then it went wrong. I'm sure Mr. Prince will sort it all out once he's acknowledged."

Hetty stilled. "Do you mean Mr. Ellis?"

"You'll have to start thinking of him as Mr. Ashbrook Prince."

"I'll never accept him as the heir. He's a notorious gaming hell owner and scoundrel."

"Why do you dislike him so intensely when you don't even know him?"

Let her count the ways. He stared too boldly. Kissed too passionately. Paraded around in towels and made her think . . . thoughts.

Bad, wicked thoughts.

The sight of his large and heavily-muscled body covered only by a small towel was indelible, etched in her memory like a cupid's arrow carved into an oak tree.

"I only ask you to use logic and caution," she urged. "A legitimate heir never would have attended our ball uninvited."

"It was the most expedient way to make his point. I admire a man who makes things happen, a man of conviction and action. A man with the Midas touch, who turns everything to gold."

"Does our financial predicament have anything to do with your eagerness to have Mr. Ellis acknowledged as the heir?"

"I'll admit it's very good timing."

"But you weren't aware of his claim before the night of the ball?"

"Of course not. But now that we do have an heir, I'm quite pleased about it. Higginbottom assures me that Mr. Ellis has never run afoul of the criminal courts, and that's good enough for me."

"Such high standards, Papa. He hasn't been to prison. Give him a dukedom."

"Tut-tut, m'dear. You've already judged the man without reviewing his evidence."

She'd seen his crimson-velvet-and-vice-laden place

of business. And she'd seen his hedonistic chambers filled with explicit love letters.

And most damning of all, she'd seen his plans for tearing up her vineyards and using the land to breed racehorses.

"According to the scandal sheets, he's deliberately ruining certain noblemen, such as the Duke of Westbury, at his gaming hell. And there are other rumors about by-blows, and nefarious activities on the Continent."

"Did you know that your great-great-grandfather was known as a notorious roué? He was purportedly so dissolute that he left dozens of bastards strewn across the realm."

"But you can't seriously be considering Mr. Ellis's claim. It's not just his scandalous reputation. Did you know that he's planning to convert my vineyards into a breeding ground for Thoroughbred horses?"

"I know you love those vineyards, Hetty, and you're tending to them as a tribute to your mother's legacy, but it's all just an impractical dream. As I said, we're on the brink of ruin. We need a savior."

"You must marry an heiress, then. I'll revise my list of duchess candidates."

"I don't want to marry anyone other than . . ." He clamped his mouth shut.

She searched his face. "You already have someone in mind?"

"I may as well tell you everything. I'm in love. Have been for some time. Madam Bianchi is well past childbearing age, and I knew you wouldn't approve. Now that we have an heir, I plan to make an honest woman of her."

So there'd been a reason behind his obstinate wish not to marry any of the duchess candidates. "Marry your Italian opera singer mistress?"

"Don't sound so shocked. It's my second marriage. You'll love Giovanna too, once you meet her."

Was everyone in the world lying to her? Hetty spooned more sugar into her tea. Everything was falling apart.

"I wish you'd told me, Papa."

"I know I haven't been easy to live with these past years. I should have seen to your marriage prospects."

"I'm quite happily unmarried."

"You can't hide away at Rosehill forever. I won't see my only daughter pass her life with only vines for company. Hosting that ball made me realize that you must marry. I want you to be happy and fulfilled."

"I'm happier tending the vineyards than I ever would be hovering on the edge of a ballroom."

"Preposterous. My daughter would never be a wallflower. You may be a trifle long in the tooth, as they say, but you're a beauty and—"

"And I don't wish to marry, and that's that. I enjoy my freedom. But Mr. Ellis will crush my dreams."

"I'm very sorry, my dear, but if he's the heir, then he's the heir. End of story."

Her composure shattered like a sparkling wine bottle with too much sugar added. "This man is a complete unknown. You mustn't acknowledge him as the heir without a proper and thorough investigation."

"Higginbottom told me that he has new evidence to present today. And there's the family resemblance. You can't deny that his portrait would look at home in our familial gallery."

"I'll admit there's some slight resemblance." She set down her teacup with such force that it almost cracked the plate. "It's not enough."

"You're too independent-minded, Hetty. You never did learn life's limitations. Even as a child, you rushed headlong into everything, skinning your knees and outrunning the neighbor boys. You didn't like to be told no. You thought you could do anything. Your mother encouraged your self-reliance."

Hetty sighed. "I may be independent, but I've put the best interests of this family before my own. I hope you'll do the same."

"All I ask is that you consider Mr. Ellis's claim with an open mind. And you may wish to retire to your boudoir before the meeting to do whatever ladies do to refresh themselves for company. Your hair is disheveled, and you have purple shadows under your eyes."

"Certainly not!" She had no desire to make herself more attractive for the meeting.

"A Mr. Ellis here to see you, Your Grace," announced their butler, Dobbins, whom they'd brought with them to London from Surrey.

"Excellent. He's early," said the duke. "Send him in."

Moments later, Mr. Ellis strolled into the breakfast parlor as if he already owned their townhouse.

He looked as disreputable as ever, the cut on his lip still fresh, his huge, bruised hands ungloved, and the crimson waistcoat cheekily embroidered with playing cards only adding unsubtle insult to injury.

"Come in, do come in," the duke said jovially.

"Your Grace. Lady Henrietta." He made a bow but there was nothing courtly about his movements. Every movement, every bow he made, every time he caught her eye with that seductive stare, all of it was calculated to unnerve her.

"Mr. Ellis," she said icily.

"Have a seat, m'boy. We're waiting for Higginbottom to arrive. He's always late, as a rule. Come and have some breakfast."

"Thank you, Your Grace."

Mr. Ellis seated himself in the chair proffered by a footman, tucked a serviette into his collar, and nodded his thanks as his cup was filled with coffee.

"How are you today, Lady Henrietta?" he asked. "Have you bribed anyone yet?"

"I've been better, Mr. Ellis," she replied coolly.

Her father's brow wrinkled. "Is there something I'm missing?"

"I believe I have something of yours." Mr. Ellis reached into his pocket and pulled out the jeweled hairpin she'd used to prop open his window.

Her cheeks flamed. What a bungler she'd been, dropping her reticule and hairpins all over his apartments.

The duke raised his bushy white eyebrows. "And how did that come to be in your possession?"

"Lady Henrietta must have dropped it while we

were conversing on the night of the ball. I pocketed it, determined to return it at the first opportunity."

How easily he lied. How professionally.

He held out the jeweled hairpin. When she reached to grab it, his fingers closed around hers for a moment.

"You should be more careful with your diamonds, Lady Henrietta," he said huskily. "There are unscrupulous mountebanks about."

The glide of his fingers along her hand set her pulse racing. She retracted her hand but couldn't stop the memories from flooding back. Their kiss on the balcony. The fluttering feeling in her stomach.

"I think it's safe to assume we might begin calling you Cousin Ashbrook soon, eh, my boy?" the duke asked.

"I don't think that's safe to assume at all," Hetty muttered.

"I've been known as Ash my whole life. Suits me better than Ashbrook." He tucked into a plate of coddled eggs and bacon, eating ravenously, and with little finesse.

Everything he did was too big and bold.

She must assert some measure of control over this breakfast parlor. It was all too convivial between her father and Mr. Ellis, as if they'd conspired behind her back and already decided her fate.

"Please do elaborate upon your history, Mr. *Ellis*," she said. "We know that you were raised in an orphanage, and then . . . ?"

"I worked at a London bottling factory." The words were simple and straightforward, but strong emotion marred his face and twisted the words into a curse. "I left the factory and supported myself by . . . various means."

"Such as . . . ?" Hetty prompted.

"You've read the gossip sheets. You know my checkered past."

"More than checkered, Mr. Ellis. You were a member of a roving gang of juvenile pickpockets. Then a gambler."

"I'm not proud of my past." That, at least, was said with absolute sincerity. "But I'm proud of how far I've come. Mr. Smith and I worked our way up. We traveled to the Continent, where we had quite a successful career as professional gamblers."

Card sharps, more like.

She'd met Mr. Smith and found him to have far more elegant manners and a more cultured demeanor than Mr. Ellis, but there'd been a watchfulness to him, a wariness, as though he'd been standing by to ensure that his friend didn't make any mistakes.

Mr. Smith had been poised to jump in and smooth things over.

She could well imagine the two of them had made a formidable pair abroad. One swaggering, the other suave.

Both unscrupulous scoundrels.

"I've been an entrepreneur, just like you propose to be, Lady Henrietta."

"My Hetty is quite dedicated to her wine concern," the duke said.

"Which, I might emphasize, is a legitimate and legal venture," Hetty added.

"My gaming establishment is legal."

"That's debatable."

"Have you been studying law, Lady Henrietta?"

"I know men like you, Mr. Ellis. You think attractive females, or females in general, aren't supposed to use our brains. We're supposed to have no other interests or ambitions outside of marriage and child-rearing."

"Marriage is a noble pursuit, Hetty," said her father. "To perpetuate a family line."

Hetty chose to ignore that. "I'll have you know, Mr. Ellis, that I'm a member of a ladies' society dedicated to the advancement of females in nontraditional roles. Our members number an archaeologist, a chemist, an etymologist, and a symphonic composer. And we have new members from around the world joining every month."

She couldn't tell him about her friend Isobel Mayberry. She was perhaps the most daring member of their club. She was nearly finished with a degree in law, but she was attending under the guise of her brother, a homebound invalid who had given her his full permission to go out and conquer the world in his name.

"Excellent," Mr. Ellis drawled, finishing his coffee. "I'm glad to hear that the bluestocking army is on the march. Are all of your like-minded friends as pretty as you?"

"What's that got to do with anything?"

"Nothing. Just wondering. I might put on a female disguise and sneak into one of the meetings."

"Your shoulders are too wide and your Adam's apple too prominent for such a disguise."

"And you're far too beautiful to be a bluestocking."

"Ha," said the duke. "That's what I always tell her. It's high time Hetty found a husband. I want a grand-child to dandle upon my knee."

Not that again. Why was her father so fixated on the subject?

"Why haven't you contacted our family before now, Mr. Ellis? The timing of your claim is suspect, in my opinion."

"Leave the interrogation for the solicitor, Hetty," her father remonstrated.

"I don't mind at all." Mr. Ellis threw his serviette on the table. "I've nothing to hide."

"Would you like some brandy in your coffee?" the duke asked.

"Need you ask, Your Grace?"

Hetty harrumphed loudly. The two of them were already thick as thieves.

She had to find a way to pull back on the reins, take control over the conversation.

After his brandy was poured, Mr. Ellis returned to her question. "The answer is that I had no idea of the connection. As I mentioned in the gardens, I have memories of my mother speaking in Spanish and telling me that I was a prince. And then I read the humorous piece in the gossip sheets about His Grace hunting for a new duchess. It mentioned a secret marriage and a lost baby descended from a junior line of the family that split off long ago. The baby's mother was rumored to be a scullery maid from Spain. That's when I began to connect the dots, so to speak." He buttered a roll and ate half of it in one bite.

Here we go, thought Hetty. She listened intently, seeking incongruence between his facial expression and his words. Something to give him away.

A slip of the tongue. A cold, avaricious gleam in his eyes.

"I went back to the orphanage and asked them more questions about my origins. One of the matrons finally admitted to me that there was an item on my person when I arrived at the orphanage. She'd kept it all of these years, but it had been weighing on her conscience, and now that she was an old woman, and not long for the world, she wanted to come clean and give me back my legacy. She left the room and returned a few minutes later. With this."

He pulled a gold signet ring out of a waistcoat pocket and handed it to the duke, who held it to the light.

"By Jove, Hetty. This is the Prince family crest."

"And the matron will corroborate your story?" Hetty asked.

"Of course."

"One ring doesn't prove your claim. Why, you could have come by that ring in any number of ways. From a pawnbroker, or you could have won it at cards. It doesn't prove anything."

"I have more evidence, as well. When all of the pieces are fit together, I believe my claim will be incontrovertible, Lady Henrietta."

Nothing she said made a dent in his arrogant demeanor. He was so certain that things would go his way. Try as she might, she couldn't detect any evasion or insincerity in his words or his face.

Either he was an actor worthy of playing Shakespeare's great characters, or he truly believed that he was the heir. Though she had the distinct feeling that he'd rehearsed his part. It was too practiced, too precise. The answers to her questions were ready and delivered without any forethought or hesitation.

Perhaps the proof of his perfidy lay in that. Most people would at least stumble a little or search for the right words to convey their meaning.

He delivered his lines with absolute conviction, every word designed to solidify his claim, and to build doubt in her mind.

"Your past misdeeds make this far more perilous than it would be otherwise," Hetty said. "How are we to be assured that there is no one from your past who holds sway over you, who could blackmail you, or harm the reputation of our family?"

"I give you my word that there is no living person that wishes me harm and could cause you or your family name any embarrassment at my expense."

Was she to trust his word on this? She was about to continue this line of questioning when the butler arrived.

"Mr. Higginbottom is here to see you, Your Grace," Dobbins announced. "I installed him, and his guest, in the Gentian Parlor."

"Guest, Dobbins?" the duke asked.

"A Mrs. Goddard, Your Grace."

The name meant nothing to Hetty. She rose, and her father and Mr. Ellis followed her from the room.

"Your Grace," said Higginbottom in his booming voice when they entered the parlor. "Lady Henrietta. Mr. Ellis." He folded his hands over his rotund belly. "I brought Widow Goddard from Cambridge today for a reason." He nodded at Mrs. Goddard. "Is this man, Mr. Ellis, known to you?"

The widow was middle-aged and red of cheek, her round figure clothed entirely in black, her hair covered by black lace. She gave Mr. Ellis a thorough perusal from his overlong brown hair, down his crooked nose, pausing to widen her eyes at the cut at the side of his lips, taking in his scarred knuckles, and ending with the playing cards embroidered on his waistcoat. "Not at all."

"And were you aware of a secret marriage between your brother, Ashbrook Prince, and a scullery maid in the Prince household by the name of Dolores Vela?"

Now Hetty understood. This woman was related to her—the sister of the distant relation Mr. Ellis was claiming as his father. She was in a position to corroborate or disprove Mr. Ellis's claim. Hetty hung on her next words, holding her breath.

"A very unfortunate business, Mr. Higginbottom," said Mrs. Goddard. "There was a marriage between them, yes. But it was conducted in secret and hidden from our parents for years. Dolores confided in me; I think she was looking for a sympathetic ear. She asked me to help her hasten the announcement of their marriage to the family. I certainly wasn't going to take it upon myself to break our parents' hearts with the news of my brother's inferior match."

Mr. Ellis's expression hardened for a moment, displeasure stamped on his handsome features.

If Dolores Vela had been his mother, then Mrs. Goddard had just insulted her.

"I see, Mrs. Goddard. And so you kept their secret?" Higginbottom asked.

"I did. Ashbrook installed her in a country cottage, promising to send for her when the time was right. I visited her there occasionally. I felt sorry for the girl, as Ashbrook had abandoned her and was carrying on with debutantes and courtesans as if he weren't already secretly married."

"A common tale, I'm afraid. The folly of youth," said the duke. "This is all most interesting. Most interesting, indeed."

Hetty was beginning to feel light-headed. She could feel her chances of persuading her father to deny Mr. Ellis's claim slipping away with every word Mrs. Goddard spoke.

Mr. Higginbottom clasped his hands behind his back and paced the floor of the room, as though he were in court. "And was there a child born to their union, Mrs. Goddard?" he asked.

"There was. Ashbrook had paid his wife a visit, and there was a resulting babe. Unwanted, poor thing. Unloved by any but his mother."

Mr. Ellis closed his eyes briefly, as though her words pained him.

"And did you witness the birth of this child, Mrs. Goddard?" the solicitor asked.

Hetty's heart thudded. This moment would decide her fate.

Mr. Ellis stared intently, waiting for Mrs. Goddard to speak.

"I did," said Mrs. Goddard. "I arrived one week before the birth out of pity for the poor childlike bride who'd done nothing wrong other than fall in love with my brother. I knew that after the child was born, the marriage would have to be made public."

"And the babe, you saw it clearly?"

"As clear as day, sir. The boy was the usual color of red, squalling lustily. He had a great gusty pair of lungs."

"And were there any distinguishing characteristics you noticed on the child?" asked Mr. Higginbottom, clearly reaching his closing arguments.

The widow nodded. "There was a rather unfortunate birthmark on the babe's right hip. A splotch of angry purple in the shape of a spade. I remember thinking at the time that it was the devil's mark on an unwanted babe who would bring only suffering and shame to the Prince family."

Hetty watched Mr. Ellis. He was fighting for control of some strong emotion, his jaw clenching and unclenching, his fists curled by his sides.

"And what happened after that, Mrs. Goddard?" Higginbottom asked.

"A tragic turn of events. A carriage accident stole the lives of my parents and of Ashbrook. Our brother, Gilbert, rest his soul, inherited the house in Cambridge, or rather, believed he'd inherited. Until

Dolores Vela made her claim that her babe was the legitimate heir."

Higginbottom snorted. "I'm quite certain Mr. Gilbert Prince didn't take kindly to such a notion."

"He was livid. He cast her from his sight, telling her never to return and denying all knowledge of her, or her babe."

"And why did you not speak at that point? Why did you not come to her rescue?"

"I had taken ill with a fever; I was on my death-bed, the physician said. I was too delirious to come to anyone's aid. And after I recovered, it was too late. Gilbert would hear no more on the subject. I tried to find Dolores, but they said she'd gone to London. I heard a rumor that she died a pauper's death, poor thing. Brokenhearted and alone. I always assumed the child died with her."

"The missing child. Presumed dead," the duke breathed. "My dear boy." He dashed what appeared to be a tear from his eye. "What an unfortunate beginning you had."

"But I didn't die," said Mr. Ellis, speaking for the first time in clear, ringing tones. "I survived against all odds."

"Blood will tell, Mr. Ellis. You have the family resemblance, and the family spirit and determination," said the duke.

"You, Mr. Ellis?" asked Mrs. Goddard. "You are that lost baby?"

"I am."

"And I will prove it to you," said Higginbottom.

"Ladies, I apologize for the indelicacy of this demonstration, but it's necessary to prove his claim. Mr. Ellis, would you be so kind as to expose your right hipbone?"

Hetty tensed. The duke leaned in. Mrs. Goddard sniffed. "Such goings-on. And in the parlor," she said indignantly. "Though I suppose it's necessary if he's claiming to be the heir."

Mr. Ellis caught Hetty's eye as he shifted his coat out of the way and loosened the flap of his trousers. Sliding the fabric down, he exposed his right hipbone, one of the only areas of his anatomy she'd never seen before. It was covered by a birthmark the color of Burgundy wine, in the rough shape of a spade.

"Is this the birthmark you saw, Mrs. Goddard?" asked the lawyer.

"The very same," she breathed, her face registering astonishment.

And that's when Hetty realized that Mr. Ellis was actually going to win.

Oh, dear God. Her fate, and the fate of Rosehill, were in a scoundrel's hands and nothing she said or did would make any difference.

He rearranged his clothing and flashed her a triumphant grin. "Well, that was all rather dramatic, I must say."

"Dolores named you Ashbrook, of course," said Mrs. Goddard. "And I was named your godmother."

"My dear boy," cried the duke, clapping his hands onto Mr. Ellis's shoulders. "Welcome to the family!"

Chapter Nine

❧ 🌹 ❧

ASH COULDN'T BELIEVE he'd actually won. His plan had worked. He would become a duke. Mrs. Goddard had played her part to perfection. Granville was clasping his shoulders, and everyone except Lady Henrietta was congratulating him.

She clutched the diamond hairpin he'd returned to her as though she wanted to embed it right between his eyes. Her dark hair was swept into a simple knot on top of her head with loose tendrils framing her face. There were roses in her cheeks, a pink flush caused by fury.

She'd fought a good fight, but he was the expert.

He'd won. She finally knew it.

He'd have the title and the power that went with it. He'd use that power to change England's labor laws; in return, he'd restore the family fortune.

Lady Henrietta couldn't see it right now, but everyone won in this game.

Ash smiled at the duke. "I'll be a good heir."

"And not only my heir," the duke cried. "My son-in-law!"

"What did you say, Papa?" asked Lady Henrietta,

the flush in her cheeks deepening to crimson and her brown eyes heating with emotion.

"It's perfectly obvious that you two must marry," said the duke.

"Now wait one moment," Ash said. That hadn't been part of his plan.

"You've gone mad, Papa." Lady Henrietta brushed a wavy lock of brown hair away from her eyes impatiently. "I'm not marrying anyone, especially not Mr. Ellis."

"Mr. Prince, I think you mean," said Mrs. Goddard.

"Capital idea, Your Grace," said Higginbottom. "It's customary for cousins inheriting estates to marry the firstborn daughter, if she's eligible."

Mr. Prince. That was him now. He'd have to become used to the name.

"Mr. Prince is a seventh cousin," said Mrs. Goddard. "The connection is slight. The marriage would be most propitious."

"Propitious it is not," said Lady Henrietta, desperation laced through her voice and scrawled across her lovely face. "I've no idea what put such a ridiculous idea in your head, Papa."

"What I saw on the balcony," the duke replied. "The night of the ball."

Damn. Ash had thought he'd cleared that up. "It was a dark night, Your Grace."

"What did you see, Your Grace?" asked Mrs. Goddard.

The duke smiled gleefully. "They were kissing. Quite passionately."

Mrs. Goddard ducked her chin. "My word. Lady Henrietta, is this true?"

"I, er, that is we were conversing, not—"

"This is very hasty, Your Grace," Ash broke in, before Lady Henrietta dug them a marital grave. He had to find a way out of this thorny new development. He could refuse to marry her, but he didn't want to cross the duke on the very day he'd been unofficially acknowledged. "Please allow us some time to think it over."

"This is unhinged!" said Lady Henrietta.

"You'll thank me someday," said the duke. "Hetty, this is the best and most expedient way to secure your future. Have you thought about what might happen if Cousin Ashbrook were to marry? His new wife might not take kindly to having an attractive cousin living on the estate. Pardon me"—he nodded at Ash—"for insulting your hypothetical future wife's character. Jealousy can make enemies of the closest of friends."

"I'd be happy to sign papers stating that Lady Henrietta could stay on at the estate in perpetuity," said Ash.

"No, m'boy, my mind's quite made up. You're precisely the stubborn fellow to go head-to-head with my daughter. She needs taming. You'll be married as swiftly as possible. Of course you'll have to sell your share in The Devil's Staircase. I know Hetty would never approve of such goings-on—isn't that right, m'dear?"

"I don't approve of *any* of these goings-on," she said with a wild look in her eyes.

"And then you two must immediately set about producing grandchildren for me," continued the duke. "Ho then, Higginbottom, let's get to the *bottom* of these legal documents, what? And then the bottom of a whisky bottle." He chuckled as he started to lead the solicitor and Mrs. Goddard out of the room.

"Don't leave, Papa. I beg of you to reconsider this insanity. You can't force us to marry. This isn't the Dark Ages."

"Father knows best, m'dear," said the duke, dragging Higginbottom and Mrs. Goddard, who'd been watching the proceedings with interest, from the room.

Ash dropped into a chair, his shoulders hitting the blue brocade with a thud.

He'd been completely caught off guard, which didn't happen often, as he made it his business to anticipate every opponent's next move. "Well, that was unexpected. This is where you say, 'I wouldn't marry you if you were the last scoundrel on earth.'"

"You took the words right out of my mouth. This is a nightmare." She began pacing the length of the room, then whirled on him. "Was this your plan all along? Kissing me, being declared the heir, and then marrying me?"

Ash smiled. "I believe that *you* kissed *me*, Lady Henrietta." And what a kiss it had been. He'd been reliving it ever since in glorious detail. "You're ravishing, but I've no wish to marry you. You or anyone else. I wasn't planning to marry for another decade, if ever."

"Now that you've been proved to be the heir,

though I still have my doubts, you'll have to marry and sire an heir."

"No one tells me what to do."

"And no one tells me what to do, either. Do you think I'd marry the man who wants to turn my vineyards into stud yards?" She paused her pacing, narrowing her eyes. "He can't force us to marry."

"You're right. I'll flatly refuse."

"No, *I'll* refuse."

She resumed her pacing. "I would only be a possession to you. A symbol of wealth and power, like the dukedom. The highborn wife. The ancestral pile. I'll never be relegated to such an untenable position. I'm not some trinket to be purchased, then discarded and ignored."

"Er . . . did you hear what I just said? I have no desire to marry you."

She continued on as if he hadn't spoken. "I've enjoyed a gratifying amount of freedom in my life, and today I've seen it all taken away. The news that my father is insolvent, and that you are, ostensibly, the heir to the dukedom. It's all too much."

"I'll say it once more. I have no designs upon you."

"But you have designs upon my vineyards."

"They're not profitable enough. If I'm to replenish the family coffers, I'll only invest in lucrative ventures."

"They can be profitable. I only need a little more time to make them so." A wistfulness washed across her face, like rain misting a window. "You haven't seen the vineyards yet. The way the sun dances through the bright green leaves, and the wind sets them trembling. Rosehill is renowned for its gardens and vineyards. It's a magnificent estate." Her gaze focused on him again, sharpening from dreamy to derisive. "Why, oh why, wasn't I born male? Then I would be the heir and you'd be only a wicked scoundrel the scandal sheets warned me against."

"I didn't make the laws of England, Lady Henrietta." Though he was going to change some of them.

"Males hold all the power in the world when female shoulders are just as capable of bearing loads, and female intellect is more than equal to that of males. I always knew that my uncle would inherit one day, but I explained the duties I'd assumed on the estate and he'd agreed that I could stay on and manage the vineyards."

"I'm not asking you to leave, Lady Henrietta. I'm only proposing a more profitable use for the lands."

"If you think I'll silently stand by while you make sweeping changes, while you undo all of my arduous work, you'll be sorely disappointed."

She was prickly, but he understood why. She'd been forced out of necessity to assume the role of both her father's caretaker and the manager of his affairs.

She'd been given a freedom that few women of her class ever experienced. And she'd grown powerful with it.

A qualm touched his heart, something like regret. He didn't like to lie to her, even by omission. A woman so powerful, and so magnificent, deserved honesty.

Some lies were necessary for the greater good.

"I promise you that I won't make any changes without consulting you first, and I'll bear the welfare of both servants and tenants in mind. My improvements and investments can only benefit the entire estate."

She turned her face away. "You sit there making these glib promises, while I stand and prepare to fight."

"I know it's not the gentlemanly thing to do. Please don't mistake me for a gentleman. I may be a duke's heir, but I'm every inch my own man. I've grown my success in life from stony soil. I know adversity and I know poverty. I will be a good landlord because of those origins."

"That doesn't settle the matter of my vineyards."

"I've done the calculations, Lady Henrietta." He softened his voice. "Your vineyards may be magnificent, but they're not making any profit."

"They're all I know. They're the life I've built for myself."

"Your debut was cut short by duties," he said gently. "You never had a chance to know any other life."

"I did what I had to do."

There was an entire universe of hurt in those words, in the curt way she said them.

Her mother had died. And her father had slid into grief and then into near ruin.

"You've lived an unconventional life, Lady Henrietta. And you'll continue to do so when I inherit."

"Forgive me if I find that difficult to believe."

"Perhaps your father does know best."

"Are you suggesting that we marry?" she asked with a horrified expression that, truth be told, did little for his vanity.

"Of course not," he said hastily. "I'm only suggesting that your father wishes to see you comfortably settled and secure."

"Ah." Her eyes turned stormy. "So now you're suggesting that I marry someone else, instead."

It would take the pressure off him. Though for some reason, the idea of Lady Henrietta shackling herself to some unworthy fop made his blood boil.

"I've absolutely no wish to marry," she said. "And even if I did, you're the very antithesis of every quality I would require of a husband. I made a list of requirements before my debut. You fulfill precisely none of them."

"Oh, I'm sure I could fulfill a few of them. Judging by that kiss, we'd suit each other in *some* pursuits, at least."

She crossed her arms. "I'm a spinster and happy to be one."

She could say that, but she didn't mean it. There was a soft, romantic, and intensely passionate heart beating inside the nettlesome Lady Henrietta.

There was still a part of her that yearned to be loved and admired. She never would have kissed him with such abandon if she hadn't been giving in to some deep-seated longing.

"You're hardly a spinster. Have you looked in the glass lately? You could have any man you chose."

"I choose no man." She lifted her chin in a stubborn movement. "Is that so difficult to understand, Mr. Ellis?"

"Not at all, Lady Henrietta," he said. "I've no plans for marriage, either. We are in complete agreement on this."

A small smile played about her lips. "I think this is the first time we've ever agreed upon anything."

For just a moment, Ash glimpsed what she would look like if she were happy. She was so vividly alive. Somehow more filled with life than anyone he'd ever met. She attacked him as she tackled life, with resourcefulness and conviction. With ambition and cleverness.

Make no mistake, the vibrant and stunning Lady Henrietta Prince would make some man a spirited and passionate wife.

Just not him.

Chapter Ten

❧ 🌹 ❧

*E*VERY TIME HETTY walked through the doors of the Boadicea Club for ladies on the Strand, she felt a surge of pride and pleasure. Despite the matters weighing her down, she knew that beyond this threshold was a safe and welcoming haven.

No one questioned her ambitions here.

No one spoke as if her only function in life was to marry and bear children.

She left her bonnet with Mr. Coggins, the dour and doddering old doorman who was the only male allowed upon the premises, except by special invitation.

A lively game of shuttlecock and battledore between Miss Ardella Finchley and Lady Beatrice Wright was in session in the back courtyard.

"Henrietta!" Her friend Isobel greeted her at the door.

"Isobel." They clasped hands for a moment. It had been months since she'd seen most of her friends. Today wasn't a scheduled meeting, which were usually long affairs, beginning in the afternoon and ending sometimes well into the evening.

Hetty always supplied the libations for these

meetings, and the subjects ranged from the ambitions and goals of the society members to interesting topics such as bawdy books, marital relations, and what went on inside men's clubhouses, something Isobel was able to regale them with because she lived half her life in disguise as a man.

They had lessons in defending themselves with pistols or improvised weaponry such as hat pins or knitting needles from the Duchesses of Ravenwood and Thorndon, and they could play games in the back courtyard.

There was a chemistry lab off the kitchens where Ardella concocted potions with noxious fumes, a reading room upstairs for quiet scholarship, and this large sitting room downstairs where they conducted their meetings at the table or sat around the fire to discuss their lives.

It really was the most wonderful, welcoming place for independent-minded women in all of London.

Isobel led her into the central room, where Viola was sitting by the fire reading a book.

"I see there's another embroidery over the mantel." Hetty grinned as she read the words stitched so prettily in curving vines and flowers over white muslin: *I do not wish women to have power over men; but over themselves.* "Another Mary Wollstonecraft quote to add to our collection."

"Philippa's been busy of late. It's her way of rebelling. She sits in her home of an evening, quietly embroidering, and no one ever asks to see the result."

"Hetty!" Viola jumped up when she saw her. "Have you found a way to disprove Mr. Ellis's claim?"

"Far from it."

"Come and sit down," Viola said. "I'll gather the others and ask Mrs. Kettle for some of her famously restorative tea."

"Thank you." Hetty suddenly felt teary-eyed, and she wasn't given to weeping.

Isobel led her to a chair and made her comfortable, and Viola went off to gather the other club members and order the tea.

When the five women were gathered in a semicircle of chairs, Hetty began. "I know Viola may have told you some of what's been happening, about Mr. Ash Ellis, The Devil's Own Scoundrel, making a claim to my father's dukedom."

"She did tell us," said Beatrice, her abundant flame-red hair windswept. "And we are most indignant on your behalf."

"Well, you've heard that Mr. Ellis attended my father's ball under false pretenses and laid claim to the dukedom. What you don't know yet is that he's now been proved to be the heir."

"And how did he manage to do that?" Isobel asked.

"My father's solicitor brought a distant relation, Mrs. Faye Goddard, to the house, and she testified to the secret marriage between her brother, Ashbrook Prince, and a scullery maid. She was also present at the birth of the child of that union and stated that the babe had a distinguishing birthmark shaped like a spade. At which point Mr. Ellis lowered his trousers over his hips." She closed her eyes. She would *not* picture that with anything other than censure.

"And revealed the very birthmark she'd described. I swear to you it was like something out of a Daphne Villeneuve novel."

Miss Villeneuve was their favorite authoress. She published one Gothic romance per year, and the ladies all looked forward breathlessly to the latest volume. Though this year's romance was quite late, and the publisher could give them no news on the arrival date yet.

Mrs. Kettle, the kindly housekeeper at the club, arrived and poured tea for all of them.

"Thank you, Mrs. Kettle," Beatrice said.

"Oh dear," said Viola sympathetically. "Perhaps we ought to add a spot of brandy to our tea?"

"Viola," Beatrice remonstrated. "It's half two in the afternoon."

"Yes, but it's five o'clock somewhere in the world."

"I should have brought some wine," Hetty said. "But I'm so flustered, I hardly know whether I'm coming or going. My life's been turned inside out."

She felt like a vine that had been pruned too violently, and too early, and she was withering from the suddenness of the wound.

"We'll help you set it to rights." Isobel poured a little brandy into the tea, and they all had a calming drink.

"So there's proof," Isobel muttered.

"Why do men scour their family trees for distant male cousins and find that preferable to daughters inheriting?" Beatrice asked. "The archaic laws of primogeniture make not one jot of sense."

"It's because property is power," Isobel said. "Plain and simple. Men want to keep the power for themselves."

Viola sighed. "I'm so sorry, Hetty. I know how much you loathe Mr. Ellis."

"It gets worse, ladies," Hetty said. "Much, much worse." She sipped her tea. "My father has squandered our fortune. And he's demanding that I marry Mr. Ellis."

"That's preposterous. You can't be forced to marry someone you don't want to," exclaimed Isobel, nearly apoplectic with outrage.

"Is he suggesting you marry the man, or decreeing it?" Ardella, whom they all called Della, asked. She was a brilliant chemist, but her clothing was always in a state of disarray.

"I'm not sure yet, but it feels like a betrayal on the grandest of scales. Throughout Papa's decline, he never did anything to curtail my freedom. Quite the opposite—his disappearance from the day-to-day chores of life gave me free rein over the estate. Which is a great responsibility and has become my greatest joy. But now he wants to make this momentous decision over my life. He actually said, 'Father knows best.'"

"Ugh," Isobel groaned.

"He wants me to wed a scoundrel who calls me girlie," said Hetty.

"No," breathed Beatrice. "Mr. Ellis didn't call you that."

"He did. Viola is my witness."

"I was there. He called her girlie," Viola confirmed.

"And she called him about ten rude things. They may as well have drawn their sabers in the middle of the gaming hell. I felt as though I were witnessing a duel."

"What were you doing in a gaming hell?" Della asked.

"It's a long story," said Hetty. "I'm still attempting to make sense of all of the twists and turns of the past two days. I've no intention of marrying Mr. Ellis."

Viola's brow wrinkled. "What makes the duke think that you two should marry?"

"He came up with the plan while Mr. Ellis and I were arguing this morning. He said he thought we were perfect for one another and that we must marry swiftly and produce an heir. I protested, of course, but he was being so obstinate, and Mr. Ellis just sat there with a smirk on his face."

"Odious man," said Beatrice. "He might have made some objection."

"He did," Hetty replied. "But only later, when we were alone. He said he had no wish to marry in general, and no wish to marry me in particular."

"He sounds perfectly dreadful," said Della.

"I can't marry him."

"You certainly can't," Beatrice agreed.

"What was Papa thinking?"

"I suppose," ventured Viola, "perhaps he was thinking of your future? Because if Mr. Ellis were to remarry, then you would be second best on the estate."

"And if I marry him, he'll own me. Such are the

marriage laws of England. I've heard your horror stories, Isobel. The women who were declared insane and committed to asylums against their will, to convenience their cruel husbands, and allow them to control the estate."

"The laws are in desperate need of reform," Isobel said fiercely. She specialized in helping females inherit and retain property.

"I'm willing to admit that my father might mean well," Hetty said, "but this isn't right. Mr. Ellis runs a gaming hell, for Heaven's sake! And he covets the land by the river at Rosehill for Thoroughbred stables. He says my vineyards aren't profitable."

Beatrice pursed her lips. "The scurrilous scoundrel!"

"I have to tell you, ladies, I'm considering desperate measures. I'm actually thinking about marrying the man in order to increase my chances of influencing him to allow me to keep the vineyards."

"What's he like?" Della asked.

"Rude. Domineering. Arrogant. He wears bombastic waistcoats embroidered with playing cards. He forced me to waltz with him." Hetty paused. She was among friends. "And then I kissed him."

"Pardon?" asked Isobel.

"Kissed him?" asked Beatrice. "Do you mean that you kissed him in your thoughts? That's exactly what happened to me with Ford. He climbed into my library window and forced me to have wanton imaginings about kissing."

"This was no imagined embrace. I was remembering my debut, and all my girlhood dreams, and I rose onto my tiptoes and I placed my lips against his."

At their shocked expressions, she hastened to add, "I didn't know he was The Devil's Own Scoundrel when I kissed him. I thought he was a rakish cousin of one of the ladies I'd invited to the ball. I certainly didn't know he was after the dukedom."

Della regarded Hetty with curiosity. "Was he gentlemanly about it?"

"Ha. He's no gentleman," Hetty replied. "I joked about crossing kissing off my list and never thinking of it again. Then he told me that I couldn't cross anything off my list because that hadn't been a real kiss and then he . . ."

"Yes?" several of the ladies spoke in unison, gazes transfixed.

"He backed me up against the wall, hauled me into his arms, and kissed me so thoroughly and with such authority that I melted against him, I'm ashamed to admit, like a complete ninny."

"Right then," said Isobel. "You can't marry him. I won't allow it."

"Perhaps she can reform him," said Beatrice. "My Ford was a rogue, and he fancied himself irresistible to ladies. But now only one lady will do."

"Ford is a good, honorable man," said Isobel. "And Mr. Ellis is a cheat and a scoundrel."

"Hetty, this is horrible," said Della. "You're the most staunchly independent woman I know."

All of the ladies nodded their agreement.

"Yes, but I need him more than he needs me." And it was killing her. "I feel as though all of the power has been taken away from me. I don't know how to regain my footing."

"Let me sharpen my quill," said Isobel, rising from her chair. "I'll make a list of pros and cons. We'll approach the topic rationally."

"Thank you, Isobel. I usually love making lists," said Hetty. "I've been so distraught about all of this that I haven't been thinking clearly." Her brain had been scrambled ever since the kiss. It was high time to reassert control over her thoughts and her life.

Isobel returned with her writing desk. "Give me your arguments for and against marrying the man."

"I know next to nothing about him except what I read in the scandal sheets, and what he's told me," Hetty said. "I have some details gleaned from my father's solicitor. A shady past that includes bare-knuckle boxing, gambling, and working in a wine-bottling factory when he was a child. He could have skeletons in his past that could prove disastrous for the family name."

Isobel wrote that down. "He's a scoundrel: con. Potential skeletons in his past: con." She raised her head. "Hopefully not literal skeletons."

"One would hope," said Hetty.

"He's remarkably handsome," said Viola.

Isobel snorted. "Is that a pro or a con?"

"Well, it would help in the heir-begetting scenario," said Viola with a guilty little smile. "I'm only saying that he's quite easy on the eyes."

"I find that to be a con," Hetty said. "He uses his good looks like a weapon. He thinks he holds sway over me."

"His pleasing appearance is a con, then." Isobel added it to her list.

"And there is the small matter of the fact that I don't love him," Hetty said.

"Yes, there's that," Beatrice agreed. "I can vouch for a marriage based on love and mutual respect. Ford and I are very happy."

Almost annoyingly so, Hetty thought, though she'd never admit as much to her friend.

Several of the members of the club had married for love, and whenever Hetty saw them with their partners, they looked so . . . connected. Their lives woven together by love and by a mutual trust and desire.

"It's not that I was hoping for a love match," she said. "I'd given up on any such foolish notions, but to marry someone I not only don't love but can't trust . . ."

"Lack of love and trust: con," said Isobel, her quill scratching across the page.

"Yet it's still quite common in society, these marriages of convenience," said Viola. "One can't always marry for love. There are family obligations, monetary issues, dependents to consider."

Isobel's pen flowed across the page.

"What are you writing?" Hetty asked.

"The fact that you don't love him deserves a longer entry. Marrying him means that you can't marry anyone else, thus eliminating your chance for a love match. As we've learned from watching several of our friends make such matches, true affection between partners can make marriage a pleasant occurrence."

"Love and chemistry," said Viola.

"Chemistry?" Hetty asked.

"Della explained all about it at our last meeting, the one you missed," Beatrice said.

"I gave a lecture on the role of scent, and its chemistry, in attraction between the sexes," explained Della.

"And then Lady Philippa gave a lecture on attraction and repulsion in the animal kingdom based on her observations when she accompanied her father on one his naturalist expeditions," Viola said.

"Oh. Well . . ." Hetty took a sip of tea. "There is, if I'm being honest, perhaps a slight element of attraction."

Skin-deep only. She responded to his virility, his self-assuredness.

"You would make very handsome children," said Viola.

"I'd given up on the idea of motherhood," Hetty said. "I'm not sure how I feel about it now."

"I'll add 'motherhood' to the neutral column then, shall I?" asked Isobel.

"Well . . ." Hetty paused for a moment. She'd once wanted to be a mother. "I think I would make a very good mother."

"I'll add it to the pro column, then," Isobel said with a gentle smile.

"Of course, to have a child, I would have to share his bed."

"A con?" Isobel asked.

"Sharing a marital bed with him does seem rather . . . daunting."

"I'll add that to the neutral column," said Isobel with a decisive nod. "Marital relations with The Devil's Own Scoundrel could be a con, or a pro."

"As his wife you might be able to influence him to allow you to keep your vineyards, Hetty," Viola reminded her.

"A pro." Isobel added this to the growing list.

"But there would be the loss of independence," said Della. "Of freedom."

"Or you might fall in love and live happily ever after."

"Beatrice!" Hetty remonstrated.

"Well, I'm just saying that it's been known to happen."

"You're a romantic."

"I wasn't before I met Ford. Love changes everything. Is Mr. Ellis a bad person, do you think?"

"He's done bad things," said Hetty. "But I don't suppose I feel that he's truly evil. He's infuriating. And he makes me want to scream. And he makes me feel so . . . so flummoxed."

For some reason, an image of his cat sprang to mind, licking her paws and wrapping herself around his boots. The fact that he'd kept the cat was one of the reasons she didn't think he was entirely bad.

"There is one other item," she said. "He has a cat. An enormous fluffy princess of a cat named Lucy. Although he calls her Lucifer and curses at her, but I think he secretly adores her."

Isobel gave her a puzzled look. "And that is . . . ?"

"A pro. I didn't expect it of him in the least."

"And you know this how?" asked Viola.

"I . . ." Drat. She hadn't planned to admit her folly. "I snuck into his apartments to search for evidence, and he caught me."

"Hetty! You promised me you wouldn't do anything dangerous," chided Viola.

"I know, it was reckless. And I made a mess of everything. That's how I discovered his plans for my vineyards."

"What's the result, Isobel?" Della asked.

"Inconclusive. It's almost evenly divided between pros and cons."

Hetty sighed. "I know."

"What does your heart tell you to do?" asked Beatrice.

"My heart says to keep my vineyards and my position at the estate no matter the cost."

"You shouldn't have to give up your dreams, Hetty," Della said.

"I think some of what you're feeling is stemming from the fact that the choice has been taken away from you," Beatrice said with a catch in her voice. "If it were your choice, and if you could impose your own conditions, it might not be so objectionable."

Hetty finished her brandy-tea. "You could be right. I've been feeling so out of sorts because all of this was being done *to* me, not *by* me."

"You could draft your own list of marital conditions," said Isobel. "I'd help you."

"I've been considering myself to be the victim in all of this, but perhaps . . . perhaps I could be the victor?" Hetty wondered.

"And why not?" Viola said. "You're the most clever, driven, and ambitious woman I know."

"He could be nothing more than a means to an end."

"I think you're right," said Isobel. "If he signs a carefully worded marriage contract, you'll still maintain control."

"The only problem is that he doesn't want to marry me. He told me in very emphatic terms."

"I think he'll marry you if you frame it in the right way," Della said. "You say that he doesn't need you, but that's not really true, is it? He has a terrible reputation, the worst, really. Even I've heard of him, and I never pay attention to gossip."

"He won't be easily accepted into society," said Beatrice. "Many people still cut Ford, and, by extension, me." Beatrice had married a handsome rogue of a carpenter who was far below her on the social ladder.

Viola sat up straighter. "You could make a bargain with him."

"A deal with the devil," said Beatrice. "You could offer to smooth his entrée into society and, in exchange, he would agree to allow you the time to attempt to make your vineyards profitable."

Isobel tapped her pen against the paper. "A bargain is a means of regaining your footing."

"I still don't like the idea of you having to marry someone you loathe in order to save your lands. Women should not be forced to make those choices," said Della.

"But this is the world we live in," said Hetty. "We seek to better the lot of women, but we must work within the system. We must create change from the inside out."

"You're right, as usual," said Della. "You've got a pragmatic and sensible head on your shoulders."

"But what if you fall in love with him?" Viola asked. "And he crushes your heart, just as he intends to trample upon your vineyards?"

"I won't allow myself to fall in love with him." Hetty squared her shoulders. "I'll remain completely in control of my heart at all times." It sounded easy when she said it here, surrounded by her dear, supportive friends.

"We'll be here for you every step of the way," Beatrice assured her. "You're not alone."

"Thank you, all. This has been overwhelming but now that I have a plan I feel much more resolute and centered. I'm very fortunate to have such loyal friends."

Mrs. Kettle arrived to refresh the tea. "Why, ladies, whatever is the matter? You look so grim, as though you'll soon be marching off to battle."

"Henrietta is going to be married," Viola announced.

"Bless my heart alive! How exciting. Congratulations, dearie." Mrs. Kettle bestowed a delighted smile upon Hetty.

"Yes, but she's marrying the very devil himself," said Della.

"Goodness. Is that advisable?" asked Mrs. Kettle with a worried expression.

"Probably not," Hetty replied. "But it's what I must do. And I'll do it on my own terms."

Chapter Eleven

TODAY WAS THE day Ash's life changed forever. Today he signed the paperwork to place him on top of the world. And from that lofty position, he would reform the laws governing child labor.

He'd worn his favorite scarlet waistcoat, and he had a matching scarlet rose boutonniere tucked into his lapel. He didn't know whether he'd see Lady Henrietta, and he wasn't trying to impress anyone, but he thought he should look the part of a ducal heir.

He'd just had some very good news from Mrs. Badger. Toby had returned to the boarding house, a little frightened, but unharmed. He refused to talk about what had happened, but Ash would coax it out of him soon. In the meantime, he'd hired a guard for the house, and Mrs. Badger was keeping a very close eye on the children.

The parlor maid who backed out of the entrance hall of Granville House upon his arrival gave him an admiring glance, and he gave her a wink.

"Dobbins, is it?" Ash asked the tall, grave-faced butler who greeted him.

"Yes, sir."

"Do you know why I'm here, Dobbins?"

"It's not my business to conjecture, sir."

"Tight-lipped, are we?"

"Discretion is my profession."

"Ha. That rhymed. A poet butler. I like it. I should think you and I shall get along famously, Dobbins."

"I'm sure we will, sir."

Dobbins showed Ash into a bright, sunny sitting room, where Lady Henrietta was bent over a desk, scribbling away at something.

Ash drew Dobbins aside. "I'm meant to meet with the duke this morning."

"Yes, sir, but Lady Henrietta asked for an audience with you first."

Interesting. Ash entered the room and Dobbins closed the door behind him.

"Mr. Ellis." She didn't glance up from her desk.

"Lady Henrietta." He made a deep bow.

"I'll be with you in one moment."

Her abundant dark brown hair had been twisted into an untidy knot at the back of her head. She wore a simple brown cotton gown with a high neckline. She looked tired. There were smudges of blue beneath her eyes and fine lines bracketing her mouth that only served to call attention to her lush lips.

Even in workaday clothing and with a lack of sleep, she was dazzling. Every time he saw her, it nearly bowled him over.

Ash glanced around the room. No footmen posted. No maids. Even more interesting.

The lady wanted an unchaperoned meeting.

"There." She set down her pen. "The guidelines are drafted."

"Guidelines for . . . ?"

"Our marital union."

The suddenness of it took him aback. He was never taken aback. He was the one who set other people off balance. Damned if he was going to stand in front of her desk like some schoolboy before a governess, being set off-kilter and ambushed.

He took a seat and propped his boots up on a footstool. "Uh . . . forgive me if my memory is faulty, but the last time we spoke, you swore you would never marry me if I was the last scoundrel on earth."

"Those were your words, but, yes, that was my initial reaction. I've since reconsidered. I have a business proposition for you."

He folded his hands behind his head and leaned back in the chair. "I'm listening."

"You've been acknowledged as the heir to the dukedom. I don't like it and I don't trust it." Her eyes narrowed. "I don't trust *you*, not as far as I could throw you."

"Which wouldn't be very far."

"I've had to make a difficult choice. You can have me as your sworn enemy, attempting to sabotage and undermine you at every step of the way. Or . . ." She rubbed a smudge of ink from her hand. "You can have me as your doting, devoted bride. At least when we are in public."

"As far as proposals go, it's not the most romantic."

"Romance has nothing to do with this. I want

security and independence. I don't want to be cast out of my own house and have my dreams trampled upon by Thoroughbred hooves. If you're looking for a love match, this won't be it."

"Love isn't on the table. It's a dangerous vulnerability. Love is what ruined my mother and sent her to a pauper's grave. If I marry you, it will be for profit."

"And that's exactly what I'm offering." She tidied her desk as she spoke, arranging the inkwell, pens, and paper in precise alignment. "My father has announced his intention to marry his mistress, flying in the face of all convention. Which means that his impending fall from grace will only add fuel to the wildfire of scandal that will be ignited when you are publicly declared heir to this dukedom."

"And scandal is what you fear the most."

"It's not good for growing a reputable wine business."

"How would our marriage prevent scandal?"

"It wouldn't prevent it, per se, but it would help to shift attention and change the story line. Don't think you will gain entrance to the exclusive gentleman's clubs and simply force the influential men to waltz with you. It won't work. The prejudice against outsiders and upstarts of unsavory origin is too entrenched."

"I know it well."

"Here's my proposal: I'll serve as your introduction to society in lieu of my father. I'll be so enthusiastically supportive of you, so devoted and glowingly approving of your rapid transformation from scoundrel to scion, and I'll introduce and recommend you to so many powerful dukes, that London's finest will have no choice but to accept you as one of their own."

"This all sounds very promising, except that you mentioned a transformation. I have no intention of changing to fit into society."

"Ha." She rolled her eyes. "Does your arrogance know no bounds? Of course you have to change. At least outwardly. You're The Devil's Own Scoundrel. The memory of your transgressions won't soon be forgotten. I thought you wanted the power and prestige that accompany the title?"

"I'll be The Devil's Own Duke. They'll have to do things *my* way."

"My father's still hearty and hale. You won't be any kind of duke for quite some time, God willing. And I'm not going to marry The Devil's Own Heir."

"You just said you wanted to marry me."

"I'll marry an astute businessman who realizes the benefit of conforming to society's expectations for the purposes of persuasion. You must be rehabilitated if you wish to have any hope of bending society to your will. You think you'll succeed by sheer brute mastery. But society requires more subtlety than that."

"And what are the stakes for you, Lady Henrietta?"

"My vineyards. If I agree to help you conquer society, then you'll agree to give me time to prove the profitability of my wine venture. Your stables are nothing but a drawing on a piece of paper and one Thoroughbred stud. I'm on the cusp of success. I've invited Mr. Ross to tour the vineyards and taste my new wines. If he gives me a favorable description in the new edition of *A World of Wines*, my reputation will be established. Your stables wouldn't be profitable for years."

Even though he hadn't thought to marry for at least a decade, if ever, he could see the sense in everything she was saying. He could allow her time to attempt to increase the profits from her wine venture. There was no way she'd succeed.

"I can see how it would be mutually beneficial," he said grudgingly. "I'll give you three months to turn a profit."

She frowned. "That's not enough time. I'll require one year."

"Six months. It's my final offer."

"It's a bargain." She drew a line across some of the text on the page before her. "You agree to give me six months."

"I can't go around being too soft-hearted. It might ruin my reputation."

"I intend to ruin your abominable reputation quite thoroughly. The campaign to rehabilitate you in the eyes of society will begin immediately upon our engagement. You'll need a complete do-over."

"That sounds ominous."

"Your outward appearance will be the easiest task."

"What's wrong with my appearance?"

"You must project *to the manor born.* You're good-looking enough but rough around the edges. You'll need a haircut. And your scarlet waistcoats." She glanced at the offending garment. "Don't get me started on those."

"I like my waistcoats. They're my signature."

"They're an affront to taste and fashion. And those old scuffed boots you're wearing."

"They're the most comfortable boots in the world."

"They have to go."

"I love these boots. You can't take them away." Ash shoved his hand through his hair. "I don't see what waistcoats and boots have to do with persuading society to accept me."

"They have everything to do with it. A true gentleman does not advertise his wealth in a vulgar manner. His worth, both monetary and of character, is evident in the cut of his cloth, the sheen and fit of his boots, and the manner in which he speaks and carries himself."

"I'll play the role to perfection."

"Once I've seen to your new wardrobe. You'll have to trust me on this matter. Believe me, I don't make this bargain lightly. That's why I wrote a list of guidelines and rules."

"Do your rules cover all aspects of the marriage?"

"They're very comprehensive."

"Even the bedding part?"

"Especially that. We must attempt to procreate. I'm resigned to the idea."

"You're going to love the procreating part."

She folded her hands together. "Is that a yes to my business proposition?" Her eyes held hope and determination.

"I haven't read all the guidelines yet."

"They're very simple. After a suitable period of feigned marital bliss wherein I facilitate your transition into the upper echelons of society, we'll lead largely separate lives, much like other marriages of convenience among my peers. The rearing of any offspring resulting from our union will be entrusted to me, and so on, and so forth."

He rose and walked to the desk, reading over her shoulder. "What's this about my by-blows? I don't have any illegitimate children."

"Really? I saw the document about the boarding house you're funding."

"Don't believe everything you read in the papers. Those aren't my children by blood."

"Oh. I thought . . ."

"You thought I had fathered a dozen children. While I'm flattered by your estimation of my virility and appetites, in this case my ill-repute is unmerited."

He read the rest of the guidelines over her shoulder. "You've thought of everything. Planned everything out. But rules are meant to be broken. Makes life more interesting."

"Rule-breakers are heedless people who care little for the thoughts and feelings of those around them."

He placed his hand over hers, guiding her finger to the page. "This rule. I don't like it." Her skin was soft and her hair smelled like roses in a rainstorm. He bent closer and ran his thumb lightly over the pulse that beat at her wrist.

The floor swayed beneath his boots, as though touching her triggered a subterranean quake.

"The guideline governing conjugal visits is most sensible," she said, but her voice faltered, and a blush rose in her cheeks.

He brushed his lips against her ear. "Is it? One conjugal visit per week, not to exceed one hour in length. I think you're going to want to revise that limit—in fact, you may want to strike this one altogether. I predict that you'll want to stay in my bed for days. You'll develop a taste for it. A craving."

"You'll never lead me down the devil's staircase. You'll never turn me into a wanton."

"And yet you think that you can reform me."

"I'm going to try."

"And I'm skilled in the art of seduction. I like my odds."

"What might work on the women of your prior acquaintance may not work on me at all."

"I've found certain techniques to be remarkably effective. I'll have you begging for my touch."

"Never."

"Care to place a wager on that, Lady Henrietta?"

"I NEVER PLACE wagers," Hetty said firmly.

His hand still covered hers. He was so formidable standing behind her, his chest touching her shoulder, his breath against her cheek. He had her trapped against the desk.

Every nuance of his behavior was deliberately and aggressively male.

"What are you so afraid of?" he asked. "That you'll enjoy yourself in my bed? I saw that passionate side of you on the balcony."

"That was an aberration. It was the memory of my debut and the wine. Not you."

"Is that so? I'd like to see you remain indifferent when we kiss again."

He set her on edge. That was the only way to describe it. As though she were a child's top and he'd launched her mind into spinning motion.

"I think you'll enjoy yourself so much that you'll want to disport every evening. Maybe even some mornings. Or some delightful afternoons, in the dappled sunlight with a glass of wine by the bedside."

Her mind produced images to go along with his words. His deep, rough voice guiding her into ever more vivid imaginings.

And in her imaginings, there was definitely no towel.

Did people really have congress in the afternoon? She'd have to ask her married friends about it.

It was difficult to think clearly when he was whispering such carnal, suggestive things in her ear.

If she turned her head, her lips would meet his. A craving built inside her for another kiss. A deeper one.

He was going to kiss her. She tensed, summoning the willpower to stop him, to run away.

Who was she fooling? She wouldn't run away. She might even turn her head, offer him her lips . . .

"You're wrong," she whispered. "You'll never corrupt me. I'll never beg for your touch."

He released her hand. "I'll corrupt you before you can even begin to reform me."

"I'll take that wager," Hetty said bravely. Foolishly. "And I'll win it."

He released her hand. "Shall we go and tell your father the glad tidings?"

"He'll want us to be married by special license, as swiftly as possible."

"I'm all eagerness." He bowed. "The sooner we reach the wedding chapel, the sooner I'll win the wager."

Chapter Twelve

❧ 🌹 ❧

"There's been a development," Ash told Jax when he returned to the gaming house.

Jax looked up from the accounting books. "A problem?"

"Same problem as before, only in a different form. The suspicious Lady Henrietta."

"Or, as I like to call her, Lady Spitfire."

"She's decided to come to terms with the inevitable—that I'm the rightful heir."

"That's a good development."

"But she's decided that her father's right. We should marry."

"You told me she refused to marry you when the duke sprang the idea on you."

"The old goat's marrying his mistress, and apparently that will make him *persona non grata* in society. She proposed a bargain. She'll play the doting wife and introduce me to a lot of pretentious dukes, and she'll stay at Rosehill and attempt to convince me to allow her to continue with her little winemaking endeavor."

"I like a lady with a plan. What's the problem?"

Ash was having difficulty articulating it to himself, let alone someone else. He sat down opposite Jax. "A woman as independent as Lady Henrietta doesn't like to have her choice taken away. This bargain she's struck is her only hope of balancing the scales. It doesn't feel right to marry an unwilling woman."

"Ha!" Jax jabbed him in the arm with his finger. "You're having qualms."

"Don't be an idiot."

Men in Ash's profession capitalized the word *Qualms* in speech as though it were a communicable disease. There were qualms and there were instincts. Ash had learned to trust his instincts above all else. He listened to the little voice in his head that told him whether someone was bluffing or not.

Qualms were something else, entirely. Qualms meant you didn't finish a game.

You folded. You lost.

"No qualms," he said forcefully, slapping his palm against the oak desk. "In for a dukedom, in for a fire-breathing bluestocking bride."

"Now that's starting to sound like my old friend Ash. And she's right, you know. The nobility is notoriously unforgiving to outsiders, especially upstarts who unexpectedly ascend into their ranks. You have too many counts against you. You're delirious if you think they'll accept you into their bosom as one of their own. She's your entrée into society. If she's willing to play the doting wife, you'll stand a much better chance."

"That's exactly what she said."

"As the lady's husband, you'll move in the highest circles, with the most glittering prize upon your arm."

"She'll look good on my arm."

And in his bed. He was eagerly anticipating the bedding part of the bargain.

"Ah . . . I thought as much." Jax smiled.

"What?"

"You're attracted to her, and you're trying to fight it. I think that's the real reason you don't want to marry her. You're afraid you'll fall in love with the chit."

"Don't be an ass."

"I know you, Ash. Sometimes I think I know you better than you know yourself. I could see that there were sparks flying between you. And where there's smoke, there's fire."

"The lady loathes me. She's made that abundantly clear."

"Does she? Because what I saw looked like a lover's quarrel. You were devouring her with your eyes. The two of you were about to rip each other's clothes off."

"There's attraction, but I'll never let her under my skin."

Jax was right, though. She'd already insinuated herself into his every waking thought. He hadn't stopped thinking about Lady Henrietta Prince since the very moment he'd met her. She'd somehow taken up lodgings inside his mind. Stealing her way into his head the same way she'd infiltrated his rooms.

"You're not going soft on me, are you, Ash?"

"Course not," Ash muttered. "I set this game in motion, and I'll finish it."

"She appeared to me to be a lady who could give as good as she got."

"She's bold and brave, but there's a vulnerability there. There's something about her that makes me feel—"

"Did you just say 'feel'?"

Damn. "Shoot me now."

Jax clicked his tongue against his teeth. "I'd hate to see it. The notorious Devil's Own Scoundrel forced to his knees by a bluestocking. Before you know it, you'll be spending cozy evenings in an armchair by the fire with her. You'll be holding her ball of yarn while she knits."

"Enough," Ash roared. "I'll never become a respectable duke's heir, reading by the fire of an evening in a velvet dressing gown, wearing fur-lined slippers. Dull. Unthinking. And I'll never be weak enough to fall in love. I've seen what it does to a man. Flays you, exposes your innards to the vultures. Makes you lose your edge."

"Good. Because you can't fall in love with her, Ash. Remember the rules. Never fall in love with a mark."

"I know the rules."

Coakley had taught them everything he knew, and at first Ash had looked up to him as a hero, a mentor. He'd gained their trust, even their admiration, before becoming a monster. That was how he'd kept his hold over them—a twisted loyalty.

He'd been the only kind of father Ash had ever known.

"Did Gus tell you what happened with Tobias?" he asked.

"He told me that you went searching for the lad and didn't find anything, but he returned safe and sound the next day at the boarding house."

"I don't like it, Jax. One of the other boys saw him leave with a man with a gold tooth, who had a playing card tucked into his hatband."

Jax stilled. "Coakley."

"That was my immediate thought. But it can't be. He's dead."

"I have something to show you." Jax pulled a wooden box out of a drawer of his bureau and unlocked it. "These have been arriving. One a week for a month now." He reached into the box and spread its contents over the desk.

The playing cards were crumpled and mangled . . . and soaked in blood.

Ash's right hand started shaking. He shoved it under his knee. "Why didn't you show these to me?"

"Thought they were from a disgruntled customer. You know we receive threats all the time. That's why we hire the bruisers like Gus. That's why we keep *you* around. But then this one arrived today." Jax picked up the torn and blood-spattered Ace of Spades and turned it over.

There was a word scrawled across the back: *Alive.*

Ash's guts twisted into a knot. "Jesus. Jax. It can't be."

"And there's something else. I've had spies watching the docks, and one of them told me they thought they saw Coakley arrive in London a week ago."

"What?" Ash exploded. "And you didn't tell me?"

"You were occupied with the duke gambit. I didn't want to worry you over nothing. It was dark, my spy could have made a mistake. Now I'm not so sure. Either Coakley's back from the dead and he's in London to exact his revenge, or someone wants us to think he is."

"But who?" Ash asked. "One of the old gang?"

"You know everyone's either left London or met a bad end. I don't think it's one of them."

This could ruin everything. And not just his ambitions. Coakley was capable of anything. Extortion. Revenge. Murder.

There'd been so much blood. The alleyway had been soaked with it. The playing card in Coakley's hatband had fallen out. Sometimes Ash had nightmares about the King of Diamonds saturated with bright, fresh blood. Grinning up at him.

"If Coakley's alive and back in London, I have to deal with him swiftly and ruthlessly. I won't have him ruining this game, making threats. I need you to find out everything there is to know."

"Don't worry." Jax gathered the blood-soaked playing cards and stuffed them back in the box. "I've already set the search in motion."

Chapter Thirteen

❧ 🌹 ❧

"Ow, BE CAREFUL with my nose hairs, if you please," Ash said as the sadistic swarm of maids Lady Henrietta had assembled plucked his eyebrows, trimmed his nose hairs, and buffed his nails.

He and Jax had spent the last week attempting to discover the origins of those threatening playing cards. They'd come no closer to finding Coakley, or the person pretending to be Coakley.

Ash had to admit that he was unnerved by the possibility of his dark past coming back to haunt him at the worst possible moment.

And now he was unnerved by the sheer number of maids being employed to transform him into something resembling respectability.

"Why did I agree to this again?" he asked the lady irritably.

"This is only what women do most days in the pursuit of beauty," she replied, her brown eyes dancing with ill-concealed merriment at his discomfort.

"Women may do these painful plucking things, but not men."

"Not men like you. Men who drink inferior gin and wear garishly embroidered waistcoats."

"Oh lord. Back to the waistcoats."

"Those waistcoats would never pass muster at White's. You've never set foot inside a top-tier gentleman's club."

"And I daresay you haven't either."

"No, but I know someone who has. You must be so buffed and polished that they accept you as one of their own even though they know you to be a gaming hell owner."

"Gaming *house*. There's a difference. Ouch!" He jerked his hand away from the petite torturer wielding a pair of bright little scissors.

"Mr. Prince. Put your hand back, please," the maid said sternly.

He laid his hand in hers. She placed his hand in warm water scented with rose petals.

Rose petals? "This doesn't feel right. Are they truly going to be looking at my nails?"

"Every gentleman of your new social standing spends more time on his toilette than most ladies."

"I don't want to be one of those foppish dandies prancing down Rotten Row."

"Never fear. No one will ever mistake you for a foppish dandy."

"They'd best not," he growled.

The maids giggled and cast scandalized glances at him. He felt like a beast in a cage at the menagerie with young ladies on the other side of the bars, gawking at him.

Ash grunted. "I'm glad someone's enjoying this. I think I'm rehabilitated enough." He struggled out of his chair.

"Not yet. This is a Sisyphean task. You're a big, rough-hewn rock, and I'm attempting to roll you up a hill. I'm very afraid you'll go crashing back down again and I'll have to start all over. Now, will you behave?"

"I'll try," he said with an ill grace. He sat back down, and the maids descended again with sharp implements and determined expressions.

He hadn't known what he was agreeing to when the lady spoke of do-overs and rehabilitation.

One of the maids headed for his brows and began plucking again.

"Ow! This is ridiculous." He half-rose from his chair. "I refuse to be primped and processed and made into some tame, sweet-smelling, coxcomb of a—"

Lady Henrietta pushed him back down and wrapped a steaming hot towel around his head from forehead to jaw, effectively cutting off his pro-testations.

Now he couldn't talk since he was muffled by a towel, which must have been her intention.

"Hold still, you big beast," she said sternly. "You agreed to submit to my transformation. I know what I'm doing. Sometimes it's best to allow the expert to take the lead."

"Mmph," he mumbled through the towel.

When the towel came off, he felt all steamy and red-faced. One of the maids used a magnifying glass to stare at him.

"What are you looking at?" he asked suspiciously.

"She's examining your skin for blemishes. We may need to blend a skin cream for you to use before bed."

"Absolutely not. I won't be using any creams. You're unmanning me," he protested to Hetty.

Her hair was damp from the steam, and it had curled around her face in little ringlets that he wanted to wrap around his fingers. "I'm certain that's not possible. A big brute like you."

Ash knew why she was doing all of this. It was her only method for retaining any dominion over him. She was definitely enjoying this.

"Ouch! That's deuced sharp."

Two more maids removed his boots and stockings. He never showed his bare feet to anyone by daylight. They weren't a pretty sight.

He felt a little embarrassed, but then the maids placed his feet into a nice warm bath in a metal bucket, where they were hidden from view by soap-suds. "Rest your feet here for a few minutes, Mr. Prince."

Ash had to admit that the foot soak was not altogether objectionable. It made him feel quite warm and relaxed.

While his feet were soaking, Lady Henrietta moved behind him and ran her fingers through his hair, gently massaging his scalp, which felt bloody good as well. Her soft breasts pressed against his back, and his cock stirred.

Down, boy. Now's not the time.

Tomorrow would be their wedding night. Thinking about it ensured that his cock grew even firmer. He wished he had a towel to throw over his lap.

A maid began to scrape the bottom of his feet with a rough stone. Could it be possible that the arch of one's foot was an erotic area?

With Lady Henrietta's breasts plumping around his neck, and his feet being massaged, he was hard-pressed not to . . . well, not to be hard.

"Now then," the lady said as she massaged her hands through his hair. "I should like to settle what we shall call one another. Given our impending nuptials, I suppose we might call each other by our Christian names."

"Do *not* call me Ashbrook." He shuddered. "Call me Ash."

"And you may call me Hetty. Everyone does. I dislike the name Henrietta because it reminds me that I should have been a Henry. Then we wouldn't be in this mess at all."

"Hetty. What are you doing to my hair?"

She was pushing it this way and that, gazing at the results in the glass. "Wondering how we should style it. Obviously, it must be shorn."

"I like my hair long. It's very thick and luxurious."

"It is," she said soothingly, "but it's also far too long for fashion. And these whiskers of yours, you never shave them close enough. What do you think, Gretchen?"

The maid with the ginger hair answered promptly. "It would bring out the noble lines of his cheekbones and jaw, milady. I believe Mr. Prince would be quite pleased with the results."

Ash sighed heavily. "I'm not going to win this one, I can tell."

"Afraid not," Hetty said cheerfully. "Gretchen, if you please."

The maid began snipping.

"Can I at least have some gin?"

"Why, certainly," his torturer-slash-fiancée replied.

A footman—which one was it? He was having trouble telling them apart—arrived with a glass of gin as if he'd been waiting for the request.

"No sudden movements, Mr. Prince," Gretchen cautioned.

He held very still. He didn't normally allow women with sharp scissors anywhere near him.

While he was at Gretchen's mercy, Hetty took the opportunity to deliver bad news.

"My friend, Miss Finchley, has created a custom scent for you. She's a chemist who works at her father's perfumery."

"Hold a moment. I don't want to smell like a flower."

"But you don't want to smell the way you do right now, either."

"What's wrong with the way I smell?"

"It's rather . . . obvious. All bay rum and musk."

"Obvious. *Obvious?* I'll have you know that women are always whispering in my ear about how delicious I smell."

"You want something more subtle. More refined."

"I'm not swanning about London smelling like a damned lily of the valley."

"You'll like the custom cologne. Miss Finchley is very talented. And the tailor will be here soon with the new dove-gray silk waistcoats I ordered to match your eyes."

"They sound boring."

There was a knock on the door. "Are you here to save me?" he called loudly. "If so, please hurry."

He couldn't turn his head to see who had entered the room because Gretchen was still cutting his hair.

"Ash, this is Miss Ardella Finchley."

A young lady walked into his line of sight. "Miss Finchley," he said, regarding her suspiciously. She appeared innocuous enough. The animated expression in her blue eyes, her brisk movements, and her bright yellow bonnet matched her name. "I heard you're here to make me smell like a dandy cavorting in a bed of roses."

She snorted. "Not at all, Mr. Prince. I created a very masculine scent. Hetty described you as a forceful gentleman."

"I didn't describe him as a gentleman at all," Hetty said.

"A bold and forceful man," amended Miss Finchley.

"That can't be all she said. She's very fond of insults." He drummed his fingers on his thigh. "Are you sure she didn't use the words *unscrupulous mountebank*?"

Miss Finchley glanced at Hetty. "I believe the words *domineering* and *arrogant* may have been employed."

"I told you that he needed to smell like old familial money," said Hetty.

"And what does that smell like?" Ash demanded.

"Like this." Miss Finchley drew a cut-glass vial out of her green silk reticule. After uncorking the vial, she dabbed a little of the contents on a scrap of yellow silk. She waved the silk under his nose.

He was prepared to object stringently . . . but damned if it didn't smell delicious. "What's in it?"

"Blackcurrant and bergamot, with a heart of juniper berries, and a base of musk and oakmoss."

"What the devil is oakmoss?"

"A species of lichen that grows on oak trees in Europe. No one else is going to smell quite like you, Mr. Prince."

"It's not too bad."

Hetty sniffed the fabric. "You're a genius, Della." She took the scrap of fabric around to the maids, and they all had a sniff.

The scent made both highborn ladies and their maids sigh and blush. Ash could work with that.

"Della is a brilliant chemist," said Hetty, taking her friend's arm and giving her a warm smile. "It's not just perfume she concocts in the laboratory when her father's away. You've done it again, Della. It's the perfect scent."

Ash wouldn't go that far, but it didn't smell like flowers, and there was something about it, something strong and seductive.

And then he saw the flare of desire in Hetty's eyes. He'd douse his whole head in the stuff if she'd only keep looking at him like that.

"Instruct your valet to apply it like so." Miss Finchley gave a demonstration by applying the scent behind his ears and at his throat. "You may wish to also touch some to your wrists."

"I have a surprise for you, Hetty," said Miss Finchley. "I prepared a scent for you, as well."

"I don't need anything . . . oh." She stopped talking because Miss Finchley waved a stopper under her nose. "Oh, that is delectable. It smells like champagne, and peaches, and . . . heaven."

"Now you two will be the best-smelling couple in all of London. My job here is finished," said Miss Finchley with a satisfied smile. "Good day, Mr. Prince."

"I'll see you out," said Hetty, taking her friend's arm.

"WHAT DO YOU think of him?" Hetty asked when they were out of earshot.

"Precisely as you described. A glowering, good-looking, arrogant devil of a man. You'll definitely have your hands full with that one."

Having her hands full of Ash had been foremost on her mind all morning, try as she might to suppress it.

"Are you quite sure you know what you're doing?" Della asked.

"I can handle him."

"You think you can manage to tame him?"

"I have to try. It's my only hope at the moment. Thank you for the scent. It truly is remarkable."

"I can't believe you're getting married tomorrow."

"Neither can I." Hetty's heart somersaulted in her chest.

"Are you worried about . . . you know. The wedding night?" Della whispered.

"I've thought of nothing else. Tomorrow night I'll be alone in a bedchamber with him."

Della's eyes sparkled. "I've heard, from Beatrice and Mina, that sometimes they spend entire days in bed with their husbands."

"Whom they are deeply, madly in love with." Hetty took her friend's arm. "I'm not in love with the man I'm marrying, and I never shall be. I'm doing this for the future of my vineyards and the future of Rosehill Park and every tenant who relies upon its bounty."

"Hetty." Della searched her face. "Are you certain you're not in any danger?"

She wasn't certain of that. Not in the least. "I'm trying to keep a stiff upper lip. Everything's happened so fast."

Della kissed her cheek. "Just remember that all of us ladies are thinking of you and sending you strength and love."

"Don't worry. I'll be all right."

Hetty walked back upstairs slowly after Della left. Her friend had every right to be worried. To tell the truth, Hetty was nearly sick with worry.

It was the fluttery feeling in her stomach every time she saw Ash. And she didn't even want to think about what happened when he touched her. However was she to maintain the upper hand when he unsettled her with only a glance?

She re-entered the chamber to find that the maids were gone, and the tailor had arrived.

She took a step backward, thinking about running away. Ash was standing before the glass, with the tailor making final adjustments to the hem of his trousers.

His outward transformation was complete.

And it was almost too much for her beleaguered heart to handle.

Chapter Fourteen

HE WAS SO handsome and debonair it made Hetty's head swim.

Gold-tinged brown hair swept back from his face in a perfect wave. Angular jaw clean-shaven and smooth, no nicks to be seen. Clothing understated and elegant in various shades of dove gray to pearly white. Not a hint of crimson. Boots polished to a diamond's brilliance.

"Your Ladyship." Mr. Beckwith, the tailor, straightened and made a bow.

"Mr. Beckwith, you've outdone yourself."

"Thank you, milady. I tailored everything to his majestic proportions."

Ash was smooth and debonair when he wanted to be. She couldn't help thinking that his ability to turn on the charm, as if touching a flame to the wick of a lamp, was proof that he was a professional dissembler.

At least today his ability to become someone else would work to her advantage. She'd almost believe he'd been born into the nobility.

Almost.

He looked the part now, but there would always be something in the way he carried himself, a challenging, swaggering edge to his demeanor, that could never be cloaked.

Mr. Beckwith took his leave, and Ash closed the door after him. He came back to stand beside her in front of the glass.

"Well? Was I right?" Hetty asked.

He turned this way and that. "I suppose I could become used to this."

"Do you like your new boots?"

"They pinch a little. I prefer my old boots."

"They'll wear in. And you'll have to have a new timepiece."

She reached for his pocket watch. He caught her wrist. "The watch stays. I won't replace that. Ever."

"But it's old and battered, and from the looks of it, it's not even real gold."

"It stays. That's not negotiable."

"You have a sentimental attachment to the piece?"

"An attachment. I wouldn't say it's sentimental." He studied himself in the mirror. "These breeches are even tighter than the ones I usually wear. Putting me on full display, are you?" He cupped his groin and made a very rude gesture. "Giving the young ladies something to dream about?"

She'd noticed how well he filled out his breeches. "It's the fashion."

They stared into the glass, their gazes locking in the frozen depths of the mirror. Her cheeks flushed, her eyes bright, his gaze penetrating.

She was having thoughts again. This time about the bulge in his breeches.

That's what the devil did, she reminded herself. He enticed, he seduced.

"You can dress me in sober waistcoats and polished boots, Hetty, but I'm still a wicked beast beneath it all. You'll never tame me. Never truly reform me."

"Don't be so sure. You may grow attached to your new appearance. You've been preening. It's only a matter of time before the man matches the tailoring."

"I was preening because I like the way you're looking at me." He reached for her and pulled her against him. "It's always going to be like this between us, isn't it? A war of wills. A battle for dominion. And I like it. We're going to burn so hot. It's going to be so good."

Blast you, Della! He smelled too delectable now. She wanted to eat him up. She turned her head, and her lips nearly brushed his. It was a compulsion. A need outside of herself.

She wanted him to kiss her. Ached for it.

He slid his fingers over the edge of her bodice, tracing the lace. He slipped his fingers lower, skimming the swell of her breasts.

He brushed a thumb over her nipple, and desire rippled through her body.

"Patience is a virtue," she said in a shaky voice. "Our wedding night is tomorrow."

Her response to his touch, this craving that resonated throughout her body, this desire, had no place in their agreement.

Perhaps she could permit herself just a small taste, an infinitesimal indiscretion.

His hands slipped inside her bodice to cup her breasts, and she did some exploring of her own, tugging his shirt free from his trousers and sliding her hand across his flat abdomen.

There was no mistaking his response to her bravery. He was aroused. She felt the rigid evidence of it against her thigh.

He parted her lips with his thumb and tilted her head back at the same time. His finger stroked her lips softly and slipped inside her mouth, the tip of his thumb touching her tongue.

Her mind went blank as his lips replaced his finger, kissing her deeply.

His hands roamed over her bodice, her waist, and grabbed handfuls of her skirts and petticoats, bunching them up and pushing them aside.

A soft brush of his fingers on the skin of her inner thigh, only a murmur of a touch, a tantalizing promise of more to come.

He coaxed her thighs apart with his hand while he kissed her, his tongue mimicking the movement of his fingers, a soft, sensual exploration.

"Hetty," he murmured against her lips. "I'm going to ravish you so thoroughly. Slide my hands all over you. You will be mine. Make no mistake. You're going to beg me for more."

"I won't." She pressed her thighs together, stopping his progress. She pushed a hand against his chest and moved him away. She straightened her skirts and slid a hand over her coiffure.

He reached for her. She danced away.

"Tomorrow," she said, and made her escape.

"WELL, WELL, LOOK what the cat dragged in," said Gus when Ash walked into 20 Ryder Street that night. He wanted to see if Jax had found anything out about Coakley yet.

"Don't laugh." Ash flopped onto a stool. "I need a drink."

"Come and look at this swell, lads!" Jax called out.

Several of the regular gamblers gathered round, disreputable miscreants, all.

"What's she done to you?" asked Gus from behind the bar. "You look blasted strange."

"He's had a haircut," one regular volunteered.

"Don't he just look pretty?" another asked.

"I can see my gorgeous reflection in those shiny boots of 'is."

Jax sniffed the air. "You smell like a pastry shop, Ash. She's running circles around you just like I told you she would."

"She wants me to look like a duke."

"You look like a bleedin' fashion plate."

The men jostled around him, drinking gin and trying to outdo one another with their jokes.

"He's already forgot us rum coves."

"I think *I* want to marry him."

"Swanning around with dukes' daughters, drinking champagne, and dousing himself in scent."

"Enough," Ash growled, shrugging them off. "I have business to discuss with Jax. Lay off or I'll rearrange your faces for you."

"I think you've forgotten how to use your fists," Gus taunted. "Wouldn't want to break one of those buffed and polished nails, would he, lads."

"That's it." Ash tore off his new coat and jumped up from the bar stool. "Come out from behind that bar, you big lug. I'll show you I haven't forgotten how to use these." He settled into a boxer's stance, distributing his weight evenly.

"Fight, lads!" the call rang out. Tables were scraped back, and wagers flew fast and furious.

The two old friends circled each other warily. Gus was enormous, but he wasn't the fastest on his feet. Ash had gone hundreds of rounds with him over the years.

He rarely won. Though tonight he had enough pent-up frustration to lay the giant flat on his back. Ash danced around him, landing little jabs.

"Face me like a man, you coward," Gus roared.

"Tap his crimson!" came a shout.

"Make 'im bleed."

"Bash him. Teach him a lesson!"

Bloodthirsty crowd tonight. They all wanted to see the fancy, sweet-smelling duke's heir taken down a notch.

"Oh look!" Gus shouted. "It's Lady Henrietta!"

Ash swiveled toward the entrance, and Gus's meaty fist smashed into his jaw. He landed flat on his back, legs akimbo, with stars dancing before his eyes. "Dirty trick," he called weakly.

Everyone stood over him, laughing.

Finally, when he could breathe again, he joined in the laughter. Gus reached a hand down to help him up and threw an arm around his shoulders as Ash hobbled to the bar.

Now that he'd definitely *not* re-established his

dominance, he really had to talk to Jax. He accepted a block of ice wrapped in a towel and held it to his sore jaw.

"Never mind them," said Jax when they were seated at their private table. "We'd all give our right arm to change places with you. A country estate and a gorgeous wife. It's the stuff of dreams."

"Have you found out anything yet?" asked Ash.

"Nothing substantial. There are rumors swirling. And sightings of someone who looks like him. But he's old and broken, they say. Might not pose a threat."

"Have you received any more threats?"

"Not since the ones I showed you. I have all my informants on high alert."

"I should be the one out hunting for . . . *him*."

"You're rather busy these days getting leg-shackled and things like that."

"You have to promise me, Jax, promise me on your life that you'll contact me at Rosehill Park as soon as you hear anything. I'll come galloping."

"You know I will. Don't worry, old friend. We'll come out on top, like we always do. We're survivors. We beat the odds before, and we'll do it again."

Ash raised a glass. "Brothers forever."

"Brothers forever. Now go get married, old friend."

Chapter Fifteen

HETTY PLACED THE bouquet of grape leaves and red roses outside her mother's stone crypt. The sun was shining, and sheep grazed placidly upon the lawns, but her thoughts were turbulent.

The rows of bright green sun-dappled grapevines usually made her feel calm and peaceful. Today the orderly rows of vines looked like they were marching away into the distance.

Was she doing the right thing?

She sat upon the ground and laid her head on the stone relief of an angel, as she'd done so many times before. "I'm getting married today, Mama," she whispered.

Her mother's face shimmered in her memory, eyes dancing with light and lips curved in a laughing smile.

"It's not how you or I imagined it would be. He doesn't love me. We don't even know each other. I'm not sure if you would approve of him. But I know you would approve of my plans for the vineyards. This year's vintage will be special, Mama, I can feel it. We had a cold and rainy spring, and I was despairing. You always told me that August makes the wine, and this one is fine and bright."

While she'd been in London, the grapes had matured, turning succulent and flavorful. Her vigneron, Mr. Renault, said the grapes were the best he'd tasted.

"The harvest won't be far off now, Mama. And soon we'll be able to open a bottle of last year's wine. I'll bring you a glass." She kissed the stone angel and rose to her feet.

It was time to don her wedding gown.

"You're so beautiful." Viola dashed a tear away from her cheek.

Isobel and Viola had arrived at Rosehill Park yesterday evening to help Hetty prepare for the wedding, which was to be held within the hour in the small family chapel on the estate grounds.

"None of that, now," said Hetty. "This isn't a sentimental occasion."

"Weddings always make me cry." Viola sniffed back more tears. "This gown is perfect."

"This was my mother's wedding gown." A clever seamstress had made alterations to bring it into vogue, widening the sleeves and adding ruffles around the bodice, but it retained the same lines. Hetty could almost glimpse her mother in the glass, a young bride, newly arrived in England, nervous and excited and terribly homesick.

Hetty's lady's maid, Gretchen, nestled a few more pink rosebuds into Hetty's upswept hair. "There, you're quite perfect, milady. Mr. Prince will be besotted."

"Thank you, Gretchen. That will be all."

"Yes, milady." Gretchen curtsied and left.

When the maid had gone, Isobel took Hetty's hands in hers. "You don't have to marry him, Hetty. There's still time to back out."

"I have to marry him, or he'll tear up my vineyards and build racehorse stables."

"You've no guarantee he won't do that anyway."

"I'm going to make him fall in love with Rosehill Park. He'll see that he should build his stables elsewhere."

"He's a ruthless man who gets what he wants, by fair means or foul," Viola warned.

"As I said, you don't have to marry him," Isobel said. "You have the choice."

"And become a scandalous runaway bride?" Hetty asked. "No thank you. I've made my bed and I will lie in it."

With Ash. Tonight. A shiver rippled through her body.

"It's your heart I'm worried about," said Viola.

"Don't trouble yourself on that account. I know the danger. I'm going in with my eyes open, and forewarned is forearmed. I know he's not the type to be true to one woman. This is a business arrangement like any other arranged marriage. I've placed limits on our marital relations, and strict limits upon my heart. I shan't let it get away from me. It's on a very tight leash."

"I'm sure if anyone can follow the rules it's you," Viola said.

Isobel smiled. "I don't fear for you. Actually, I fear

for your husband. You're so beautiful it almost hurts to look at you."

"Nonsense. I'm tired, and I have worry lines around my eyes." She'd noticed the fine lines around her eyes and lips had been deepening since the mourning period for her uncle and cousin.

"Now *that's* nonsense. Have another look at yourself."

"I look well enough."

"Oh, Hetty," Viola gushed. "You're simply delectable. He's the one in danger of falling at your feet, I predict."

"Scoundrels never stumble. He's far too confident for that. Life is a game to him, and all he wants to do is win. He doesn't care about the hearts he breaks along the way. We placed a wager, but he won't best me."

"What sort of wager?" Isobel asked.

"He says he'll corrupt me. Turn me into a wanton who longs for his touch. I maintain that I'll reform him. Transform him into a gentleman."

Viola and Isobel exchanged a cryptic glance.

"Another glass of wine?" asked Isobel.

"One more glass."

The effervescent wine helped calm her nerves. Despite her outward composure, and her brave words about her practical reasons for the marriage, she was filled with misgivings.

Nearly sick with them, really. She had to drink enough wine to lull the butterflies in her belly to sleep.

"Are you prepared for the wedding night?" Isobel asked.

"I know the general principles of the thing. It's only . . ."

"You're trepidatious, and rightfully so," said Viola. "To give your body to him when you've no feeling between you, when it's merely for the purposes of procreation. It does seem rather cold, somehow."

"I'm thinking of it as a duty, and nothing more. I have to prune back the vines for them to bear fruit the next year, and I have to share his bed in order to conceive a child."

"Lie there and think of England, as they say," Isobel suggested.

"Beatrice has told me that *it* can be quite transporting," Viola whispered. "Quite deliriously delicious, as she put it. And you know Beatrice was so buttoned up, and Ford has changed her completely. She's still the same Beatrice and she's still obsessed with language and words and her dictionary, but she laughs so much more easily now. And the two of them are always cooing at each other, building things together."

"Yes, but that wasn't the bedding. Not all of it. She's in love, Viola."

"Of course. Love. Yes, she's in love, and that, I suppose, makes the difference."

"Our marital relations might be physically pleasurable, but they won't change me. Because only love can truly change a person. And I have enough love in my life. I have my father, Bacchus, my vineyards, my work. My friends." She smiled at her friends. "I'm quite satisfied. I want for nothing."

There was a knock at the door, and her father

appeared. "It's time to go to the church. You look lovely, Henrietta."

"Thank you, Papa."

"I wish your mother could be here today."

"As do I, Papa." She wouldn't cry. Her control and composure were all she had left. She must cling to them at all cost.

As he led her down the pathway to the church, Hetty resolved once again to remain absolutely herself and not to let her impending marriage change her or take away her freedoms.

Scoundrels took love as their due, and they threw it away. They put another notch on the bedpost. She wasn't going to be another one of his conquests, his victims.

She'd never allow him to take any part of her, any small piece. He could have her body. She'd give it freely.

But her heart would remain intact.

Ash usually avoided churches. But that would be difficult in this case.

For one, he would own this church someday.

For another, he was standing at the altar, waiting for his bride to walk down the aisle.

It was a small stone chapel on the expansive grounds of Rosehill Park, built for the particular use of the Prince family and their retainers. Rosehill was some sixteen miles outside of London, and it had taken him a little under two hours to reach it in the ducal carriage they'd sent for him.

He was garbed in black silk and snowy linen, with

a collar so high that he could barely turn his neck. His hair had been tamed into one submissive wave over his forehead, jaw clean-shaven, new boots so shiny they reflected the blue and red light filtering in from the high stained-glass windows.

And yet he'd undone all of her careful rehabilitation with one bar fight. He had a fresh cut at his eyebrow, and a pronounced purple bruise over his jaw.

His jaw still ached. Trust Gus to ruin his wedding night. Kissing would be difficult . . . but he'd manage.

The servants hadn't blinked an eye when they saw the damage to his face from Gus's fist.

He hadn't seen Hetty yet. She might not be so sanguine.

But it was better for his disreputable appearance to match his bruised and battered heart.

He'd had to wrestle his fingers into signing a new signature on the legal documents—so many pages of them it had been dizzying.

Ashbrook Bartholomew Henry Prince.

If he heard that name or read it in the papers, he'd assume the owner of it was a right little prig, born with a silver spoon in his mouth, coddled by nursemaids and favored by schoolmasters, until eventually he became so convinced of his own superiority that everyone below him on the social ladder was hardly a person at all.

That's how the noblemen and businessmen viewed the laborers in their factories.

The sordid masses. The unwashed poor. Expendable animals existing only to line their pockets with gold.

Ash hadn't had an upbringing. His had been more of a down-bringing. A constant abasement and inculcation of shame and subjugation.

And yet he'd found a way to believe in himself, to better himself.

Look at me now, then, Coakley.

He refused to believe that his old enemy was alive. He'd watched him die, for Christ's sake. He'd gasped his last on that cobblestone street in Barcelona. Ash and Jax had slunk away, into the night.

The scent of blood filled his nostrils. The saints painted on the walls stared down at him with accusatory eyes.

He'd done it in defense. To save Jax's life.

He'd do it again.

He was a killer. No fit husband for a refined lady who smelled of sun-warmed wildflowers and whose kisses were like champagne, sparkling and heady.

He shifted, glancing toward the door. He half expected her to bolt for it, run away to her bluestocking clubhouse and barricade the doors against all men who sought to control her.

Anything rather than marry The Devil's Own Scoundrel.

Something perilously close to tenderness touched his heart as he remembered her invading The Devil's Staircase and showering him with insults. She was so brave.

The door to the church opened and Hetty entered, escorted by the duke, and followed by two of her friends, Miss Beaton, the dimpled one, and Miss Isobel Mayberry, a slender blonde with sharply etched features who'd cornered him in a corridor earlier, skewered him with a glare, and told him that if he hurt her friend in any way he would face her dagger, and the weapons of her friends.

His inclination had been to laugh, but he'd stayed solemn because Miss Mayberry had been deadly in earnest.

His bride walked down the aisle, glowing with life, if not with joy.

Her shiny brown hair was threaded with pink rosebuds, and there was a matching wash of pink high on her cheeks.

Wine-stained lips and brown eyes with heavy black lashes.

Creamy satin flowing over soft curves, skirts rippling as she walked.

The sunlight caressed her, spilling over gleaming skin and satin.

His mouth went dry. The stone floor swayed beneath his feet.

This is real.

As she walked slowly toward him, he heard the faint strains of a lullaby sung in Spanish. *Duérmete, mi niño . . .*

The only comfort he'd ever known. The only love he'd ever known.

As he watched Hetty walk toward him, his heart filled with the ache and wonder of her beauty. But she wasn't walking toward him. She was marrying a lie.

You're a prince, my son. Never forget it.

He threw back his shoulders.

Her face was calm and composed. She'd resigned herself to her fate, but the mutinous spark in her eyes reassured him that here was no wilting wallflower.

Here walked a strong-willed and blade-smart woman who knew what she wanted.

"You're . . ." he began, but his throat closed around the words. What was wrong with him? He always had a suave and seductive comment to make. What his heart was saying was very simple. "You're the most beautiful thing I've ever seen."

"And you've been fighting," she whispered. "You've ruined all my hard work."

"I told you I couldn't be tamed."

Her eyes swept from the crown of his head to his toes. "There's cat hair on your coat. Did you bring Lucy with you?"

"Of course. I wasn't going to leave her in London."

"And you've been holding her. Petting her. Admit it."

"I'll admit no such thing."

Though it was true. The damned cat had traveled in the carriage with him in a basket. He'd made the mistake of letting her out, and she'd been so frightened of the motion of the wheels that she'd spent the whole ride clinging to him.

"Cat hair is the most noble accessory of all," Hetty said with the faint ghost of a smile.

He wanted to bring a real smile to her lips. He wanted to be the one to make her laugh, to make her come undone with pleasure.

The clergyman read the marriage rites, and Ash's heart began to hammer. His palms went clammy, and he broke out in a sweat.

This is real.

The thought slammed into his mind like Gus delivering a right hook. This wasn't a game. He was really marrying this woman, and it couldn't be undone.

Marriage hadn't been the plan for him, or for her.

She deserved a loving partner. A man with fewer dark secrets in his past.

The second thought twisted like a blade to the ribs, sliding in with a sickening, slicing finality.

She should only give herself to someone whose heart wasn't shot through with holes.

He could never give her the love and tenderness she secretly craved.

Until this moment, he'd been proud of his exploits. He'd worn them as a badge of honor, the games he'd won, the knockouts he'd delivered, even the pockets he'd picked.

He won't miss that timepiece, lad. He's got twenty more like it. Ripe for the plucking, 'e is.

For one panicked moment, he was that boy again, the one who'd worked in a factory, until he reached the point of severe exhaustion, fingers gone numb and one thought left in his brain, one thought only: survive.

He traced the contour of the timepiece in his pocket. He'd survived near-starvation. Beatings. The factory. Coakley. He'd survived. He still had that gnawing hunger inside him. To win. To best life. To take what he was due.

And here he was. Marrying this fairy-tale princess.

She was sunshine, champagne, soft curves, a rare smile, but one that lit his mind like a stained-glass window pointing to heaven.

Something about the curve of her cheek, bathed in ruby light, made him ache with a different kind of hunger.

To be better. To be worthy.

But he knew all too well how to silence his better angels. Muzzle them tight. Go cold inside.

Speak the words. Play the game. Roll the dice.

Until it was done.

They were married. Too late for qualms of conscience now.

He walked by her side back to the great house for the wedding breakfast.

There was cake. It was sweet.

There was Hetty by his side, not meeting his gaze. Her hand shaking slightly as she lifted her fork.

There was sparkling wine, the sound of the cork popping and the foam spilling over the side accompanied by ribald comments from the duke, who was already half seas over. "Empty glasses should be filled, eh m'boy?" Winking and nudging Ash with his elbow.

Hetty bore the bawdy teasing stoically, her expression unreadable, her back straight and head unbowed.

Her friends took turns glaring at Ash, silently

warning him that they had Hetty's best interests at heart, and he'd better have the same.

He and Hetty never had a moment alone until the duke led them out of the room, proclaiming loudly to the guests that he'd personally see them to the marriage bed.

Back through the main hall, to the curving staircase. Ruby-red carpeting. Dark wood paneling and oil paintings of officious ancestors.

The duke staggering, his whisky glass tumbling over the galleried landing and shattering on the flagstones below.

"I want a grandchild. And be quick about it," the duke slurred as he pushed them through the doorway of a bedchamber.

Ash nodded to the footman who'd accompanied them a few steps behind and shut the door of Hetty's chambers in the duke's blotchy face. "Well," he said, clearing his throat. "That was awkward."

Hetty moved to the window. "My father's not known for his subtlety. I'm not sure why he delivered us to my chambers instead of yours. Your rooms are through that door."

The door separating their rooms was massive, stretching twice his height, carved from solid oak and embellished all around with carvings of grapevines and other fertility symbols.

"My father moved out so that we could have adjoining bedchambers. I'm in my mother's room."

"He didn't have to do that."

"He insisted. I hear a faint mewling coming from

behind the door," she said, pressing her ear against the oak.

"That would be Lucifer."

"You mean Lucy. It's best to keep her in your chambers for at least a week so that she can become accustomed to her new surroundings and not run away and get lost in the woods."

"She doesn't need coddling."

"Don't lie to me. I saw the receipt for those kippers. You treat her like a princess."

He raised his hands in a gesture of defeat. "You caught me. If I don't feed her the finest cuisine, she makes her displeasure known with her claws. She's shredded several of my waistcoats."

Hetty smiled. "Cats are very sensitive and they definitely keep score of grievances."

"Are you keeping score, Hetty?" He cupped her cheek with his hand. "Have I earned claws or a kiss?"

She ducked away from him. "I'll need some time to prepare."

"Of course. I'll be next door. If you need me for anything." *She knows that, Ash.* "I'll knock on your door in a few hours."

"No! I'd rather knock on your door. When I'm ready."

"Very well."

She was drawing another line between them. He was all for re-establishing boundaries after the disturbing meandering of his mind during the ceremonies.

"I look forward to your knock." He bowed and left her.

The cat was sleeping on a cushion and she glanced up when he arrived.

"Are you still angry with me about the basket?" he asked. "You had to travel somehow."

A servant arrived in his room moments later with gleaming kippers on a real silver platter.

"See that, you furry demon? You've moved up in the world. You're a princess now."

"Mrrow," she replied. Which meant that she'd always been a princess, thank you very much.

After her meal, she hopped up onto the imposing bed that occupied the center of the room and settled atop one of the pillows for a grooming session.

She was quite pleased with herself, licking her paws most assiduously and combing them over her brows. She'd already taken to her opulent new surroundings.

It would take Ash more time to become accustomed to the idea that this room was his; it was simply too big.

He could have fit three of his rooms at Mrs. Dougherty's into this one. One man didn't need this much space. It would be difficult to heat a cavern of this size in winter, even with two fireplaces, one so large he could stand inside it.

He almost got lost exploring the adjoining wardrobe, which stretched the length of the chamber and was stuffed with clothing, boots, top hats still in their boxes, gloves, riding costumes, and everything else a high-and-mighty duke's heir might wish to clothe himself.

The servants kept coming and going with food,

wine, and offers of more food. They built him a fire though it was a fine summer's evening, and then they lit an enormous standing candelabra with dozens of beeswax candles.

The extravagance and waste were astounding.

This was her world, peopled by her friends and family. He had no one here. No one except a managing sort of feline.

"What do you think of all this, you little monster?" She ignored him.

"Ungrateful imp. Look what I've provided you with, chambers fit for royalty. You're not still cross with me, are you?" He tried to scratch under her chin, but she swatted his hand away with claws distended.

"Wretch. I hope my bride will treat me better."

He climbed onto the bed next to the cat with a bottle of Hetty's excellent wine and drank deeply. Soon he'd be back on familiar ground.

He knew pleasure in all its many forms . . . and positions.

He would have preferred to remove that silk wedding gown himself, but now he lived in a world where there were servants for every small task.

She'd be in his bed soon enough. He'd slide whatever silky thing she wore off those opulent curves and learn the shape of her, the sound of her.

The pursuit of bliss would clear these dark clouds from his head, at least temporarily.

Chapter Sixteen

❧ 🌹 ❧

*H*ETTY WAS AS prepared as she'd ever be. Gretchen had helped her select a peignoir in a pale shade of shell pink, gathered under her bosom with silk ribbons and embroidered rosebuds.

The silk slid over the tips of her breasts with a delicious friction every time she moved. Over the peignoir, she'd donned an ivory silk wrapper that tied at the waist.

Her feet were bare. Her hair loose and brushed until it shone.

Anticipation frothed inside her mind. *Are you really going to do this, Hetty?*

For all her fine resolutions to remain impassive and indifferent, there was a naughty little voice that said she would enjoy herself tonight.

There wasn't anything wrong with enjoying it. What would be wrong would be to mistake it for anything other than what it was: a duty.

One hour of conjugal relations. That's what she'd negotiated. She had a wooden hourglass under her arm. When the last grain of sand slipped away, she'd return to her own room.

There was a schedule to keep. There were boundaries to maintain.

She knocked softly on the door separating their chambers. No answer. She knocked louder. Still no answer.

"Ash," she called. "Let me in."

They both had the option to lock the door from the inside. She had made sure her side was latched as she had a bath and Gretchen had prepared her for the wedding night.

She tried the knob, and it turned easily. Swinging the door wide, she took a deep breath before walking over the threshold and into the arms of the wicked scoundrel who would take her virginity tonight.

The scoundrel who was . . . fast asleep?

He lay curled up on the bed with Lucy nestled in the crook of his arm, holding her as if she were a baby. The two of them were snoring lightly. Lucy's paw was draped over his forearm.

They had matching contented smiles on their faces. Though Hetty could never be certain if cats really smiled, or if humans only assigned them this personifying trait.

Lucy looked as though she were dreaming of kippers.

Ash had an expression she'd never seen before on his ruggedly handsome face: vulnerability.

She gazed down at him, and her fingers wanted to run through his golden-brown hair. He'd fallen asleep fully clothed with a bottle of her wine, empty, beside him on the bed.

She didn't know whether to be insulted or relieved

that he wasn't ready and waiting, eager to have his way with her. She placed the hourglass on the mantel and had a look around the room.

He'd made himself at home, strewing clothing over chairs and piling books on tables. His shiny new boots already had a scuff and had been discarded in a heap by the fireplace.

There was a half-eaten plate of food on the table. He must have dismissed the servants and told them not to return.

She could tiptoe out of the room and let him sleep. He'd wake up when the room was pitch dark. Then he'd remember. This was his wedding night.

Maybe he'd knock on her door, but by then she'd be slumbering, her door latched.

Lucy opened her eyes, regarding Hetty with an indignant expression as though to say, *This is my source of warmth and affection, not yours. Move along now, human woman.*

Ash stirred in his sleep. "Hetty," he murmured, rolling over, grabbing one of the pillows and hugging it tight.

She stifled a giggle. Was that pillow supposed to be her? He must be dreaming about conjugal relations.

Lucy yawned and stretched her paws out, giving her owner's back an affronted glare before hopping down from the bed and settling in a chair by the fireplace.

Hetty sobered. If she woke him, he'd replace that pillow with the real thing. Was she prepared for that to happen? Maybe she should take this opportunity to scurry back to her room and bolt the door. She could leave him a note. *You had your chance.*

None of that. She'd made a deal with the devil. There was a price to be paid. She would follow the schedule and consummate this marriage.

But first she had to wake her bridegroom.

"Ash," she whispered.

"Mmm." He nestled into the pillow. "Hetty."

She laid a hand on his cheek. Even though he'd been clean-shaven during the wedding ceremony, there was already stubble shadowing his jaw.

She shook his shoulder, softly at first, and then harder.

He shot upright, eyes wild. "What is it? Have you found Coakley?"

She took a step backward. "It's Hetty. Your bride. And who is Coakley?"

He blinked. "Never mind."

"I knocked, but you were asleep."

The confusion left his eyes, and the seductive smolder flared to life. He grabbed the tie of her robe, tugging her closer to the bed. "What are you wearing under that robe?"

She grabbed the tie and resisted his attempt to pull her toward him. "You said my name, in your sleep," she blurted. "And then you hugged your pillow."

"Did I?" He pulled harder on the tie of her robe. "Must have been dreaming about you. Let me see if I can recall what it was. Ahh . . . yes." A sultry smile. "I remember now. It was a very, very good dream. Let me show you what I was doing to you."

He reeled her toward him using his superior physical strength.

She wasn't going to win this fight. She dug her heels into the carpet. "I'm at a decided disadvantage here."

"And you don't like being out of your depth. You like to be in control of everything."

"It was my only way of imposing order in a life that had gone far off course."

"Don't be nervous, Hetty. We'll find our rhythm together. Your pleasure, my pleasure, in equal measure. I'll make it good for you, I promise."

That's what she was afraid of, she realized. That it would be too good between them. Too right. And she wouldn't be able to maintain a core of indifference, of independence.

She hovered indecisively, half of her wanting to know what he'd been doing to her in his dream, the other half frightened and considering leaving him with the silk robe and escaping back to her room.

"Are we going to play tug-o'-war all night, sweetheart? Or are you coming to bed?"

"I-I thought . . ." She bit her lower lip. "I thought we might converse a little first?" Her nerve had deserted her. She needed to buy a little more time.

"Don't think I'm going to allow you to talk our allotted time away. I see that hourglass you set on the mantelpiece."

"The time we spend talking won't count toward our agreement. I . . . I don't know if I'm ready."

"Fair enough. Let's talk, then. We can reset the hourglass when it's time for bed." He relinquished his hold on her robe. Swinging his long legs over the side of the bed, he padded over to the wardrobe, tugging off clothing as he walked, first his cravat, then his waistcoat. He had the practiced efficiency of a man who was accustomed to disrobing without the aid of a valet.

When he was wearing only trousers and a loose white shirt, he pulled a chair out from the table. "Sit."

She tucked herself onto the chair, feeling small and vulnerable.

He sat opposite her. "Have a few sips of gin." He poured a small amount from a bottle on the table. "It might take the edge off."

"I'd rather drink Rosehill sparkling wine."

He glanced at the empty bottle by the bed. "Afraid I finished the bottle. It certainly goes down easily. And I sent the servants away and told them I didn't want to be disturbed until late morning." He pushed the glass of spirits closer. "This is high-quality gin. Jax, Mr. Smith, distilled it himself."

"Can you even use the words *quality* and *gin* in the same sentence?"

"Just try it."

Hetty took a tiny sip. It wasn't as harsh as she'd anticipated. There was a strong juniper scent and a bitter taste that dissolved into something almost pleasurable. "What is it flavored with besides juniper?"

"This one's distilled with licorice, almonds, Seville oranges and lemon peel."

She coughed. "It's quite strong, isn't it?" she sputtered. "It singes the senses."

"It's the big bad wolf of spirits."

Just like him. He was a wolf, a predator. But she was no meek lamb. No shrinking violet. She could hold her own with the devil. The gin heated her belly and gave her a shot of courage. Firelight bathed him in a warm glow, casting his skin to bronze and teasing hidden warmth from his cold, gray eyes.

She swallowed the rest of the gin and placed the glass on the table. "Take me to bed, Ash. I'm ready now."

He searched her face. "Not just yet. I think I'll teach you a card trick."

"I don't gamble."

"This isn't gambling, it's sleight of hand."

He lifted the deck of playing cards stacked on the table and fanned them out into a semicircle. "Select a card. Any card."

She chose one from the middle.

"Don't show it to me," he said. "But remember which card it was."

It was an ornate Ace of Spades.

"Now place your card back into the deck, face-down so I can't see it."

He moved the cards around, staring into her eyes, not at the cards. Then he transferred the cards behind his back. "Now I'm going to shuffle the deck without looking at it and find your card." He matched his movements to his words and then he placed the deck of cards on the table and fanned it out again. He selected a card and placed it faceup before her. "You chose the Ace of Spades, and here it is."

"Uncanny! How did you do that?"

"It's very simple, really. First, I manipulated you

into choosing the card I wanted you to choose using what we call a force. Then I used a reverse trick. It's all in the way you place the cards.

"You wanted me to choose the Ace of Spades because that's your calling card. Like your birthmark."

"Spades signify strength and power. The Ace of Spades is the highest card in the deck."

"When did you learn your first card trick?"

"After I left the factory."

"What was your job at the factory?"

"I was one of the boys employed to examine the empty bottles and reject flawed ones. I washed bottles, pasted labels, and fitted corks. There was always more work to be done. The bottles kept coming at breakneck pace."

"Your years in the factory gave you a hard casing, Ash, as though you're encased in solid oak and you never let anyone see inside to the real you."

"That's because there's nothing to find. This is me. Solid oak. Nothing aging to perfection inside me. I was dealt a losing hand at birth, but I found a way to manipulate my own fortune. I transformed a losing hand into a winner."

Was he trying to tell her something? The way he'd used the word *manipulation*. She still had her doubts about his legitimacy as the heir.

They were married now. Like him, she had to take the hand that life had dealt her and find a way to win.

"My childhood wasn't pretty, Hetty. I'm sure yours was much more congenial."

"I have happy memories. My mother is a blur of motion in my memory. She was always doing something, always talking. She used her hands when she talked to illustrate her points. Her last words to me were, 'Take care of your father, Hetty. He'd be lost without you. And continue my work with the vineyards. I shall look down on you from Heaven and feel so very proud.'"

Ash poured her another finger of gin. He was listening. She could see it in his eyes. And she wasn't quite sure why she needed to talk. Only that it meant she didn't have to go to bed yet.

"When I was nine, my mother took my hand and led me into the vineyards. She asked me a question: 'Hetty, what would you do if today were your last day on earth?' I had no idea why she would ask me such a question. I said that I supposed I would want to spend the day with her. And that I'd like to be allowed to taste some of her sparkling wine and eat a whole frosted cake by myself. She laughed and said that her answer would be much the same as mine. She'd spend her last day with the ones she loved, eating good food, and drinking wine made by her own hands. 'You are my heart, Hetty, and wine is our life,' she said. 'When I see people drinking my wine and their eyes light up, all of my struggles are forgotten.'"

"You're very lucky to have known such a mother for seventeen years," he said quietly. "My mother died in an unmarked pauper's grave, cast aside and destitute. I wish the world had been different. That she hadn't given me away. That she had lived, and I'd been able to care for her, give her a good life."

"We can't bring them back, Ash, but we can honor

them with our actions. What of your mother's family in Spain?"

"The strange thing is that I spent two years in Barcelona. I very well could have crossed paths with a family member from my mother's side. But I never would have known it."

"Perhaps now that you know your mother's name we can search for her relations."

"Perhaps." Shadows striped his face and his eyes.

Hetty's heart surged with sympathy for the young boy Ash had been.

Unwanted. Unloved.

It was a heavy stigma for a child to shoulder.

When he spoke about his childhood, the emotion was real and raw. Though she still sensed that he wasn't telling her everything, and that he had ominous secrets in his past.

She had to trust that he was the heir, with the birthmark proving his claim, but he was still a closed book.

His confident mask slid back into place. He smiled teasingly. "I know exactly what I'd do if today were my last day on earth." He held her gaze. "I've had my wedding feast, my wedding cake, and my wine. The only thing left to have is . . ."

He rose from his chair. Bending down, he lifted her into his arms.

Startled, Hetty threw her arms around his neck to keep her balance.

"You, Hetty," he whispered in her ear. "The only thing left to have is you."

He carried her to the fireplace and she held on to his neck as he supported her body with one hand, and flipped the hourglass over with the other. "Our hour begins now." He carried her to the bed and laid her down reverently.

"Now, let's see what you have on under that robe." He slipped the robe from her shoulders and slid it off her body.

His nearness flooded her body with heat, and set her atremble, like a grape leaf in a strong breeze. If she weren't careful, she'd break free and answer the invitation to abandon all control.

The desire wouldn't have to be feigned. It was there, crouching inside her, waiting to pounce and take over her mind.

He kissed her neck. Every time he touched her, a little more of her resolution to remain separate slipped away.

Hetty knew pleasure. She knew sunsets over the vineyards. Veins of red in a bright green leaf over her head. She knew her mother's hand on hers, teaching her how to prune a vine, so delicately, so gently, that the vine wouldn't die.

She knew the taste of young wine that hadn't matured yet, that was just a promise.

This was somehow all of those things, and none of them. Something entirely new but something that had grown from every experience in her past.

Ash's large, scarred hands exploring her body gently, delicately, so she wouldn't have a shock.

Savoring her slowly, running over her lips, her throat, slipping beneath her peignoir, cupping her breasts and squeezing her nipples so softly she had to hold her breath to feel it.

He wasn't in a hurry. He lay beside her, still clothed in trousers and a shirt, and every new curve and hollow he explored was a revelation, a promise.

Her mind tried to assert control, but her body had other ideas.

Surrender, her body whispered, undulating under his expert touch. *Surrender completely.*

No, her mind replied. Unacceptable. Dangerous. Surrender nothing.

The two sides of her warred for control, the sensual surrender and the cautious control.

It was seductive to have this rough, bold man so focused on her, as though nothing existed except for this bed, her body.

He explored her in a leisurely, unhurried way, stoking the warmth in her belly.

With a smooth, sudden movement, he peeled the silk peignoir up her thighs and over her shoulders, slipping it easily off her head.

He's quite good at that, her mind said. *He's very practiced. You're nothing special.*

You're naked, shivering under his touch, and you want to arch your back and offer him your body.

"Why don't you relax," he whispered, as he had when they'd been waltzing. "I know what I'm doing."

"And sometimes it's best to let the expert take the lead," she said, finishing the line for him.

His face was all shadows and angles and glinting silver eyes in the darkness. "Exactly."

He trailed his fingers down the center of her stomach, stopping to swirl a circle around her navel, and resuming his exploration. He held her gaze, as he had at the ball, with that singular focus and intensity that sent frissons of awareness between her shoulder blades.

Lower. And lower still. Over the curls between her legs, with a target in mind. He dipped his head and kissed her lips deeply as he gently inserted a finger inside her body.

She gasped, but his lips swallowed the sound, his tongue filling her as he added another finger, stretching her open.

Just when she thought she might not want this, that it was too much, too soon, his fingers left her body and moved upward, only a few inches, but he found just the right place.

She moaned.

His lips left hers, and he lifted his head. His fingers moved over the sensitive spot. "There?" he asked.

She nodded, wordlessly, ducking her head because she didn't want to look into his eyes while his fingers were doing . . . *that*.

Sensing her shyness, he nuzzled his lips into her neck, hiding from her view, allowing her to breathe and allowing the pleasure to build and ripple outward up her belly, down her thighs, and into her mind.

No more rules about keeping herself impassive. Something was happening here, and she wanted to know what the outcome would be.

She'd anticipated their coupling, but how could she have known about this? That a man so brash, who took command of the room, would be so gentle? Would focus so completely on her pleasure, not even attempting to take any for himself.

He was still clothed, even. And, somehow, she knew that it was a deliberate move on his part to put her at ease, an unspoken message that this was about her pleasure, not about his needs.

He wasn't showing her how it was done; he was listening. And listening intently. When he brushed his finger over her core, he listened, his ear near her mouth.

When she sighed, he stayed there, at precisely that angle and with the same pressure. Stayed there in the perfect place, gently brushing across her flesh, pausing sometimes to dip his finger into her for the wetness that waited there, to ease his movements.

It was impossible to remain impassive to his min-istrations.

She struggled to remain distant, above her body, not in it. *Don't let him win.*

But her body wanted release. Craved the pleasure he could give. Her belly clenched tight, and her breath began arriving in gasps. There was no controlling it. She could have rolled over, closed her legs, pushed him away.

But a release was so close now, nearly upon her.

"Let it happen, Hetty," he urged. "It's all right. Let yourself go."

He listened, and his fingers made the right choice, moving slightly to the right. She lost control com-pletely, spilling into sensation. Pulsing with it. Bright and hot.

Pleasure bubbling, effervescing like wine in her mouth. She wanted to savor it, drink it to the dregs. Capture the taste and the feeling of it.

A soft, salty smell. The scent of her own body.

The taste of juniper and orange on his tongue.

A rush of emotion, something unexpected, a lump in her throat and a slight itch behind her eyes. Pleasure still pulsing and breathing inside her.

"Good work, Hetty. You did it."

But what had she done? She'd given some part of herself to him by allowing him to make her feel so much.

Slowly, as the sensations grew dimmer and faded away, her mind reasserted its mastery. She closed her legs, trapping his hand.

"Don't think you've won," she said, her voice shaky. "I'm not corrupted. I won't start begging for your touch."

"Mmm. If you say so." He was still lazily touching her, drawing light circles around her belly. She was sensitive everywhere.

He stripped off his clothing in swift, practiced movements until he was naked. He climbed over her, replacing his fingers with his phallus, rising above her on his muscled forearms.

Tentatively, she ran her hands down his hips, testing the hard muscles. His birthmark was dark purple in the candlelight.

The devil's mark.

He guided himself into position. She took a sharp breath as the crown of him opened her, stretched her.

Too much.

She squeezed her eyes shut, her body taut and trembling.

She heard his breathing, harsh and labored. Felt his strong, heavy body quiver above her, his arms like iron bars forming a cage around her.

Ash clenched his teeth, his jaw, his entire body, quivering with the strain of holding back when he longed to sink into her silken heat.

"Hetty, are you here with me?"

Her eyes were tightly closed, arms held rigidly by her sides. "Of course. I'm here." She opened one eye. "What are you waiting for? Do the deed. Consummate the marriage. And be quick about it."

"Possibly the least erotic sentence ever spoken." It certainly cooled his ardor.

The women in Ash's bed were hot and ready and primed when he took them. They moaned his name, scratched his back with their fingernails. Bit his shoulder. Urged him forward. Hetty had reached her pleasure quietly, half-battling the sensation. She hadn't let herself go completely.

She was still frightened. She was an innocent, sheltered young lady who'd been kept in the dark about many of life's experiences, both good and bad. He couldn't expect her to suddenly abandon the restrictions she'd placed upon her emotions, the inflexible rules that governed her conduct.

"I'm not going to take you unless you're an equal participant," he said through gritted teeth.

"Why should you care? You're a big bad wolf and I'm your prize. Claim me. Have your wicked way with me."

He took a deep, shuddering breath, and rolled off her, landing with a thud by her side. Not tonight. Soon, though.

"What's the matter?" she asked.

"This is a mutually beneficial business arrangement. And it will be mutually pleasurable, as well. I'm not going to bed a passive cipher of a woman. I want my partners here with me, body and mind. I'll accept nothing less than your total surrender."

"You'll never have it."

"I will. But not tonight. You may have branded me a scoundrel, Hetty, but I do have one hard and fast rule: I have never, not once in my life, bedded an unwilling woman."

"It's our wedding night. We are expected to . . ."

"Do the deed. I'm well aware of that."

"I'm willing, or I wouldn't be here."

"Sometimes willing and ready are two different things." He rolled onto one elbow so he could see her face. "If you're not fully present, if you're not enjoying it, then I wouldn't be able to enjoy myself either."

Her brow wrinkled. "I hadn't considered that you might have such compunctions. I was under the impression that men were governed by needs and urges and would slake their thirst if an offering was made."

"An offering. There you go again. You're not some vestal virgin offering, Hetty. We're in this together now." He softened his tone. "I understand what you're doing, and I won't consummate anything if you're going to turn it into some kind of martyrdom."

"What am I doing?"

"I think you've made a plan to share my bed but remain as distant and controlled as possible. You're thinking you're going to lie back and remain passive while I have my wicked way, which would give you all the more reason to resent me. Am I close to the truth?"

She turned her face away, which was all the answer he required.

"You need some time to get used to me. I understand that. Thankfully, this isn't our last night on earth. You'll beg for my touch soon enough."

"You're overconfident."

"And you're shivering." He found her silk robe on the floor and tucked it around her. "Time to go back to your room now. And take that hourglass with you. We won't be needing it tonight."

She left in a huff, clearly put out that he hadn't fulfilled her expectations of a rutting beast who ravished frightened virgins.

Think again, Hetty.

He'd take her when she was ready and willing. Should only be a matter of days. In the meantime, more gin. And maybe a dousing with ice cold water.

Tomorrow he'd begin exploring his new kingdom. Jax had promised to send word if there were any new developments with the Coakley threat. Hetty could never know the truth about his past. She could never know the lies he'd told or the dark secrets he hid.

This game he'd set in motion was a house of cards, balanced edge upon edge, and he'd nearly reached the top. He was prepared to deal swiftly and ruthlessly with any perils to his new position. He hadn't plotted everything so meticulously only to see it come crashing down.

He'd won the dukedom. And he'd win over his bride.

That body of hers . . . his cock swelled again. She was all luxurious curves and long limbs. Ripples of dark brown hair spread over the white bed linens. Her full lips red and beestung from his kisses.

He wanted her badly, he'd never wanted anything more, but he could wait. His patience was forged from a lifetime of delayed gratification. He knew how to bide his time, planning the perfect moment to make his move.

She would surrender willingly, and when she did their passion would blaze hotter than Hades.

Chapter Seventeen

❦ 🌹 ❦

"Mr. Prince was so attentive yesterday," Hetty told Gretchen as the maid brushed her hair the next morning. She didn't have to feign her blush. She yawned and stretched luxuriously. "I'm simply exhausted. I don't know how I'll find the strength to do anything except laze about in bed."

Gretchen smiled. "Only as it should be, milady."

Hetty's wedding night hadn't gone exactly as planned, though Gretchen could never know it. Her maid was obviously dying to know the details. She had a cousin who worked for a newspaper office in London. Hetty didn't mind if Gretchen supplied a few details to him, if Hetty was the one to control the flow of information.

Once the news of Ash's inheritance and their hasty wedding reached the scandal sheets, they would be a great curiosity, and their every move would be conjectured upon and debated. She had no doubt that bets were being placed about them in the betting book at White's on whether their marriage would be amicable. When he would take a mistress. That sort of nonsense.

The bargain had been that Hetty would play the doting and devoted wife. Society must believe that Ash had been reformed by the love of a good woman.

It would be a lie, of course. After last night, Hetty had grave doubts about winning the wager. She'd been thoroughly pleasured, but Ash hadn't been in any hurry to claim his prize. It vexed her that he'd remained so fully in command of his emotions and urges, while she'd succumbed so easily and eagerly to his expertise.

"What will you wear today, milady?" Gretchen asked after Hetty's hair was fixed into a simple chignon.

"My light blue day dress. I'm giving Mr. Prince a tour of the estate."

"Very good, milady."

If Hetty had any hope of reforming Ash she must make him fall in love with Rosehill Park. If he cared about the estate he wouldn't be so eager to carve it up. The plans she'd seen in his chambers had indicated that he planned to tear down the Temple of Bacchus and replace it with stables. Her job today was to convince him that the estate was perfect the way it was, and he should find another location for his stud stables.

"Please ask cook to prepare a light luncheon in the wine tasting room. Mr. Prince has expressed an interest in tasting the various wines on offer."

"Very good, milady."

Hetty entered the breakfast parlor and stopped just inside the door. Her father had a companion: an older woman with a towering mound of dark hair streaked with gray. She wore a gaudy day dress of pink and green stripes that was altogether too close-fitting and low-cut to be proper.

The two were engaged in feeding each other bites of flaky pastry.

She'd never met her father's mistress before, she'd only heard rumors of her existence before her father confessed his attachment. "Good morning, Papa."

"Hetty, allow me to introduce Madam Giovanna Bianchi."

"Oh, my dear. I'm so very pleased to meet you," cried Madam Bianchi. "Finally, my Henry and I can bring our forbidden love out into the open. I've hated the sneaking around."

Ash strode into the breakfast parlor looking entirely too handsome and suave in his new gray silk waistcoat and crisp white cravat. "Good morning, all."

"Cousin Ashbrook," said the duke, "this is Madam Bianchi."

"Please call me Ash." He lifted Madam Bianchi's hand and kissed her knuckles. "Enchanted, madam. I saw you perform many years ago. Your voice is sublime."

"Fie, what a charmer," she replied, giggling.

"He's only speaking God's truth, my little Vanni." *His little Vanni?*

Hetty had never seen her father look like this, not since her mother was alive. He was glowing. He was in love. How could she have been so ignorant of his amour?

"The newlyweds. It's so romantic!" said Madam

Bianchi. "Felicitations on your marriage. I begged Henry to introduce me to you, Lady Henrietta, many times, but he didn't think it was prudent. Now we're throwing caution to the winds, aren't we, darling dear." She tickled his white whiskers.

"We certainly are, my buxom bottle of Chianti." The duke captured her fingers and nibbled at the tips of them. "We're off today, to Rome. We'll be married posthaste."

"You're leaving today?" Hetty stopped slathering butter on her toast.

"I can't wait another moment to make this adorable creature my wife," the duke said.

"Oh, Henry. Finally, we can be together." Madam Bianchi sniffed.

"I leave my Hetty in your care, Ash. I'm certain that you two will find something to occupy yourselves with while I'm gone." The duke winked at Ash, who was attacking his bacon with the ferocity of a starving cat.

"You could have told me about your desire to marry, Papa," said Hetty.

"Alas, I'm of a certain age, Lady Henrietta," said Madam Bianchi. "And I knew that dear Henry must do his duty to the family and produce an heir."

"But now I don't have to!" her father said gleefully. "I have an heir, and a son-in-law. Now all I require to make my happiness complete is a great brood of grandchildren. You must begin work on that endeavor immediately and I'll expect a babe in the nursery upon our return to England."

Hetty stared at her toast instead of meeting Ash's gaze.

You'll beg for my touch soon enough.

She shivered. With her father leaving, she'd be alone on the estate with Ash.

"I wanted you to be here for the visit of Mr. Ross and Monsieur Chabert, Papa. You know I've been corresponding with them in your name. They'll expect you to be here to show them the vineyards and give them a wine tasting."

"Ash will serve in my stead, won't you m'boy?"

"I don't know much about wine," said Ash, his voice gruff. "Only that I like drinking it."

"Hetty will instruct you in the finer pleasures, I've no doubt," said the duke with a hearty laugh.

"I look forward to becoming better acquainted with the both of you," Madam Bianchi said, "but really, dear Henry, we must hurry. We have an elopement to enact!"

"And then we're going to take Hetty and Ash's honeymoon, my sweet."

"Our honeymoon?" Hetty asked.

"You're too busy to travel abroad. We'll send you letters from every place we visit, never fear." The duke kissed his lover on the cheek. "Every bed we christen."

"Oh," Madam Bianchi fluttered, "you naughty man."

"Your carriage is ready, Your Grace," Dobbins announced with a bow.

The duke and his paramour hopped up from the

table and skipped out of the room with their arms wrapped around each other.

"I wasn't aware that my father had plans to leave England," she said to Ash. "I've been so occupied with growing my wine business that I didn't see what was before my own eyes. My father had a secret life I knew nothing about."

"The sly old fox."

"He could have waited a week to be here to conduct the wine tour. Mr. Ross has no idea of my involvement in the vineyards."

"Ah, the infuriating Mr. Ross, a charlatan of a wine expert, he of the poison-pen."

"Things have changed on the estate since he last visited. And this time I also invited my mother's visiting cousin, Monsieur Chabert, of the champagne House of Chabert."

"Visiting from France?"

"Yes. I was hoping that with the Chabert connection to our vineyards, and the superior flavor of our new wines, Mr. Ross would have no choice but to rectify the erroneous characterization of Rosehill Park in the forthcoming edition of *A World of Wines*."

"You'll charm the trousers off them."

"I'm quite worried about what they'll say when my father isn't here. They won't be expecting a woman to be in charge."

"Wear a low-cut gown," he said.

"I want them to take the Rosehill Park vineyards seriously. *I* want to be taken seriously."

"Stuff that. Make a grand entrance wearing something seductive, silk the color of grapes poured over those dangerous curves of yours, flash your décolletage, and bat your eyelashes at Mr. Ross, and it will all be over before he even tastes your wine. He'll fall at your feet."

"What a typically male and typically offensive thing to suggest." She rolled her eyes. "I'm not going to flash my décolletage, as you so crudely put it."

"I'm only saying that you should use every asset at your disposal. Hook him with your curves, reel him in with your impressive knowledge of wine, and then club him over the head with the excellence of your wine."

"Mr. Ross is not a trout."

"He's a man. And most of us are easily landed by a beautiful woman. You hold power over us. If you have a goal, you should try to win by any means necessary."

"Is that what you do?"

"I'm unscrupulous, you know that. I'll find a way to win."

"You shouldn't give me your secrets, Ash. Maybe I'll make my wine the toast of London."

"You can try."

"But you don't think I have any chance of success. Isn't that right? That's the only reason you agreed to the six months."

He shrugged. "Your words, not mine."

"Well, I'm not comfortable using my physical appearance to gain my way in the world. My father used to say something similar. 'Your face is your fortune,' he'd say, whenever I bemoaned the fact that I wasn't born male and the laws of primogeniture prohibited me from inheriting. It used to make me so angry."

"It's the way of the world, unfortunately."

"For my whole life, people, men, have been telling me I'm beautiful. And it became a kind of duty, a liability. When I made my debut, I felt I had to be as physically perfect as possible, to live up to this impossible image that people had of me. And if I fell short, it was almost as if I was personally letting them down. If I had a blemish on my cheek, or I stumbled as I danced, I felt ashamed, as though I wasn't this graceful goddess they wanted me to be. It was very hard work."

"Your beauty isn't a liability, Hetty. It's a gift. You're like the ceiling of the Sistine Chapel. A breathtaking work of art and a window into heaven."

"Beauty fades. I was almost relieved to give it all up, in a way, after my mother died and my father declined. Here at Rosehill, I don't have to uphold some impossible physical standard. I'm not being judged or measured against anyone but myself and my ambitions. Here, my duty is to grow grapes, to give them the conditions and the love they need and then to press them, put them into barrels, and give them the time and space they need to mature."

"Make a speech like that to Mr. Ross, then. You're so impassioned and articulate on the subject of wine. Why don't you take a risk and reveal that it's your talent and vision behind the wine venture?"

"I'm not going to reveal my true role in the vineyards to Mr. Ross, or the world. Not yet. Not until the reputation of the wine is secured. Maybe I *will* seduce Mr. Ross."

His slate-gray eyes darkened to wet ash. "I didn't say you should seduce him. Only dazzle him."

"You wouldn't be jealous, would you?"

"I'm never jealous."

Hetty smiled. She'd recognized the flash of possessiveness in his eyes. "You've eaten the whole platter of bacon. You might wish to take some exercise now, or those new waistcoats won't fit for very long."

He threw his serviette onto the table and rose from the table. "Lead the way, my bride. Show me these famous pleasure gardens of yours."

HETTY WAS DETERMINED to make Ash fall in love with the estate. Who could remain impassive to such radiant natural splendor?

"Rosehill Park was developed by my great-great-grandfather, Henry, the fourth Duke of Granville. He carved this remarkable series of landscaped gardens out of the unpromising Surrey heathland. You'll already have noticed the Gothic tower on the western boundary, it's impossible to miss, and there's the ruined abbey overlooking the lake, a grotto, a Turkish tent, and a mausoleum containing antiquarian objects brought from Italy. He was a fanciful man, and very well-traveled."

She led him through a series of gardens, each new scene unfolding like a series of natural picture frames.

"He liked to utilize the elements of concealment and surprise. He wanted to integrate nature into his designs, instead of taming it into contrived symmetry. There's a certain quiet and peace you can only find in a well-designed garden. The stillness of forests is dense, and dark, and hushed with moss, ancient, and not quite human. These gardens have a purpose to them. He wasn't trying to impose his vision on nature, but he wanted us to see nature in a new way, revealed in all her glory."

Ash stopped, shading his eyes with his hand and looking out over the vineyards. "At least he wanted a select few noblemen and ladies to see his vision. These are pleasure gardens for only the privileged to see."

Hetty cocked her head. "I've never thought about it that way."

"Of course you haven't. You were born with every advantage. You view these magnificent gardens as your right and your due." His gaze swept over the rolling hills, the rows of vines, and the sparkling lake. "We're from such different worlds, Hetty. I was raised with a view of soot-darkened bricks and destitution."

She'd always been so proud of the estate, her heart gladdened by the sight of so much unspoiled natural artistry.

She'd seen Ash's architectural plans. Where they were standing had a direct vantage point down to the area where he planned to build his stables, on the flat land beside the lake. She could tell he was measuring things with his eyes, placing the stables, the paddocks, and the practice courses.

"The nobility is a dying breed, Hetty. You won't hold power forever."

"You're a member of the privileged class now, Ash."

His laughter was short and bitter. "We'll never see these gardens through the same eyes."

"You can't deny their surpassing beauty."

His gaze met hers. "No, I can't deny they're pretty to look upon."

"It's profit you seek, though, is that it? You'd demolish my ancestor's artistry for the sake of quick and easy monetary return."

"Isn't that the point of the vineyards?"

"The fourth duke planted five acres of vines on this steep slope overlooking the artificial lake fed with a waterwheel from the nearby river. He did it as an experiment, without thought for profit. It was my mother who began the work of expanding the vineyards into a business."

Hetty resumed walking down the hill toward the vineyards and Ash followed. "The fourth duke started with two grapes from Burgundy—the Auvernat, which is delicate and difficult to grow in England, and the miller grape, sometimes called the black cluster, which is hardier and more suited to our climate and soil."

The vines were planted in orderly rows, and the grapes hung heavy and purple on the vines. Hetty picked a few grapes and handed them to him. "Taste. This is the miller grape."

He bit into the fruit, licking the juice from his lips. "Very nice. But it's purple. And your wines are white."

"The outside is purple but the inside"—she crushed a grape and showed him—"is pale greenish-yellow. We'll harvest the grapes on a cool morning in early September and convey them to the barns as swiftly as possible. When we crush them in the press, we filter off the skins and seeds. The juice will be a golden color, like liquid sunshine."

"Where's your vigneron?"

"Mr. Renault will be in the barns, turning the bottles and making sure the wine is aging properly. I'll take you to meet him."

"He came over with your mother?"

"And he stayed on after her death. He married an Englishwoman, and they have three children. These vineyards are a labor of love. With too much humidity, mildew will grow on the vines, and we must drop fruit—go through each row by hand and clip any grapes affected by mildew. Good pruning is fundamental and necessary. Still, we try to do as little as possible, to be as gentle as possible, and allow nature to sing."

"A poetic turn of phrase." His gray eyes reflected the blue skies, appearing lighter and more teasing. It was warm, and he'd loosened his cravat. This was the first time she'd seen him in full sunshine. It teased more gold from his hair and gave his already tanned skin a warm glow.

He undid his cravat and opened the top buttons of his shirt. "It's quite warm, isn't it?"

Hetty's straw bonnet hid her face from him, a useful trick when one's cheeks were flaming because one was watching a man disrobe in broad daylight.

"Let's continue the tour," she said hastily, moving ahead of him.

"In its heyday, there were thirty to thirty-five thousand vines at Rosehill—more than some vineyards in France, but unfortunately my grandfather allowed the vineyards to suffer neglect and even planted a grove of Scotch pines over parts of them. My mother was the one who reclaimed the vineyards when she arrived from France to marry my father."

She stopped to examine a vine that was drooping. They'd have to water more frequently if the sun continued as hot. "My mother used to say that the soil here in the southern part of England is very similar to where she grew up in France. The Champagne region is so far north, and the soil is a bright white chalk with ancient seashells mixed into it. She believed it was our chalky soil that gives Rosehill sparkling wine its crispness, and its clean, dry properties."

"I thought the dastardly Mr. Ross insulted your soil."

"Shows what he knows," Hetty said, moving along the rows, her fingers searching for insects and imperfections. There were several farmhands working in the vineyards, and she waved to them.

"Maybe this time he'll be more open-minded," said Ash.

"I do hope so." She popped a grape into her mouth. "It's very near harvesttime now. We have to watch the grapes very closely. We're praying for this sunny weather to continue."

"What happens if it rains?"

"A period of sustained rain could cause the fruit to

swell and dilute the juice. The wine would be weaker and less flavorful. I do hope you won't pray for rain, Ash."

He clapped a hand over his heart. "I'd never do such a dastardly thing."

"All I ask is a seat at the table for English wines. We build the reputation, and once it's established, then we plant ten more hectares, then twenty. I want to open a wine cellar in London. The profits will start to flow, and with the capital, I can complete all of the projects on the estate that I've been waiting to accomplish."

"What type of projects?"

"I redistribute all earnings from the vineyards into upkeep for our cottagers. I've helped finance a great number of improvements on the estate, and I have very ambitious plans for the future. There are hundreds of servants and tenants at Rosehill Park, and every last one of them relies upon the Prince family for their livelihood. As my father descended into drunken disorderliness, I had no choice but to forge relationships with the tenants. Their respect has been hard-won, let me assure you."

"I don't doubt it."

SHE WASN'T ANYTHING like what Ash had branded her: a privileged, thoughtless rich lady. She'd led a sheltered life on her vast country estate, but she was striving toward worthy goals, and that made him want to like her.

He wasn't supposed to like her or feel a kinship with her.

She seemed to absorb the sunlight as she spoke, her smile glowing, eyes alight with passion.

There would be one way to make Lady Henrietta Prince smile—plant her more vineyards.

But Ash had to be clearheaded about this. His plans for the estate were far more practical. It was a crime to own all of this land when so many children in London were starving, were laboring their lives away . . . and dying for the enrichment of landowners.

Strolling through these tranquil gardens, he could almost believe that the grime, poverty, and desperation of London didn't exist. Except he knew that they did. This was an oasis for the privileged only. The rulers. The oppressors.

He would take the financial rewards from his racehorse business and fund more schools to keep destitute children out of factories. He'd use his wealth to force the aristocracy to do his bidding. Give them a taste of their own bitter medicine.

Hetty stroked a grape leaf, tracing the ruffled edge. "I told you when I met you at the ball that I created the wine. But really, if you think about it, I don't create anything. The vines and the sun and rain do the work. All I can do is give the vines the conditions they require. We nurture the soil, ploughing and plucking any weeds because they would compete with the vines. We grow oats and clover between the rows, then plow them back into the soil, to feed the vines. We check the temperature of the soil. Watch for excess water that could kill the leaves. Vines need love. They need warmth and attention and care to grow."

He saw it so clearly. She was speaking of herself. She was the one who hadn't gotten enough love or attention, not since her mother died. Her life had withered on the vine with that tragic occurrence. She'd turned to the vineyards, pouring all the love and pain in her heart into creating a tribute to her mother.

"I know what you're attempting to do, Hetty."

"You always seem to think you know everything about me, Ash."

"You're trying to make me fall in love with the vineyards and with these pleasure gardens."

"Well, of course that's what I'm trying to do. I don't want Thoroughbreds trampling my chalky soil."

"Profit rules my world, Hetty. My promise to your father was that I would restore the fortunes of this dukedom."

Thoroughbred breeding was a far more practical use for the prime piece of flat land positioned next to the lake. He could see it now—sleek racehorses gleaming in the sun, flying over hurdles.

Investors and buyers having luncheon under pavilions erected on the lawns.

Who knew? He could even rival Tattersalls someday as an auction house for the most exclusive champions.

"Six months, Ash," Hetty said. "You promised to give me six months."

"And I'll honor that promise."

"I want to show you one more sight: the Temple of Bacchus," she intoned with pride. "Inspired by the fourth duke's grand tours."

He had to admire her determination. She'd seen the plans he'd drawn up. And the Temple of Bacchus was standing in his way.

Her plan wasn't going to work. He couldn't be swayed by elegant shrubbery, fake Roman ruins, and sensuous curves . . .

She raised her hands, as if worshiping the sun. "And now we've traveled to ancient Rome."

A classical building rose before them, white columns gleaming in the sunlight.

"The relief above the doorway depicts the parade of Bacchus."

"Bacchus looks foxed," Ash observed. The potbellied and bearded god of wine was being helped onto a horse by a strapping young fellow.

His lovely tour guide led him through a tall doorway into a cool, spacious room.

The ceiling was ornate plasterwork in a simple eagle-and-vine design. There were Greek statues set in niches along the wall, and twelve busts of Roman emperors in a row.

The middle of the room was dominated by an enormous statue of Bacchus holding a cluster of grapes and leaning on a thick grapevine.

"Isn't he grand?" Hetty asked. "He's seven foot tall."

"He's a lot younger in this statue. And a lot less clothed," said Ash. There was a sash draped across his chest and nothing more. "His endowments leave something to be desired. I wouldn't be so cavalier about displaying myself to maidens if that was all I had to offer."

A large tiger-striped tomcat ran into the temple and rubbed his chin against Ash's boot. "Hullo there, fine fellow. And who might you be?"

"That's Bacchus," Hetty said. "He's my Chief Rodent Catcher."

Bacchus swaggered over to Hetty and rubbed up against her skirts, purring loudly.

"It's a good name for him. He walks as though he's seven foot tall."

"We'll have to introduce Lucy to Bacchus," she said.

"Are you sure that's a good idea? He looks like a bit of a scoundrel."

Hetty laughed, scooped the cat up, and planted a smacking kiss on his nose. The cat yowled in protest but made no real struggle to escape from his fair captor.

Ash had never been jealous of a cat before.

"He is a scoundrel, but he's a dear, sweet boy. Aren't you, Bacchus? You're my good boy." She nuzzled the top of his head.

Bacchus stared balefully at Ash, but Ash could tell he was secretly enjoying his captivity.

Who wouldn't?

The cat began to struggle, and Hetty released him. He raced out of the temple as if he'd caught sight of a field mouse.

"He never does let me hold him for very long. He's not the most affectionate of cats. He wouldn't be caught dead sleeping in my room like Lucy sleeps in yours."

"And she wouldn't be caught dead eating mice.

She only eats fresh silvery kippers arranged in a precise row."

Hetty grinned. "It should be interesting to introduce them. We'll allow her some time to settle in, and then we'll see how it goes. Speaking of dining, are you hungry yet? I've asked cook to prepare a light luncheon in the wine tasting room."

"I could do with some refreshment." He closed the gap between them. "But I'd rather taste your lips."

"Ash," she remonstrated.

"What? You can't lure me into a temple dedicated to the celebration of hedonistic pursuits and not expect me to pay obeisance to the flesh-and-blood goddess before me."

He dropped to one knee on the marble floor.

"Ash, what are you doing?" she breathed.

"Lifting your skirts." He burrowed under her petticoats in search of the warm, sweet woman beneath the muslin.

She swayed above him, listing as though standing on the deck of a ship. She wasn't wearing any drawers. Hallelujah! He reached his hands around to grab her firm bum, steadying her and tilting her pelvis toward his lips. It was damn hot under all these skirts, but he wasn't going to let that stop him.

His tongue found the seam of her thighs, licking softly, persuading her to open for him. He was nearly to his goal when a loud male voice interrupted him.

"Lady Henrietta. Are you in the temple?"

"It's Renault," came Hetty's muffled voice from above him. "He's coming this way. Hurry, Ash."

"Damn Renault, and may the devil take his soul to hell."

"Ash!"

Reluctantly, he extricated himself from her skirts and rose woozily to his feet.

"I'm in the temple, Mr. Renault," she called, as Ash adjusted the fit of his breeches and smoothed down his hair.

Mr. Renault entered the temple. He was a small man, about fifty, with wizened features and skin tanned to leather from working in the vineyards.

"Mr. Renault," Hetty said, "this is Mr. Prince. My new husband, and heir to the dukedom."

Renault doffed his cap. "Mr. Prince. What do you think of this earthly paradise?"

The estate was nice enough, but Ash had been about to taste heaven when he'd been so rudely interrupted. It didn't make him disposed to like the man. "It's lovely," he said, looking at Hetty instead of Renault.

Her cheeks were rosy and her eyes were bright with laughter. So she thought it was funny that he'd been interrupted. He'd have his revenge later.

And he'd take his slow, lingering time about it.

"I'm afraid I have some bad news, Mr. Renault," said Hetty.

"Is there rain coming? You found mites, didn't you. We're sunk. All is lost."

Cheery fellow, Mr. Renault.

"There's nothing wrong with the vines," Hetty hastened to assure him. "My father won't be here for the visit of Monsieur Chabert and Mr. Ross. They were expecting him to be here to give them the tour since, as you know, I've been corresponding with them in my father's name."

"Mr. Prince can give them the tour."

"I might not be available. I might have business dealings in London." The moment he received a summons from Jax, Ash would ride for the city.

Renault's already wrinkled brow creased further. "And what's more important than this visit, Mr. Prince?"

"I don't know anything about wine, Renault. I've tried to convince my wife that she should lead the tour and show them how passionate she is about sparkling wine."

"I'd like to," said Hetty. "But I think it would decrease my chance of receiving a favorable review from Mr. Ross. Actually, I agree with Mr. Renault, Ash. Mr. Ross would be far more disposed to give the wine a favorable review if you gave the tour."

"I hope they don't come on harvest day," said Renault. "Could be soon if this weather holds. Or it could rain buckets and turn everything to muck. Then everything would be ruined."

"Don't even think it," said Hetty.

"I'll be going back to work now," said Renault. "This is the most precarious time for the vines."

"I know I've been gone too long," Hetty said. "I'm here to help now."

"It's your honeymoon, milady. I can manage. Though I only have two hands. And it could rain. Torrents of rain. And the grapes could drown." He gave a dour shake of his head. "Best make an offering to Bacchus, milady. We'll need all the divine help we can get."

Mr. Renault walked away, grumbling to himself in French.

"A delightful man," Ash remarked.

"Don't mind him. He always gets this way around harvesttime. He's nervous, and being nervous makes him cross."

He moved closer. "That's what I was trying to do, before we were so inconveniently interrupted. Make an offering to the god of hedonism and ecstasy." He ducked his head, avoiding her bonnet brim, and kissed her lips. "It might help the harvest."

She lightly pushed him away. "We can't just go around making offerings wherever you decide. There are rules to follow. I agreed to one hour per week."

"We don't start counting until after the week of our wedding."

"I don't recall writing that guideline."

"I'm adding an addendum."

A smile curved her lips. "Perhaps you'll receive a knock upon your door tonight . . . or perhaps not. Now come along, it's time for luncheon."

She danced away, a curvaceous goddess come to glorious life.

Escaping her stone pedestal, free to wander the world of men and bewitch their poor souls.

Chapter Eighteen

❧ 🌹 ❧

"*Three* BOTTLES OF wine?" Ash chuckled. "Are you trying to make me drunk?"

A cold repast of charcuterie, cheeses, and various garnishes was laid out on a wooden table in the barn where the oak casks of wine were stored for aging.

Amethyst-colored wineglasses and wines were laid out, ready to be opened.

Three bottles of wine and Hetty.

He could get used to this.

She guided him to the bench by his hand.

"Close your eyes," she said when he was seated.

"Why?"

"Just close your eyes."

She tied a velvet blindfold around his eyes. His body stiffened for a moment, but then he relaxed. "I'm usually the one tying velvet blindfolds onto women, not the other way around."

"This isn't for bed sport. It's for the wine tasting. You're going to tell me what you taste.

"This is one of our finest," she said, handing him the glass. "The 1828. This is the one I'll serve to Monsieur Chabert and Mr. Ross. Ash! Don't gulp it like you do your gin. That's sacrilege! Swirl it in your glass and then taste it. Slowly."

He followed her instructions and took another sip. "It tastes expensive."

"Doesn't it? I remember when this one was maturing. It's always a time of great anxiousness. But there's really nothing I can do. I've had to learn the trust and faith not to intervene. Not to do anything. Not to manipulate it. To allow it to mature and change. I've had to accept the risk. If I wanted to undertake something easy and certain, I would do something different. With more certainty of outcome."

"This one certainly was worth the risk."

"Every now and then we strike gold. It has a good amount of fruit to it. It's crisp and refreshing and light. You'll notice that the aftertaste lingers for a full minute. Tell me what you taste."

"Ripe grapes and . . ."

"Yes?"

"I taste you, Hetty. Your lips. Your kiss."

He couldn't see her, but he felt her behind him. Her fingers brushed the nape of his neck. He smelled her new scent, warm peaches and lemon flowers.

"Open your mouth," she commanded.

She held something cold and smooth to his lips and he bit down, tasting a ripe strawberry, sunny and sweet.

"More," he said.

She fed him more strawberries. Then a lemon cake with frosting which he licked off her fingers.

"When do I taste more wine?" he asked impatiently. First the wine, then Hetty.

"Drink some fresh well water, to cleanse your palate." The touch of cool glass on his lips. A little awkward to drink without seeing. She guided the cup to his lips, and he tilted his head back. The water was cold and tasted slightly of earth, cool and damp, just drawn from the well.

Some dripped down his chin, and she patted it dry with a cloth. Could he manage to spill some water lower?

He was desperate to feel her hands on him.

"On my fifteenth birthday, my mother opened a bottle of champagne that she'd brought with her from France as part of her wedding dowry. A bottle she'd been saving. It was sublime. Sometimes a bottle of wine, sometimes one glass of wine, can be the equal of a book of sonnets, or a symphony. Sometimes it changes you, filters through you and colors your blood, your vision, and you become something new. That's my goal, Ash. I want to produce wine that works a kind of magic. I've come close before, but not close enough. I'm hoping this year's vintage will be the one."

"You're making me thirsty, Hetty."

"Now then, of these three bottles, two are French champagne, and one is my sparkling wine."

Another hard glass rim against his lips. He drank deeply, throwing back his head and bringing the glass with it.

"No! You must sip and savor."

He sipped. "It's fizzy."

"Yes."

"It's tart."

"Yes. Anything else?"

He wanted to please her. What would she want to hear? "Um . . . it tastes like ripe pears?"

A sigh. He'd disappointed her.

He tried again, dredging up every ounce of poetic fervor he hadn't known he possessed. "The bubbles are like pearls poured upon my tongue, seductive and sparkling, bursting with notes of . . . sun-ripened fruits and newly blossomed pale flowers."

A delighted little laugh. "Very good. That will do nicely. Now the second wine."

It tasted slightly different. It had the same fizz, the same pop on his palate, the same tartness, but it was sweeter.

"I like this one better because it's sweeter. I taste honey."

"You're right, there was more sugar added during the second fermentation to this wine."

More cool spring water. The sound of wine being poured. He followed that sound and grabbed her wrist. He pulled her toward him and settled her into his lap, wrapping his arms around her shapely curves.

"Hetty," he nuzzled her ear. "I want to taste you."

"Drink this first," she said breathlessly. She didn't attempt to free herself or leave his embrace. He settled her rounded bum against him, desire spreading through his body like flames consuming wood.

She turned in his lap, holding a glass to his lips and he sipped slowly. This one was definitely different. There was the fizz and pop, the tart bursting on his tongue, a little lemony? And then something like a freshly opened vanilla pod. Something comforting. Vanilla and frothy egg whites. Cream. Strawberries.

A pang in his heart as he remembered the cook at the orphanage, Peggy. The one who'd sneaked him biscuits if she had any extra.

"You're silent. This one is bringing back a memory?" she asked.

He swallowed. "Yes. A memory from the orphanage. The wine reminds me of a dessert the cook used to make for the matrons using cream and strawberry jam layered with vanilla biscuits. I was a favorite of hers. She often remarked with a sniff that I reminded her of her own dear boy who'd gone off to war and never come home."

He hadn't thought about Peggy in years. He wondered if she was still alive.

"This one is yours, isn't it?" he asked.

"Yes," Hetty whispered with a catch in her voice. "There's hope for you yet, Ash."

Her words were said lightly, yet he heard what she was really saying. That she hoped he might learn to love her wine enough to want to nurture the vineyards with the care and attention she lavished upon them.

Maybe some part of her even hoped that he might fall in love with her and become the staid, boring husband of her fantasies, reading books by the fire with her and tending the vines together.

An ache started in his chest, a desire to hold her close to his heart like this forever. Wrap his arms around her and never let her go. Her approving whisper, the smile he heard in her voice, his only benchmark of success in life.

She made him thirst for more than wealth, more than the power to change the world. Holding her made his life before he met her seem hollow and cold, like an empty wine glass.

She was everything effervescent and tart-sweet, everything intoxicating.

Never fall in love with a mark.

He could thirst for her lips and her body only. Never for her heart.

"I'm blindfolded and at your mercy, Hetty," he whispered, kissing her neck. "You can have your wicked way with me."

Hetty longed to taste him, to kiss him. Here? In broad daylight. In the barn.

Yes, here.

She poured more of the Rosehill sparkling wine into her mouth and brought her lips to his.

He kissed her greedily, until she could barely breathe, his large hand cradling the back of her neck, keeping her pinioned as his tongue entered her mouth with sweeping, velvety strokes.

Breaking away, she ducked her head into the haven of his neck, allowing herself a moment to breathe.

Don't lose control.

"You spilled a drop, Hetty. We wouldn't want any of this wine to go to waste." He kissed the tip of her finger.

"You spilled wine down my gown when you grabbed my wrist as I held the glass."

"Where did the wine spill?" He turned her to face him, sliding her skirts up and positioning her limbs on either side of his hips. "Here?" He kissed her collarbone.

"Lower." She held her breath.

His lips dipped lower. Her head fell backward as he slid her bodice down with his mouth and claimed her nipple.

"Yes," she murmured. "There."

Longing flooded her body as he moved to the other breast, circling the nipple with his tongue before closing his lips and suckling gently but insistently.

Tingling awareness lapped at her mind, flowing down into her belly, pooling between her legs where a delicate pulse had begun.

A wanting.

She knew the pleasure he could wring from her body.

The hard contour of his arousal was inescapable. She sat right upon it. She shifted on his lap, and he wrapped his arms more tightly around her. His hands slid to cup her bum, squeezing and lifting, rocking her core against his stiffness.

Was she still in control here? It felt like the balance had shifted, even though he was blindfolded. He was moving her where he wanted her to go. Sliding her body against his arousal.

"You're more intoxicating than any of these wines, Hetty."

She was having the most wanton thoughts. She wanted him inside her. The knowledge shocked her. Did that mean he'd won the wager?

Only if she begged for it.

"Ash, we shouldn't. Not here. Wait until later, I'll knock on your door tonight."

He moaned. "I want you now. On top of me. You can set the pace."

He still wore the blindfold. She could see him, but he couldn't see her. His throat worked with emotion. If she reached down and undid his trousers . . .

It would mean she'd been thoroughly corrupted.

She broke his clasp and slid off his lap.

There was a knock at the door of the barn and a discreet clearing of a throat.

Ash ripped off his blindfold and shifted the table-cloth to hide his lower half.

"Yes, what is it?" Hetty asked.

Dobbins entered the barn. "It's a delivery for you, Mr. Prince. Your Thoroughbred stallion has arrived, and the deliveryman is wanting to speak with you."

"I'll be right with you, Dobbins," Ash replied.

Dobbins left the barn.

"You're already having racehorses delivered?" Hetty asked.

"Only the one. But he's to be the sire of a noble bloodline."

And the destroyer of her dreams.

She busied herself with tidying the wineglasses, though a servant would be along any moment.

"Hetty, I—"

"Go see about your horse, Ash. I'm obviously wasting my time here."

"You're not wasting your time. Your wine is delicious. I'm a convert."

"You don't care about the wine at all. You were only humoring me. Well, you can stop it. I don't want to be pandered to, and I won't be played like a pawn in some secret game of yours."

"Does this mean I won't be hearing a knock upon my door this evening?"

"Just leave, Ash."

Chapter Nineteen

❧ ✿ ❧

THE NEXT MORNING, Hetty proposed a visit to the tenant farmers. And then she stayed silent through the remainder of breakfast. Ash couldn't coax a smile, or even a word from her lips.

She was still angry about the unceremonious end to their erotic wine tasting.

Having the racehorse arrive at that moment had been spectacularly bad timing. And he only had himself to blame. Perhaps he could have kept the horse in London, eased her into the idea, instead of springing it on her.

Now she was marching ahead of him through the woods on the path that led to the cottages, and he had to rush to match her pace. "You're still cross with me," he observed, catching up with her.

"You might have at least *pretended* to give me a chance at keeping my vineyards before purchasing your stud horse."

"I'd already purchased him before we reached our bargain. I'd been paying for a stall in London, but here I have an entire mews at my disposal."

"Humph," she retorted, her face set in disapproving lines.

"It's only one horse, Hetty."

"The father of a new line of racehorses."

"I've promised to give your wine venture a chance, and I will keep that promise."

"You have a funny way of showing your sincerity."

"Do you want me to send Dionysus back to London? Will that make you feel better?"

"Is that the horse's name?"

"Yes. And I might add that I named him *before* I met you. You could see it as serendipity."

"Or I could see it as the symbol of your schemes which will supersede mine." She picked up her pace again, leaving him behind.

As they approached the cluster of cottages, trailed by three footmen bearing baskets laden with books, food, and other practical gifts, Ash began to have a sick feeling in the pit of his stomach.

He was no lord of the manor.

These farmer tenants would look at him in his new clothes with his polished boots, and they'd take him for a nobleman.

Someone who had the power to rip their children away from their homes and force them to labor in unsafe factories.

You're being irrational. They'll have heard about The Devil's Own Scoundrel. They'll know of your unlikely rise into the nobility. They'll know you're more one of them than one to the manor born.

But the children wouldn't know the difference. All

they'd see was someone who held their lives in his hands. The authority and arbiter of their fates.

He hung back on the pretext of admiring the idyllic view.

"Ash," Hetty called over her shoulder. "Do keep up."

"You walk ahead," he responded. "I won't be a moment. Just admiring the view."

He clenched his hands into fists. The violent emotion took him by surprise. His hands began trembling. The faint scars on the backs of his legs and hands burned as though they'd been freshly cut.

Remembering his years in the bottling factory sometimes had this visceral effect on him, as though time unspooled backward and he was eight again, small for his age, and terrified of the whippings meted out by the factory overseers.

Even more petrified of the fists and boots of the older boys, who lorded it over the younger ones.

There was nothing he could do but take deep breaths and wait it out. He'd be right soon.

Ready to keep up the pretense. Assume the role.

Duke's heir. Not a care in the world. The world is my pleasure garden.

Resting his palms against the trunk of a venerable old oak tree to stop the tremors, he closed his eyes, inhaling the fresh green scent of the moss underfoot and the oak leaves overhead.

"Ash?" A soft touch on his shoulder.

He opened his eyes to find Hetty standing next to him. "Is something the matter?"

"Nothing's the matter." He straightened his shoulders, but his damned hands were still shaking. He clasped them behind his back.

"Don't lie to me, Ash. There's something wrong. I can see it on your face. I sent the footmen ahead with the gifts. We can take our time." She gazed over the grouping of cottages with their whitewashed walls and thatched roofs, with hyacinth and roses adding splashes of vivid color. There were sheep dotted about the hillside, and children running through gates and chasing cats.

"Pretty, isn't it?" asked Hetty. "Those cottages are as snug and comfortable as any of the best estates can boast."

"Like a painting." He tried, and failed, to keep the bitter edge out of his voice. "English countryside with cottages. Something to hang in a gallery for society to ooh and ahh over."

"Ash. I know something's wrong. What is it?"

She wouldn't leave him alone until he told her. He knew firsthand how stubborn she was.

"The factory I labored in as a boy employed mostly orphans, like me, or children from the poorhouses. But sometimes the younger children of cottagers from grand estates would be sent to London to earn an extra income when they were still too young to work in the fields. My friends and I, raised in London, had it better than those tenant children. At least we knew the harsh and unforgiving way of the world. Those poor lads from the countryside didn't know anything about air heavy with coal smoke or beggars wrapped in bandages on every corner. They climbed into a cart, promising to send money home to their mamas and papas, and they imagined that they'd find their fortunes in the big city. London ground them down, reduced them to shadows of their former selves. Many didn't survive."

"None of our tenant children have ever been sent to work in factories, as far as I know. The families have a good life here at Rosehill."

"You don't know everything there is to know about this estate."

"I know every tenant, Ash. The youth attend the village school. I have a scholarship for promising children, male or female, and if any of them show a desire or aptitude for book learning, I speak with their families and offer to pay their way to a reputable institution. I try to open doors, not close them."

Every time he attempted to fit her into the box he'd defined for the heedless rich, she managed to surprise and disarm him. "Then you're the exception, Hetty, not the rule."

"Come." She took his arm. "You'll meet the tenants for yourself and judge their living conditions and prospects."

They continued walking, this time in step together.

"Oh, Your Ladyship." A girl of about sixteen flew toward them as they approached. "I'm so glad you've come. They sent me to fetch help."

"What is it, Missy?"

"It's my brother Davy. He's gone missing. He's been away for a full day and night."

"What happened?" Hetty asked.

"Some of the lads were teasing him. You know

how lads are. He ran away and shouted that he'd
never be back. We thought he'd surely come home by
teatime, but he's missing and . . ."

Hetty put her arm around her shoulders. "We'll
find him."

"He's probably gone to the fair," said Ash. "All
young boys like to see a good fair and try their luck
with the games."

"I-I hope you're right," Missy said. "Though he
hasn't any coins to spend at the fair. Everyone's out
searching the forest right now. He's so small and
young. There could be w-wild animals."

"Is your mother at home?" Hetty asked.

Missy nodded. "She's waiting there in case he comes
home on his own. I've never seen her cry like this."

"Now, Missy," said Hetty. "You go to the great
house and tell Dobbins what's happened. He'll send
over more footmen for the search and organize pro-
visions for everyone."

Missy thanked her and set out at a run.

Ash and Hetty followed the lane down the hillside
to the cottages. Ash knew the fields would normally
be filled with men working plows, but all was eerily
quiet today, the farming equipment abandoned mid-
furrow to search for the missing boy.

They entered a tidy, cheerful cottage to find an
apple-cheeked and handsome woman wearing a
frilled cap, sitting on a stool, sobbing her heart out.

"Oh, Mrs. Clapham." Hetty rushed toward her.
"We'll find Davy, don't worry. I've brought Mr.
Prince. We'll search together. And Missy will bring
more help from the house."

"Lady Henrietta." Mrs. Clapham dried her eyes with her apron. "And Mr. Prince. How good of you to come."

Ash had to ask this next question, though it wasn't an easy one. "Have they checked the well, Mrs. Clapham?"

She nodded. "They've checked everywhere."

"Would he go into the lake?" Hetty asked.

"He doesn't like swimming."

"His sister said the other boys were teasing him?" Ash asked.

"He's a target for the other boys. He's a sensitive lad, not like his father at all. Davy doesn't take to sports or hard work. He's always got a book hidden beneath his pillow. He'll ruin his eyes reading by candlelight every night."

"Show me the books he's been reading," Ash said.

"Do we have time for that?" Hetty asked.

"Trust me, it could help."

Mrs. Clapham showed them into a small bedchamber with three little beds. A bright red rug made the smooth wood floors cheerful, and there were yellow curtains at the windows.

Ash smiled as he read the titles of the tattered and worn books on a small shelf. "*Don Quixote, Robinson Crusoe, Peregrine Pickle, Gil Blas* . . . he likes adventure stories."

"That *Robinson Crusoe* is Davy's favorite book in all the world," said his mother fondly. "Why, he must have read it a hundred times. He's always pretending to be a buccaneer and capturing imaginary loot."

Ash took Hetty's hand. "I think I know where to find young Davy."

HETTY RUSHED ALONG beside Ash, who held her hand with a firm grip. "Where are we going?"

"Any child who pretends to be a buccaneer will be searching for treasure. We passed a mausoleum near the lake, and you said that it held ancient artifacts."

"All the way there? He'd not stray so far, would he? The children are told not to play too near the house. They have a whole wood to explore behind the village."

"He was being bullied. I have an instinct about this, Hetty."

He hurried her along, his shoulders set in a tense line.

"We'll take a shortcut through the woods," she said. "I know the way."

Within a half hour they'd reached their destination. They entered the dark mausoleum.

"Davy!" she called. "Davy, are you in here?"

"No," a small voice replied. "Go away."

She sighed with relief and squeezed Ash's hand. "Oh, thank God."

He placed an arm around her shoulder. "Let me talk to him. Man to man."

"All right."

Ash moved in the direction the voice had come from, the back left corner, behind a stone sarcophagus. Hetty could barely see him in the dark space.

He knelt down. Hetty could just make out the boy huddled in the corner, holding a gold chalice in the cradle of his cloak.

"Davy, is it?"

"Y-yes," Davy sniffled. "Who're you?"

"I'm Ash Prince."

Davy tilted his head up. "The Devil's Own Scoundrel?"

Ash laughed. "That's me."

"I'm a scoundrel."

"What name would I know you by?"

"They call me the Scourge of the Seven Seas."

"A very good name. It's sure to strike fear into the hearts of your enemies."

Hetty's heart swelled until it felt like it might burst in her chest.

"Are you, by any chance, hungry, Mr. Scourge?" he asked.

"Might be."

"Lady Henrietta has some fresh-baked rolls at the house. And big platters of bacon. That's my favorite. Do you think you might like some?"

"Might do."

"What's that?" Ash asked, pointing at the chalice.

"My pirate treasure." Davy lowered his voice to a whisper. "Course I know it's not really mine, but I can pretend."

Hetty walked toward them. "You may pretend all you want," she said. "But you mustn't run off and worry your parents."

Davy's small shoulders hunched. "I know. I . . . I didn't mean to fall asleep, and then it was morning, and I couldn't go back there. Not after what they said to me."

"What did they say?" Ash asked gently.

"I'm not a tattletale."

"Do you know, Mr. Scourge, I used to be bullied by

the other boys for reading books. There's no shame in loving to read. Devouring all the books you can find will make you a clever boy, and you'll have a very bright future. That's the sweetest revenge on those dimwitted boys who bothered you."

"Do you think so?"

"I know it to be true."

"My father says reading will give me airs and graces. But Mama says I might be clever enough to go to school."

"Should you like that?" Hetty asked.

"I want to be like Mr. Prince, and marry a beautiful lady like you."

Ash chuckled. "We'll have a word with your parents, shall we?"

"My father won't like it."

"I never knew my father," said Ash.

Davy sniffed. "Y-you didn't?"

"He died when I was only a baby. I think you're very lucky to have a father and mother who care about you."

"They're very worried about you," Hetty said. "Shall we go back?"

Ash held out his hand. "Up you go, Mr. Scourge. And leave that chalice where you found it."

They walked with him back to the house, Davy holding on to Ash's hand and peppering him with questions.

"You're very good with children," she whispered to Ash.

"Does this mean I'll hear a knock on my door tonight?" he asked with a wicked smile.

"Perhaps," she replied, her heart hammering with anticipation.

DAVY HAD BEEN safely delivered back to his house, and Ash had had a little chat with his father and mother. Everything was decided. Davy would begin living at Ash's boarding house in autumn and taking his lessons with the other boys, none of whom would tease him for loving to read.

After their evening meal, Hetty gave Ash the fourth duke's memoirs and they sat reading together by the fire in a cozy parlor.

"Did you know that your ancestor was a cheat?" he asked Hetty.

She lifted her head from her book. "He wasn't."

"He was. It says right here that he sold his sparkling wine to merchants for fifty guineas a hogshead, and then they sold it as French champagne. He says he fooled many venerable judges of wine, who thought his wine superior to any champagne they'd ever tasted, but he thought it prudent not to divulge his wine's origins until after they'd passed their judgment because of the prejudice against English wine."

Hetty groaned. "The prejudice remains the same today, even though we British invented the method for producing sparkling wine."

"We did?"

"The French think it was Dom Perignon in 1697, but it was a fellow named Christopher Merrett who presented a paper to the Royal Society about adding sugar and molasses to make wines brisk and sparkling and that was thirty years before Mr. Perignon made his experiments."

"Fascinating." He yawned. "But isn't it time for bed yet?"

Hetty flipped a page. "Just one more chapter." She returned to her book. Ash would rather study her.

As she read, a blush colored her cheeks and her bosom rose and fell more rapidly with every page.

The memoirs were tedious. And she was stimulating.

He couldn't sit across from her without feeling aroused. But there was more. Simply a desire to be near her, to listen to her, to speak with her.

"What are you reading?" he asked.

"*The Wicked Earl's Wishes* by Daphne Villeneuve." She turned another page.

"Sounds exciting."

"It is. I have to find out what happens."

"So, you're reading a boudoir novel and I'm supposed to be content with these dry memoirs? I'd rather be drinking wine than reading about it."

No response. She was engrossed in her book, flying through the pages. Was she even reading them? No one read that fast.

"I knew it!" she cried. "I knew that Lord Valdemar was really the villain."

"With a name like Valdemar, he'd have to be, wouldn't he?"

"Sometimes the heroines do make bad choices, but they end up with the right person." She sighed. "It's very romantic. But now I need to know what happens to Sophronia and Ethelinda's youngest sister, Vespera. Only her book has been delayed and the publisher can't tell us when the manuscript will be delivered. Miss Villeneuve is cloaked in mystery. No one seems ever to have met her."

"Could be a man writing those books, have you ever thought of that?"

"Oh, I doubt that very much. She has a way of describing things that is entirely from a feminine perspective. And the books are always focused on the journey of the heroine. And the poor heroine, who has to endure so many trials, always triumphs in the end."

"Is this what you normally do when you're not working in the vineyards?"

"I read books, yes."

"Don't you ever invite your neighbors over?"

"Sometimes. Lord Ryland is elderly and has a host of physical ailments and complaints. Sometimes I invite him and his daughter over of a winter evening and we sit by the fire."

"Sounds stimulating."

Ash felt a little like he'd stepped into the pages of a book by Miss Austen, one of those mannerly tomes where passions simmered far, far beneath the surface and nothing was ever out in the open.

It wasn't right to bottle up your passions. Ash was a fan of letting them out. Fanning the flames.

"I also spend time whenever possible with my friends in London," she said. "We have a wonderful library at our clubhouse on the Strand. We have a significant collection of works by female authors."

"Why does that not surprise me? And I suppose males aren't allowed in your clubhouse to peruse the titles."

"Only by special invitation. Perhaps . . . one day on one of the occasions where males are allowed to attend a lecture, or a fundraising event, you'd be welcome."

"Perhaps," he said neutrally. They weren't supposed to make too many plans for the future. Secure an heir and then . . . separate lives.

That had been the agreement.

"Do you miss your wild companions and your London life?" she asked.

"Not at the moment."

Jax's mocking words echoed through his mind.

The notorious Devil's Own Scoundrel forced to his knees by a bluestocking. Before you know it, you'll be spending cozy evenings in an armchair by the fire with her.

There was only one reason Ash was sitting here, and that was to kill the hours before the bedding began. At least that's what he told himself.

"Now that you've read your naughty novel, it's time for bed, Hetty."

"You may join me in my chamber at precisely eight o'clock. Don't be late," she said sternly, but there was a saucy glint in her eyes.

He'd have to buy her more boudoir novels. That Villeneuve woman needed to write faster.

Chapter Twenty

❧ 🌹 ❧

GRETCHEN BRUSHED HETTY'S hair until it was smooth and snarl-free. "Shall I leave your hair down, milady?"

"Yes, please."

"The white nightgown is most becoming."

"Thank you." Hetty's gaze sought the clock. "Oh, is it almost eight? That will be all, Gretchen."

"Don't forget your new perfume," said Gretchen with a sly smile, handing Hetty the bottle. "I've heard that a dab of scent behind the knees can be delightful."

As soon as her maid left, Hetty climbed into bed, pulling the covers up to her chin.

No. She sat up. Why should she be waiting under the covers like a timid maid?

Maybe the only way to wrest back any modicum of control and maintain a proper emotional distance was for *her* to seduce *him*. That way she wouldn't be surrendering anything other than her body, and on her own terms.

She didn't know the first thing about seduction,

but how difficult could it be? He'd said that she should wear a low-cut gown to influence Mr. Ross.

What would happen to Ash if she weren't wearing any clothing at all?

Her fingers curled around the lace-trimmed hem of her nightgown and she lifted it over her head in one quick movement, before she over-thought anything.

She dropped it over the side of the bed where it pooled in a shimmering white heap.

She shivered, the hairs on the backs of her arms standing straight.

How should she arrange her limbs? She slid both knees to the side and sat up like a mermaid on a rock. With one hand covering her most private place, and an arm over her breasts, she wasn't completely exposed.

She was as ready as she'd ever be.

His loud rap upon her door came at precisely eight o'clock. Her heart pounded. No backing out now.

"Enter." Her voice barely trembled.

He entered, carrying a candlestick, and stopped just inside the room, staring at her.

He made a noise in the back of his throat, a strangled sound. "Bloody hell, Hetty. Are you trying to kill me?"

"No, I'm trying to seduce you. You can't corrupt me if I'm the one who seduces you."

"Oh, is that how it works?"

"I just added it to my schedule for the day. Item number nine: seduce Ash."

"I like that item."

She felt very exposed. Perhaps she should have left her nightgown on. But he'd seen her now. "Do you like what you see?"

Another strangled sound and an affirmative nod. "If you're seducing me, and all bets are off, that means we don't need to use the hourglass."

The hourglass! She'd forgotten about it completely. "That will be acceptable. Just this once."

She closed her eyes.

Against her eyelids she saw what he must see. Her substantial curves, round, heavy breasts. The inflection of her waist and the emphatic flare of her hips.

Thighs soft and overlapping.

Dark hair over her sex.

"Hell's bells, Hetty." A ragged pronouncement, a prayer.

She opened her eyes.

He stared hungrily, his gaze heating her like wine in a barrel, beginning to fizz, to expand.

Making her blood simmer.

He hadn't even touched her yet and the warmth was spreading through her body. The tips of her breasts tingled under his gaze.

"Touch your breasts," he ordered. "Lift them."

She lifted her own breasts, felt the weight of them in her palms, firm and soft.

"You're ripe and ready. I want to eat you up." His voice was gruff. "I'm going to taste you, devour you."

A thrill along her spine and melting warmth between her legs.

"Spread your thighs. I want to see all of you."

"As you wish." She was in control here. She wasn't doing his bidding. She was seducing him into wanting more.

Needing more.

She inched her thighs apart.

"Raise your knees and spread them."

Bared for his gaze. Her secrets exposed.

Her body glowing against the covers, lush and full. Her breasts round, belly rounded, thighs spread wide, knees apart.

"Take your clothes off, Ash," she said, trying to match his domineering tone.

"With pleasure." He set the candlestick down and stripped off his clothing so swiftly his hands were a blur.

She swallowed, feeling her throat working, feeling the rise of emotion in her chest, some trepidation, mostly longing.

He was naked.

He was everything she desired.

Soft firelight flickered over his hard body. She drank in the sight of him. His rugged face and sensual lips. His wide shoulders and muscled chest. He kept his hands at his sides, making no attempt to hide the thick phallus that jutted at a right angle from his body.

"Looked your fill?" he asked.

She swallowed. "I find your body to be . . . attractive."

He cocked his hips forward. "I definitely have more to offer than that statue of Bacchus."

An understatement. His sex was huge. She imagined it entering her. There. Where her body pulsed with longing. She wasn't afraid.

She was tempted.

Tempted to invite the devil into her bed and beg for his touch.

She'd never beg.

There was such power in seeing the evidence of how much he wanted her, how his flesh strained and quivered.

The intent look on his face as he stared at her.

She should feel shy, or protect her modesty, or something like that, but all she felt was powerful and seductive.

HETTY TOOK HIS breath away. She lay, naked, in the center of the bed, knees up and thighs spread for him.

Thick, silky ropes of brown hair swerving over her shoulders.

Extravagant breasts, large and plump, with an enticing shadow down the center.

He wanted to slide his tongue between her breasts and then between her legs.

She wanted him to jump on her, ravish her, have done with it. A few minutes (if he were being honest—it had been months since he'd had any female companionship) and he'd fall asleep by her side. And she'd be . . . unsatisfied. And in control.

"Take your nipples between your fingers, Hetty," he commanded, knowing that if he was the one giving the orders, he held the advantage.

She obeyed, and he nearly lost all control.

"You like my breasts, don't you, Ash?"

He loved them. He wanted to play with them and make friends with them. Fondle them and kiss them forever.

"Touch yourself, Hetty."

"Where?" she whispered.

"You know where," he said gruffly.

HETTY BROUGHT HER fingertip between her thighs, lightly touching, questing. Finding the right place and lingering there, so soft and sweet.

She imagined that Ash was touching her. She was almost willing to beg for it. That was the game he was playing.

Make Hetty beg. Drive her wild with desire.

Drive him wild. Make *him* beg.

She caught his gaze and held it, allowed the pleasure to seep into her eyes, as her fingertip continued gently circling, a pressure building. A clenching and a drumbeat starting inside her.

He moved closer to the bed, until he was standing above her. He gripped his phallus with his fist and gazed down at her with such intensity in his gray eyes that she thought his gaze might mark her somehow.

This was beyond anything she'd ever imagined. This man standing over her, palming his hard flesh, stroking up and down with his fist, as she sought her pleasure.

Who was controlling this? Who was winning?

Maybe it didn't matter.

This was awkward and strange, but it was thrilling as well, because Ash was touching himself too, and she knew he wanted to be inside her, that he was imagining the act.

"Are you . . ." she began, not sure if she was brave enough to say the words. "Are you imagining that you're inside me?"

His breathing turned guttural and harsh. "Christ, Hetty. I want to be inside you so badly. I want to slide inside you, fill you up, make you mine. It's going to be so perfect. We're going to move together, mount each other. I'll be on top of you, and then we'll change, and you'll be on top."

"I think . . . I think I'd like that," she said huskily, her breathing shallow as she neared her crisis.

With her body's moisture slick over her fingertip, she bit her lip as she found the gathering of nerves, the most sensitive place, and she softly slid her finger from side to side.

The warmth from the fire was nothing compared to the heat inside her. The growing pressure to find release.

He stared at her finger moving over her sex.

"I want you to make yourself come, Hetty."

She was soft, and she was wet. She ran her fingers along the sides of her sex, and it was delicious. He leaned forward to watch, and the expression on his face, the intensity, made her even more bold.

She dipped her fingers inside, into the wetness, and then back to the center of her craving.

He moaned hoarsely, watching her, his fist moving faster up and down the hard length of him.

"Don't stop touching yourself," he commanded.

As if she'd stop now. She was nearly there. Existing only for pleasure, teasing at it, holding back. Soon it would burst inside her, flooding her whole body with sweetness.

Ash dropped to his knees beside the bed and stroked his hand up her inner thigh.

"Keep touching yourself," he said. "Don't stop."

It was a thrilling and triumphant sensation, knowing that she'd brought him to his knees, that he was worshipping her with his eyes.

He gazed at her reverently as he pleasured himself with one fist, using his free hand to slide two of his fingers inside her in a pleasing rhythm, making fluttering motions, while she continued stroking herself, delicately, knowing that her crisis was close now.

There was nothing delicate about what Ash was doing to himself. While his fingers were inside her, his other hand pumped up and down his phallus, faster and faster.

Veins stood out on his neck and sweat beaded on his forehead. The muscles of his arm bunched and rippled as he worked himself.

It was too much.

Hetty came, softly crying her release and arching her back off the bed.

She heard his harsh cry, felt his fingers thrust deep inside her as he reached his climax.

He withdrew his fingers.

She peeked at him from behind the curtain of her hair. He'd risen from his knees and was using his shirt to clean himself.

He slid the bedclothes down and climbed into bed beside her. She'd never had a naked man in her bed before.

What would he do now?

Apparently, what he was going to do was fall into a deep, immediate slumber. She curled up against his warm body, watching his chest rise and fall.

There was a scratching at the door and muffled mewling. Poor Lucy. She didn't like being locked away from her father.

Hetty slipped out of bed and wrestled with the bedclothes, and with Ash's heavy body, until he was covered. She used the privy and washed her hands and face. Donning a clean cotton nightgown, she brushed the tangles from her hair.

More scratching at the door and pitiful mewling.

"Oh, very well," she whispered, opening the door. "But don't disturb your father," she told Lucy sternly. "He's resting after our exertions."

Lucy hopped up on the bed and promptly nestled into her favorite spot in the crook of Ash's arm. Hetty climbed into bed and cuddled up against Ash's back, suddenly exhausted.

He was so much less intimidating when he was asleep. She held her hand over his heart.

She was in trouble. She felt it deep in her bones.

He was still the same man she'd waltzed with, domineering and ambitious, but she'd glimpsed so many other facets of his character in the short time she'd known him.

There was no preparing, or protecting, her heart against such an unfair onslaught.

She was doing her very best to maintain her distance, and then he described her wine with poetic perfection, or encouraged a vulnerable child to keep reading, which was custom-designed to seduce both her mind and heart.

She knew him now, knew that he would come to her aid, and to the aid of her tenants, in a time of crisis. Knew him to be, if not honorable, at least well-intentioned.

Think about when he leaves and goes back to London and takes another mistress.

Think about that, Hetty. Do you really want your heart to be entangled when that break happens?

Maybe she didn't have a choice. Maybe it was already too late.

Chapter Twenty-One

❧ 🌷 ❧

$\mathcal{A}$SH WOKE WITH a start. There were soft things in the bed with him. Two soft, lightly snoring things. Hetty was wrapped around him from behind, her arm over his arm, her breasts pressed against his back.

And the damned cat was curled up in the crook of his neck, her head resting on his pillow.

"How did you get in here, you little demon?" he whispered to the cat. She made one of those adorable noises she made when disturbed in the middle of a serious slumber.

Hetty nestled closer, sighing in her sleep.

He was well and truly trapped.

All curled up and warm and cozy. Hetty cuddling him from behind, her breath fanning his cheek. The vanilla and lemon scent of her, her delicious curves cradling him.

He reached around and ran his hand over the contour of her hip. She'd put on a nightgown but he was still naked. Under the bedclothes, his cock was at full mast. Maybe he should do something about that.

First, he'd have to get rid of the cat—set her on the floor.

Then he'd roll over and wake Hetty with kisses. She'd smile and wrap her arms around him, gathering him close to her swiftly beating heart.

They'd have sleepy languid sex in the golden morning sunlight. He'd bring a pink flush to her cheeks. He'd feast on her soft lips, her nipples . . . and then he'd find his way home, to the heart and heat of her. Clasped tightly by her body.

He groaned aloud. What in God's name was wrong with him? He was losing his edge, just like Jax had predicted. All he wanted to do was wake her with tender kisses, but that was too close to breaking the first rule: *Never fall in love.*

Theirs was a marriage of mutual convenience. She was his ticket to the top.

He could desire her, find pleasure with her, but he could never, ever mistake her for his salvation.

Nothing could wash away his sins. He'd risen from poverty and deprivation using his wits and his fists. She'd never had to work for anything in her life.

She'd been kept ignorant of the origins of her family wealth, and the cruel consequences of the stranglehold the nobility kept upon their privilege and their superiority.

Hetty cared for the welfare of her tenants, but she was a rare exception. Her class had been heedlessly ruining lives, imprisoning innocent children in factories and workhouses for their own enrichment for too long.

He was going to change all of that. He'd need to be canny and ruthless, he must keep his wits about him, and sharpen his edge, not blunt it.

He'd spent enough time at Rosehill touring ornamental gardens, drinking fine wine, and reading books by the fire.

She was dangerous to his plans, she dulled his ambition. Made him begin to think that waking up with her arms around him was a goal worth fighting for.

Leave this bed, Ash.

He lifted her arm off his chest. She stirred, then rolled over, her eyes fluttering open. "Ash? You're still here."

"I'm still here," he said grimly. *But not for long.*

"Then I won," she said with a sleepy grin. "You fell asleep in my bed and slept the night away. I've definitely reformed you."

He left the bed and found his trousers. The shirt would need to be laundered.

"Ash?" she murmured.

"Go back to sleep, Hetty. It's early yet. I'm taking the cat out for her morning necessities."

"You love Lucy, admit it," she said sleepily, rolling over and burrowing back into the covers.

Admit nothing. Don't look at her.

If he even so much as glanced at the tumbled mahogany curls spreading over the pillow, the teasing light in her brown eyes, those perfectly kissable lips, he might lose his resolve to leave.

If he didn't leave now, he might never leave her side again.

He scooped the cat into his arms and entered his chamber, closing the door behind him.

There was a fresh plate of kippers waiting under a glass cover. The cat scrambled out of his arms and set to with gusto.

A knock sounded. For a moment, Ash thought it was Hetty at their adjoining door, but then he realized it was the external door. He opened it to find Dobbins standing there with an envelope on a silver platter.

"A message sent by special delivery for you, Mr. Prince."

Ash's throat constricted. This was news of Coakley. "Thank you, Dobbins."

He opened the envelope and read the coded message from Jax.

Dobbins cleared his throat. "Will there be anything else, Mr. Prince?"

"I'll need my horse saddled. I ride for London immediately. Please have one of the maids take Lucy—take my cat out for a walk around the enclosed garden after she's finished eating."

"Very good, sir. Shall I send His Grace's valet to help you dress?"

"That won't be necessary. I've been dressing myself my entire life." And he wouldn't be wearing any of the custom-fitted new clothing Hetty had ordered for him. He couldn't look like a soft and polished nobleman where he was going, with what he might have to do.

His old comfortable battered boots. A simple neckcloth instead of a fancy waterfall of a cravat. And his pistol.

There wasn't a moment to lose. Jax's code had been crystal clear: Coakley was back from the dead.

Ash's hands trembled as he buttoned his waist-coat. This was his worst nightmare. His past had come back to haunt him, just in time to threaten all of his carefully laid plans, right at the moment when he could almost taste victory.

He searched for his comfortable old boots and couldn't find them. What had the minx done with them? She'd probably thrown them out. He'd have to wear the new ones that pinched his toes.

He'd defeated Coakley once before, and he'd do it again. How he'd survived that gunshot was a mystery. But Ash would put another bullet into his dark heart if he had to. Now he had Hetty to protect.

She could never know about this, never know that he'd brought this grave danger to her door. She'd be safe at Rosehill as long as he dealt with Coakley swiftly in London.

He scrawled a note to her before he left, telling her that he had urgent business in London. She had much to keep her occupied, thankfully, with the visit of Mr. Ross and the impending harvest.

Before he left, he made Dobbins promise not to let her out of his sight, and then he mounted his horse and set out at a breakneck pace for London, to face his past.

To conquer his demons once and for all.

HETTY AWOKE TO a maid opening the curtains. For a moment she had the fear that a stark-naked Ash was still in the bed with her. That would be quite a tale for the maids to tell. But then she remembered their morning conversation. He'd gone to take Lucy for her morning walk in the walled garden. He was devoted to that cat, even though he was too gruff and proud to admit it.

She smiled and stretched her arms over her head, still feeling pleasantly satiated from last night's exertions. She'd thought the seduction had gone rather well. A quiver trilled through her body as she remembered Ash's reaction when he saw her arranged upon the bed in her altogether.

He'd dropped to his knees on the floor, his expression filled with devotion.

Bringing big bad beasts to their knees. Another skill to add to her list of accomplishments.

Speaking of lists, she had a long one for today. Mr. Ross and Monsieur Chabert were arriving for their visit in a matter of days. Everything must be perfect for the tour and the wine tasting.

She rose and went to the windows. The sun was shining brightly and the vineyards glowed emerald-green in the distance. Ash had said that he might not be here for the wine tour, that he might have urgent business in London, but he was still here now, and she'd find a way to persuade him to stay a few more days.

As reluctant as she was to admit it, it would be helpful to have a male tour guide for Mr. Ross. The wine critic was far more likely to take the Rosehill wine seriously if it was proffered to him by a ducal heir, even one who was still rough around the edges.

She was beginning to like his rough edges. His gruff commands.

Careful, Hetty. Don't let him steal your heart. It can only end badly.

Pushing the warning to the recesses of her mind, she crossed the room, intending to ring for Gretchen, until she saw the note slipped beneath the adjoining door.

She read the brief missive. Ash had been called away to London on urgent business. He was sorry he couldn't be there for the wine tour. He knew she'd dazzle Mr. Ross.

She knocked on the door between their rooms but there was no answer. He was already gone. She tried the knob and it opened easily.

Lucy was sleeping on Ash's bed. Hetty gave her a scratch between her ears and she began purring.

"Where did your father go? What could be so urgent?" Hetty asked her.

She looked around the messy room. While he was gone she could at least take the opportunity to have his room tidied. She noticed a crumpled piece of note paper lying in the grate. It looked like a recent addition.

She shouldn't be snooping through his room, but she'd done it before. The man she'd married had too many secrets.

She uncrumpled the note.

Two words: *Diamonds high.* Signed by Mr. Smith.

What could that mean? Something to do with gambling, but she could make neither heads nor tails of the message. He'd most likely gone to meet Mr.

Smith at The Devil's Staircase. What were those two up to?

If she hurried, she could be to London and back before supper time. Dobbins and Renault could see to the preparations for Mr. Ross's visit. She'd take Leland for protection.

She kissed Lucy's head. "You'll have to stay with Dobbins, Lucy. He's very softhearted, despite his impassive exterior. I'm quite certain he can be persuaded to scratch beneath your chin and stuff you full of kippers, just like your father does."

Following Ash around London was probably a foolish and dangerous plan, but she had to know the truth about the man she'd married.

The man she was very afraid that she was falling in love with.

She'd known he had secrets when she'd married him. She also knew that it was time for the secrets between them to end.

Chapter Twenty-Two

❧

Ash and Jax arrived at the house Jax's informant had named in Seven Dials and kicked in the door, pistols raised.

Ash swiftly noted all the details. A cigar still smoldering on a table. A deck of tattered and blood-spattered playing cards. An empty bottle of gin.

A curtain fluttered in the breeze. "He must have escaped through the window," Ash said. "He'll have disappeared into the crowd by now."

"Who tipped him off that we were coming?" Jax wondered.

"No idea, but I have a bad feeling about this." His stomach churned. "It might be Coakley, Jax."

"Or it might be someone impersonating him to intimidate us."

"What's the end game? Why not attempt to black-mail us already?"

"If it's someone pretending to be Coakley, some-one who knows about our history with him, their power lies in keeping the mystery, building the anxiety and fear, until we're jumping at our own shadows."

"I watched him bleed. He was lifeless."

"We left that alleyway before we made absolutely certain."

"Why hasn't he come back before now, then?"

"I don't know." Jax kicked a chair. "This is getting inside my head. I don't like this game of cat and mouse. I don't like being the mouse."

"We've worked hard to become the hunters, not the prey," Ash agreed.

Jax placed his pistol in the holster beneath his coat. "Whoever is toying with us will reveal himself when he wants to. In the meantime, I have a business to run. And aren't you supposed to be on your honeymoon? We can't live our lives in fear."

Ash noticed a movement of the curtain that hadn't been a breeze. *Someone was out there.*

He lifted his finger to his lips and jerked his head toward the window to show Jax what he'd seen.

Jax saw the silhouette and nodded.

"We were too late," Jax said loudly. "He's gone. We should leave now, Ash." He stomped toward the front door, making a lot of noise, while Ash stole noiselessly to the window.

In one abrupt motion, he thrust the curtain aside and grabbed their spectator under the armpits, bodily hauling them over the ledge and through the open window. The person struggled but Ash soon had them pinned onto the floor in a tangle of limbs and . . . curves?

Wait a moment. Ash knew those curves. *"Hetty?"*

"Ah, Lady Spitfire," said Jax, standing over them. "We meet again."

"Unhand me," Hetty said indignantly.

Ash hauled her to her feet. "What the devil, Hetty? You followed me into Seven Dials. Do you have any idea what kind of danger you're in here?"

She brushed off her sleeves and straightened her bodice. "The only danger I noticed was the peril of being injured or crushed by *you*."

"How long have you been following me?" Ash asked.

"Since you left the gaming house. Don't worry, I have an armed footman with me."

"Where is he, then?" Ash glanced around, folding his arms and glowering at her. "I don't see him."

"He's posted around the corner. We rehearsed a bird call that would have brought him running to the rescue. And I have my pistol." She patted the pocket of the gray cloak she wore.

"Is it loaded?"

"No," she admitted. "But I could use it to frighten someone. And I have a very sharp hat pin stuck through my bonnet. I'm trained to use it as a weapon."

Jax chuckled. "Maybe we should hire Lady Spitfire as our security at the gaming house, Ash."

"Not funny. This is serious, Hetty. You are in grave danger. I told you to stay at Rosehill. Don't you have a wine critic coming to visit? And grapes to harvest?"

"Yes." She sniffed. "But you left so suddenly and it was so mysterious. I want to know what secrets you're keeping from me, Ash. Who's this Coakley

you two were going on about? He poses some manner of risk to you."

He flinched, hating to hear his enemy's name on
her lips. "I'll tell you in the carriage. It's not safe here.
You didn't see anyone lurking nearby when you were
skulking outside the window?"

"I did not."

"You're going back to Rosehill, Hetty," Ash said.
"And that's an order."

"Humph. You don't have the right to give me
orders."

"I do when your safety is at stake." Ash turned to
Jax. "I'll meet you at the gaming house in one hour."

"Good luck," Jax said with a cheeky grin. "Lovely
to see you again, Lady Spitfire."

Hetty regarded him suspiciously. "I'm not sure
whether I like that title."

"Trust me, it's a compliment," Jax said. "You're
more than a match for The Devil's Own Scoundrel."

Ash was beginning to scare Hetty. He was gripping
her arm too tightly. His face was set in rigid lines.

"You want to know my secrets?" he muttered.
"You won't like what you hear. Best for you to remain
in the shiny protective bubble of your noble rank and
your ignorance."

The people they passed on the street were dressed
in ragged clothing, their faces coated with grime.
A woman grinned at Hetty, her mouth full of rotting
tooth stumps.

"Leland," Ash said when they reached the footman. "You are never to allow your mistress to go gallivanting around the worst neighborhoods of London armed only with a hat pin and an erroneous belief that she's invincible."

Leland bowed. "Understood, Mr. Prince. I'm heartily sorry." He wouldn't look at Hetty.

"He was only following orders," Hetty said.

"And those orders were harebrained and foolhardy in the extreme," said Ash.

"You needn't shout at me—oof!" Hetty exclaimed as Ash lifted her into the carriage, none too gently, and deposited her on the seat.

She heard him giving instructions to Leland and the coachman, but the words were indistinct.

"Are we going back to Rosehill?" she asked when he joined her in the carriage.

"We're taking a detour first," he said grimly. "And then you're going back to Rosehill, and I'm staying in London."

Those were the last words she could coax from his lips before the carriage stopped along the docks. Ash handed her down. She didn't recognize her surroundings. The windows were all broken or patched. The doorways gaped open like festering wounds, giving glimpses of miserable, cramped rooms where babies squalled, and men shouted obscenities.

Thin, raggedy children with hungry eyes clustered around her, hands outstretched.

Ash handed out coins to the children and they ran away with their loot, whooping with delight.

"This way," Ash said.

Hetty placed a hand on his arm. "Where are we going?"

"Down the real devil's staircase."

She picked her way gingerly across the broken glass and filth clogging the street, Ash urging her along. She stumbled and he righted her, but he didn't slow his pace. She held her sleeve over her mouth to block out the stench of refuse and urine.

He led her down a narrow, rickety flight of stairs leading toward the docks. He stopped halfway down and tugged her into a dark doorway. It took several moments for her eyes to adjust to the gloom inside the warehouse.

It was a wine-bottling factory. Hetty realized it first by the smell of rotting grapes, heavy and putrid. Then she saw the bottles piled everywhere. From their vantage point on a landing halfway up from the floor to the ceiling, she watched the laborers sorting bottles, examining them for flaws, or washing and setting them into crates.

"How old are those children?" asked Hetty.

"As young as seven. I began working here when I was eight." His face was impassive, though his voice held wrenching emotion barely kept in check. "The children labor fourteen to sixteen hours a day with only water and scraps of bread for sustenance. Only the strong ones survive. Many perish from the diseases spread by the rats scurrying everywhere, or the vile, damp air."

A heavyset man in a battered black top hat emerged from a rickety counting house perched with a view of the floor and bellowed at one of the children below. The lad staggered back to his feet, and began sorting bottles, his eyes glazed and head hanging low.

"That charming gentleman is Mr. Hornsby," Ash said. "It was his father who gave me these." He held out his hands, palms facing down, and Hetty recognized the faint scars crisscrossing the backs of his hands. She'd thought he'd come by his scars and bruises from the bareknuckle boxing he'd done.

Now she knew the truth. "Oh, Ash. I'm so sorry." Her eyes filled with tears. "These sordid conditions. The young children working their fingers to the bone. It's unacceptable."

"Unacceptable, you say, but it was acceptable to your father."

Her heart skipped. "What do you mean?"

"Your father used to own this factory, Hetty. He owned it when I worked here."

"That's a lie."

"The Duke of Granville used to own half the warehouses on these docks. Didn't you ever ask where your fortune came from?"

"My father's investments were in land, in shipping, and in the importation of goods and spirits from the Continent. I would have known if he owned a bottling factory." She paused, searching her memory of the accounting books.

Then she remembered her father's words about the falsified ledgers she'd read. Perhaps she hadn't been as aware of his business dealings as she'd thought.

"Ash, I didn't know. My father's not a cruel man, he wouldn't harm children."

"He probably didn't even know about the conditions of the factory. He certainly never bothered to visit while I worked here. He was just a name, a kind of deity. The exalted Duke of Granville. We pictured him living in splendor in his London townhouse, with ten servants to do his bidding at all times, stuffing himself with sweetmeats and wiping his lips with dainty lace and linen."

Ash was gripping the railing of the balcony they stood on, his eyes gone hard and distant.

"The nobility never considers the human cost of luxuries and privileges. Have you ever thought about where you would bottle your wine if you expanded the concern enough to open your own cellar?"

"I thought I would continue bottling it at Rosehill. But I do see what you mean. If I planted more vineyards and had more wine to bottle, I might have sent the oak barrels to . . ."

"To someplace like this," he finished for her.

"I would have toured the factory first, to ensure it was a reputable business that treated its employees fairly."

"Even so, you wouldn't have found a better option. Believe it or not, this is actually one of the more humane factories in London." He spat the words out, emotion harshening his voice.

"When I become the exalted Duke of Granville, I will advocate for the reform of child labor laws. I would prefer children were never forced to work under such conditions, but at the very least there must be a minimum age set for child laborers and a maximum number of hours they are allowed to work. They shouldn't be forced to work through the night. Children require sleep. They require adequate food and decent housing. They must be given an education if they are to rise above the filth and muck of abject poverty."

That's not all children required. Children required love. And Ash had never known any. Her heart bled for him. She wanted to wrap him in her arms, take his pain away.

His childhood had been a hell. Of her father's making.

She covered his hand with hers. "Ash," she said softly. "I want to help you with these goals. I'm so very sorry that I didn't know about my father's business dealings, the cruelty inflicted in his name. I wouldn't blame you if you hated him, if you hated . . . me."

"I don't hate you, Hetty," he said, but his face was still devoid of all warmth. "I only want you to recognize that you and I are from opposite worlds. You can't chase after me, trying to unearth my sordid secrets. My past is filled with this." He swept his hand over the sad scene beneath them. "This and worse. I've done terrible things. You can't reform someone whose sins are indelible."

"You're being irrational now. Why don't you confess your sins to me and allow me to be the judge?"

"You shouldn't care enough about me to even want to know the truth."

"I do care." She laid her hand over his heart. "I do care, Ash."

"Hetty." Her name was wrenched from his lips like a curse. "Our marriage can only be a business arrangement. We both signed the agreement. Right now I need to know that you're safely stowed away at Rosehill, away from the dangerous man Jax and I are hunting."

"Coakley. Tell me about him. What hold does he have over you? I thought you assured me there was no one from your past that could harm our family."

He flinched. "Do you really want to know the truth, Hetty?"

She squared her shoulders. "Tell me."

He gave a hollow laugh. "The truth is that I thought I killed him. I thought I killed Coakley with a bullet to the heart. I left him to bleed to death in an alleyway in Barcelona."

Her blood seemed to congeal in her veins, slowing her thoughts to a trickle. Ash was a murderer.

"You must have had a good reason," she said staunchly. Please God, let him have had a good, honest reason. Let it have been done in self-defense.

"Does it matter? I have blood on my hands, Hetty. While you were living in luxury at Rosehill, nurturing your vines, starting clubs for bluestockings, I was traveling a dark and troubled path. I never wanted you to know about this. The only reason I'm telling you now is so that you understand the present danger. The truth is that I believed I killed a man, but he might have survived. Or it could be someone pretending to be him. Whatever the reality, Jax and I will discover it, and swiftly. I refuse to put you in danger by proximity to me. You're going back to Rosehill where you'll be safe. I'll send word when the threat is mitigated or eliminated."

"Eliminated? You're frightening me, Ash."

"Good. Then my job here is finished." He clasped her elbow and bodily led her back through the doorway and up the rickety stairs.

Chapter Twenty-Three

❧ 🌹 ❧

"Today's the big day, milady," said Dobbins as Hetty entered the breakfast parlor. "I've no doubt Monsieur Chabert will be very impressed with the vineyards. And Mr. Ross will want to devote half of the new edition to Rosehill."

Dobbins was one of her most devoted supporters. He was particularly fond of the 1825 vintage, though it wasn't their best.

Hetty tried to eat some toast with marmalade, but it stuck in her throat.

She hadn't heard a word from Ash since he unceremoniously dumped her back in the carriage and sent her back to Rosehill. She'd asked him to be here for Mr. Ross's visit.

He didn't care enough to be here. He was off grappling with his demons. She didn't know the man she'd married, and he wanted to keep it that way. She'd tried to convince him to tell her more about his motivation for shooting Coakley, but he'd refused to say another word on the subject.

"May I say that you're looking lovely today, Lady Henrietta?" Dobbins gave her an approving smile.

"Thank you, Dobbins. This is one of Mama's frocks that I had altered. French couture never goes out of fashion." The gown had puffed sleeves and a deep neckline that showcased her bosom. The lines were simple; the allure was in the quality of the silk and the rich shade of claret. She wasn't planning to seduce Mr. Ross, though it couldn't hurt to look her best.

She paced to the window and peered up at the sky. "Do you think it looks like rain, Dobbins?"

"Not at all, milady. The sky's as blue as a robin's egg."

"Yes, but a sudden squall could blow through."

"I doubt that, milady."

She continued her pacing. First to the window, to squint at the blue sky. Then to the table, to take a sip of tea. And back to the window.

She realized she was watching for Ash. Maybe he'd had a change of heart and decided to come and help her. A carriage wound up the drive and her heart lifted for a moment, until she realized it was an unfamiliar equipage.

Her distinguished visitors had arrived. And she was on her own once again.

"Monsieur Chabert, of the House of Chabert, and Mr. Clive Ross," Dobbins announced.

The gentlemen entered the parlor. Chabert was tall and slender, with her mother's dark brown hair and brown eyes, while Mr. Ross was even more portly than the last time she'd seen him, and more bald, as well.

"Gentlemen, so good of you to come," Hetty said.

"Lady Henrietta." Monsieur Chabert bowed over her hand.

"Bonjour, Monsieur Chabert," Hetty said warmly. "It is my great pleasure and honor to finally meet you, having heard so much about you and the House of Chabert from my mother."

"Your French is nearly flawless, Lady Henrietta," he replied.

"Merci. I learned it by my mother's side."

"Let me look at you." Monsieur Chabert held her at arm's length. "It's remarkable how much you have the look of your mother," he said in French. "Such a charming girl she was, filled with verve and vivacity. I was so saddened to hear of her passing."

"Thank you," said Hetty.

"I'm afraid we don't have long this morning, Lady Henrietta," said Mr. Ross with an officious clearing of his throat. "We are wanted back this afternoon for an appointment at St. James's Palace. The Lord Steward is eager to purchase some of Monsieur Chabert's champagne and asked me to personally introduce them."

"And where is your father, the duke?" Monsieur Chabert asked, glancing toward the doorway.

"My father had to travel unexpectedly away from England," said Hetty.

"I'm very sorry to hear that," said Monsieur Chabert. "I've enjoyed our correspondence most heartily. I brought the seeds that he had requested when last he wrote. And a bottle of our finest vintage." He presented it to Hetty as though it were a precious newborn child. "Save it for a very special occasion."

"That's very kind of you. I'm sure he'll be so pleased."

"If the duke isn't here, who will show us the vineyards?" asked Mr. Ross.

"I'll be happy to show you around the estate, gentlemen," said a deep, gruff voice.

Ash. Hetty stared as he strode into the parlor looking sophisticated and handsome in the tailored clothing she'd ordered for him. "Gentlemen, allow me to introduce my husband, Mr. Ashbrook Prince."

"Such a great honor, Mr. Ross," Ash said with a disarming grin. "I'm a great admirer of your books. I've memorized whole chapters from *A World of Wines* to quote at dinner parties. You have such an elegant wit. The section on ancient wine practices was most illuminating."

Mr. Ross nodded. "There's no book quite like mine," he said with no modesty whatsoever.

"Shall we have the tour?" Ash reached for Hetty's hand and tucked it into the crook of his elbow.

As the gentlemen followed them out of the house and down the path toward the vineyards, Hetty leaned into Ash. "Why did you come back?"

"You didn't think I'd allow you to face those pompous blowhards alone, did you? You asked me to be here. I'm here."

"Does this mean you've mitigated the threat?"

"We're close now. Jax can spare me for an afternoon."

"Why are you helping me when you want my wine venture to fail?"

"I never said I wanted it to fail. I only said that racehorses would be more profitable."

"Are you staying at Granville House?"

"Yes."

"Should I send more servants?"

He gave her an incredulous look. "I'd prefer less servants. There's a cook, a housekeeper, and dozens of maids and footmen. I'm a man of simple needs."

"Thank you for coming."

"Let's dazzle them," he whispered. "Gentlemen," he called. "The vineyards."

The party stopped at the rise of the hill that overlooked the vines.

"How many hectares do you have, Mr. Prince?" Monsieur Chabert asked.

"Ten. Though we plan to expand by five hectares soon."

Oh, we did, did we? Hetty couldn't stop the wellspring of hope his words uncovered.

Hetty saw Mr. Renault working nearby and waved him over. "Gentlemen, I'd like to introduce you to our vigneron, Mr. Renault."

"Mr. Renault." Mr. Ross nodded. "We've met before."

"We have, indeed." Mr. Renault's sour expression spoke volumes about what he'd thought about their last encounter.

"Bonjour, Mr. Renault." Monsieur Chabert greeted his countryman in French. "Will you tell me about the composition of the soil?"

"Bien sur. The topsoil is made of calcareous clay

and clay marls." He launched into a technical discussion with Monsieur Chabert, leaving Ash and Hetty to entertain Mr. Ross.

"When do you plan to publish your next edition of *A World of Wines*, Mr. Ross?" Ash asked.

"Next year, if all goes well. I presume you are a wine lover, Mr. Prince?"

"I only drink wine on days ending in y," said Ash.

"Ha-ha. Quite right. 'Give me wine, women, and song,' eh, Mr. Prince?"

"I'm with Byron, Mr. Ross."

Hetty yearned to steer the conversation to the wines from Rosehill, but the two men were trading wine quips, and this could only bode well for her chances of securing Mr. Ross's endorsement. Ash was slathering on the charm and flattery, and Mr. Ross appeared to be basking in it.

"Lady Henrietta," said Monsieur Chabert, rejoining their party. "Your father wrote to tell me that he'd had some success of late with his sparkling wines."

Finally! "He's had a great deal of success. Our wines are far superior to the last time you visited, Mr. Ross."

"The duke informed me that he found the wine to have a finer flavor than the best champagne," Ash said. "You'll be the judge of that. But let me assure you that the first running is as clear as spirits, and both pressings sparkle most pleasingly. I was reading a history of the estate, and it seems that the fourth duke even sold his sparkling wine to merchants for fifty guineas a hogshead as French champagne."

Monsieur Chabert winced. "I should never be

taken in by such a trick. I would certainly know the real champagne when I taste it."

"It's a sacrilegious thought," Mr. Ross agreed. "Only the Champagne region of France has the necessary terroir to produce a sparkling wine of the finest quality."

"Quite right, Mr. Ross," said Monsieur Chabert. "It's the very heart of France. Our hills are drenched in blood from so many wars. We have the soil. And we have the passion for champagne."

They continued their tour in the barn while footmen prepared a sumptuous repast on tables covered in white cloths on the lawn. Hetty had even hired a small orchestra for the occasion, to set the ambiance for their luncheon alfresco.

"These hogsheads are left all the depth of winter in the cool barn, to reap the benefit of the frosts," she told her visitors.

Everything was going well, she thought. Now for the tasting. The most precarious moment.

"Gentlemen," she said. "Luncheon is served."

They walked to the lawns together, and Hetty's heart began to beat faster. The moment of truth was nearly here.

"While it does look most delectable," said Monsieur Chabert with a glance at the sumptuous spread. "I'm afraid we don't want to be late for our interview at the palace. We must account for the possibility of delays upon the road."

"But you must taste the wine," Hetty said.

"I'm afraid duty calls us elsewhere, Lady Henrietta." Mr. Ross made a bow.

"I insist, gentlemen," said Ash with a sharp edge to his voice. "Even if you can't stay for luncheon, you must taste our wine."

"I suppose we could have one glass," conceded Mr. Ross, with the air of someone who was doing them a great honor.

Dobbins poured the wine himself with great dignity, not willing to entrust the task to anyone else. He proffered the crystal glasses to the gentlemen in turn.

"This is the 1828 vintage, gentlemen," said Hetty. "I shan't tell you more than that. I'll allow the wine to speak for itself."

She knew the wine could stand on its own merits.

"Very nice, very nice, indeed," said Mr. Ross after a small sip. "Your father should be very proud, Lady Henrietta."

"A most excellent effort," Monsieur Chabert agreed. "Bravo."

Was that all? They weren't smiling. They had only taken small sips. "Gentlemen, perhaps if you taste the wine with some of these oysters—"

"I'm afraid we must be going," said Mr. Ross, handing his half-empty glass to Dobbins.

"You will take bottles with you, then," said Ash. "And taste them later when you have more time for the experience. You won't be disappointed."

Hetty selected two of her finest and handed one to each of the gentlemen.

"Please give my regards to your venerable father," said Monsieur Chabert.

"And if you like the wine, Mr. Ross?" Hetty prompted. "Will you consider writing a line about it?"

The blank stare with which he regarded her was like a dagger to her heart. "I've already written a section about Rosehill Park in my book, Lady Henrietta."

"Yes, but with the new edition, I thought you might make some updates."

"I will be including more descriptions of established French wine houses."

"Don't you want to promote English wine? You're English!" Hetty said.

Mr. Ross and Monsieur Chabert exchanged amused glances.

"Promote English wine, Lady Henrietta? Why, what an idea. I should be a laughingstock." Mr. Ross chortled. "English wine is but a curiosity to be tasted if there's nothing else available."

"Well said, Mr. Ross," agreed Monsieur Chabert.

"Then why did you come here today?" Hetty asked, her blood beginning to boil.

"To give your father the seeds," said Monsieur Chabert. "Mr. Ross is accompanying me everywhere on my visit to England."

"Now, if you will excuse us, we really must be going," said Mr. Ross.

"I'll show you out," Ash said. He left with the visitors, talking glibly of the delights in store for them when they sampled the wine she'd gifted them with.

Hetty could tell it was all in vain.

"The bastards," Hetty swore when they were out

of sight. "So dismissive and smug. They had no intention of giving our wine a chance."

"I agree, milady," said Dobbins sadly. "They came here with their minds already prejudiced against English wine in general, and Rosehill in particular. But perhaps Mr. Prince might change their minds. All is not lost yet."

Hetty dragged her feet on the way back to the house. She'd been planning for the visit for so long and it had fallen dreadfully flat.

"Why so glum?" Ash asked when she entered the parlor.

"What do you mean? The visit was a disaster. They won't even open those bottles we gave them." She sank into a chair and rested her chin on her fist. "What was I thinking?"

"You were thinking that your wine is good. Really good."

"Not good enough for the pompous, puffed-up, pretentious Mr. Ross. I'll have to find another way to secure the reputation of my wines."

A streak of gray and white flashed across the doorway. "Was that—?" Ash asked.

"Lucy!" Hetty cried, jumping up from her chair. She and Ash ran after the cat who bounded across the lawn and hopped up onto the luncheon table, where she immediately set about tasting the delicacies that had been meant for their visitors.

"You naughty thing," Hetty laughed as she reached the table. "Did you smell the feast all the way upstairs?"

"And how did you escape?" Ash asked.

"She must have slipped out when a maid opened the door."

"I think she wants a saucer of your best sparkling wine to go with luncheon," Ash said.

Bacchus appeared in the door of the barn, sniffing the air and shaking his tail.

"You'd better not give him a taste of this rich fare," Ash said with a chuckle. "It might put him off mice forever."

"I can't allow Lucy to gorge herself and leave Bacchus out. Come here, sweetheart." Bacchus approached her and she lifted him onto the table.

He stared warily at Lucy who was licking the juice from a platter of venison with elegant, lady-like movements of her pink tongue.

"We wanted to introduce them," Hetty said. "I think it's time to allow Lucy the run of Rosehill. She knows where her rooms are now, and where the kippers appear of a morning and evening."

Ash looked worried. "You don't think she'll run away?"

"I don't. Look at her, she's only here for the feast and then she'll probably run right back inside."

Bacchus tore into a plate of cold sliced chicken, growling and shaking the chicken to make certain that it was dead.

Lucy was most disdainful of such behavior. She licked her paw clean as if to say, *where are your manners, you uncouth beast?*

Bacchus left the chicken and approached Lucy. He circled her for a moment. She arched her back, preparing for battle.

The tomcat circled her again, and then sniffed her in a very rude part of her anatomy.

Lucy hissed and batted his nose with her claws, hard enough to draw blood, and Bacchus let out a mighty yowl, leapt from the table, and ran back into the barn.

"That didn't go very well," said Hetty. "Lucy, you must give Bacchus a chance. He's really a very noble provider sort of cat."

Lucy was not impressed by Bacchus, or her new surroundings. She meowed piteously and jumped down from the table, rubbing up against Ash's boot. He lifted her into his arms. "Had enough of the great outdoors and bad-mannered tomcats, Lucy?"

"Ash. Did you hear what you just said?"

Ash's brow wrinkled. "What?"

"You called her Lucy."

"I, ER, DID I?"

"Yes, you did." Hetty's eyes sparkled with laughter. "You can't deny it."

"I should be going back to London," he said gruffly.

"You came back to help me give the tour and now you've called Lucy by her proper name." She approached him and gave Lucy's chin a scratch. Lucy settled back into his arm with a contented expression, giving Hetty better access.

"There's hope for you yet, Ash."

There really wasn't. It was only the effect she had on him. The thoughts he'd had in the church on their marriage day about wanting to be a better man for her sake.

"I do have to go back," he said. "We're closing in on the truth about Coakley. And while I'm there I'll find a way to make Mr. Ross change his mind."

"I'd rather you didn't try. I'll think of another way, I'm very resourceful."

"You told me you wouldn't sit idly by and let a man control your life. Are you losing your nerve, Lady Spitfire?"

"Just don't do anything too brash or foolish."

"Says the lady who runs around Seven Dials armed with a hatpin."

"I know you want to help but I'll find my own way forward. On my own terms."

She was so radiant in the afternoon sun, wearing a gown the color of red wine that lifted her breasts like an offering. He wanted nothing more than to back her into the barn and find a hayloft.

Don't kiss her, Ash. Don't do it.

He had to go back. He couldn't rest yet, couldn't allow himself any indulgences.

"I'll take Lucy back upstairs." Damn, there he went again. "Promise me that you won't leave Rosehill until I come back and it's safe for you to leave."

She nodded yes. "I promise. It's nearly time for the harvest. I'll have my hands full. Don't be too long, though. Lucy and I might miss you."

He'd thought marriage would be a premature grave, but it was his old life that was the shallow grave.

He'd been buried for too long, breathing dirt, not air. Hetty made him feel intensely alive.

He'd thought no woman could change or transform him. He'd been so arrogant in his conviction of cold, hard mastery.

All it had taken was one bold, argumentative bluestocking with dangerous curves to rock the ground beneath his feet and set him permanently off-balance.

Chapter Twenty-Four

❧ 🌹 ❧

INSTEAD OF GOING straight to the gaming house for an update on Coakley, Ash decided on a brief detour through Mayfair. An idea had occurred to him on the ride back to London. A brilliant idea. Not the best idea for the future of his Thoroughbred stables, but one that just might help Hetty achieve her goals.

The butler who answered the door of the Duke of Thorndon's townhouse was dubious about Ash, until he mentioned his connection with the Duke of Granville. Then he became all obsequiousness. "His Grace is in the library. Follow me, please, Mr. Prince."

Amazing how titles opened doors.

They were met at the door of the library by a cloud of cigar smoke, the sound of clinking glasses, and loud male voices. This was Ash's kind of place.

Five large men were all crouching over a table, staring at something and commenting loudly.

"Your Grace," the butler said, raising his voice to be heard over the din. "A Mr. Prince to see you."

A tall man with dark hair waved Ash inside, and the butler left.

"Mr. Prince," said the Duke of Thorndon, "I was

wondering when you might pay me a call, as our lady wives are fast friends and all."

"Er, yes. That's why I'm here, actually."

"Mr. Prince, the one who married the delectable Lady Henrietta?" A fair-haired man resting on an ebony walking stick gave him an assessing look.

Ash bowed. "The same."

"Lucky man."

"Mr. Prince, meet my brother, Lord Rafe," said Thorndon. "Don't mind him. And this is the Duke of Ravenwood, the Duke of Westbury, and Mr. Ford Wright."

He seemed to have interrupted some sort of duke club.

Ravenwood had a dangerous look about him and hooded eyes that seemed to see directly into Ash's soul. Ash had the distinct feeling he should avoid holding his gaze too long.

"Westbury," Ash said. He knew the dissipated Duke of Westbury from the gaming tables.

"Last time I saw you at The Devil's Staircase, your name was Ellis," Westbury said, eying him suspiciously. "You've come up in the world since you last picked my pockets."

"Come now, Your Grace, it was only a friendly game of cards."

"Friendship comes dear, then. And how did you become Mr. Prince, anyway?"

"It's a long story. Had a bit of luck."

"Wish I could find some of that," Westbury mumbled. He was the very picture of a golden-haired Adonis of an English lord . . . if that Adonis was dipped in a vat of whisky, deprived of sleep for a week, and turned upside down to empty his pockets.

Ford Wright was obviously no gentleman. No dove-gray waistcoats or high collars for him. His shirtsleeves were rolled up, and his boots were battered and scuffed.

Ash had a moment of keen boot envy. The polished boots he wore had not improved with time. They still felt stiff and uncomfortable. Where had his old boots gone off to? He hadn't been able to find them before he left.

"We've heard a lot about you from our wives," said Ravenwood. "All of it bad," he added with a scowl.

Not an auspicious beginning.

Ash cleared his throat, ready to make his request and leave this room filled with more dukes than he was prepared to confront, when Thorndon cut him off.

"Never mind Ravenwood," he said. "Come and have a drink with us and see Wright's latest invention."

"It's my father's design. I'm the one producing them, is all," Wright said.

Ash could use a drink. He accepted a glass of whisky and took a place around the table, where they were examining a wooden oval, about five inches long, with lots of metal implements bristling out from its sides.

"What is it?" Ash asked.

"It's an all-in-one tool. See here?" Wright showed him the different tools one by one. "There's a file, a pick, a blade, pliers, a wrench, and a turnscrew. In this new design, we've added a tiny pair of spring-operated scissors. And it all fits in your pocket."

"Very useful. I'd like one of those," Ash said.

"What are you calling this one, Wright?" asked Thorndon.

Wright held up the contraption. "Wright's Amazing All-in-One Multiplier Versa-Tool."

No one clapped.

"The name's rather long," Westbury said.

"Definitely unwieldy," Thorndon agreed.

"That's what Miss Beaton thinks," said Wright, "but my wife, Beatrice, does love her words, and it was she who christened the thing. She was very proud of the 'All-in-One' description."

"I like 'Versa-Tool,'" said Ash. "Very clever."

Wright nodded. "That was Beatrice's idea, to combine the words."

"And 'Multiplier' is promising," Ash said. He thought a moment. "Do you know what this thing needs? A corkscrew, for opening wine."

Wright cocked his head. "That's not a bad idea. Oh, well, back to the drawing board, then."

"And definitely find a shorter name," said Thorndon. The duke clapped Ash on the back so forcefully he sprayed whisky from his lips. "Now, what did you come to see me about, Mr. Prince?"

"I need your help and advice."

"Thought you might," Thorndon said. "I suppose you want to know about the Mayfair Ladies Knitting League, or the Boadicea Club, or whatever they're calling themselves these days."

"Should be called the Spitfire Club," said Westbury. "That's about the sum of it. My sisters' music instructor, Miss Viola Beaton, is a member of that infernal virago club, and she's become quite insubordinate as a result. Might have to sack her."

"Don't be an ass, West," Thorndon said.

"All our wives belong to the club," explained Ravenwood.

"Not mine. Haven't got a wife," Westbury muttered. "Not yet at least. I'll probably have to find an American heiress to leg-shackle myself to."

"And I'm not married, either," said Lord Rafe. "You poor bastards."

"As I was saying." Thorndon glared at his unmarried friends. "You probably want to know the rules of the club, whether they're actually plotting to overthrow the patriarchal order of society, how that fits with your life, et cetera and so forth."

"Well, actually, I'm not here about the ladies' society at all," Ash said.

"You're not?"

"Perhaps, in a way," Ash mused. "If you know about the bluestockings and their goals, you'll be aware that Lady Henrietta is a vintner."

"I've tried her wine on several occasions," Wright said. "It's very good."

"It's better than good," Ash said fiercely. "It's award-winning."

"It is?" Wright looked surprised.

"Not yet. But it will be. That's where you lot come in. I want to hold a blind wine tasting at my gaming establishment at 20 Ryder Street. And I'd like you to host it, Thorndon. That is, if you're willing to help Lady Henrietta."

"I'll do it," Thorndon said in his booming voice. "Give us all the details. You can have three dukes for the price of one."

JAX WAS SLIGHTLY less enthusiastic when Ash broached the subject. "You want three dukes to host a wine tasting at my gaming hell?"

"It's not just any wine, it's Hetty's—she created it herself."

Jax gave him a sidelong glance. "And how long would I have to prepare?"

"Three days. Monsieur Chabert is leaving England soon."

"Out of the question. I can't disrupt the play to host a bunch of fops and nobs lifting crystal goblets to their lips."

"This is important to me."

"What does Lady Spitfire have to say about it?"

"She doesn't know about it yet. It's a secret. I'm not sure she'd approve of my methods, but she'll be happy about the results."

"Is it really wise to call so much attention to ourselves when Coakley might be out there?"

"Actually, I think it's the best thing we could do. If we host a public event, Coakley, or the man pretending to be Coakley, might show his hand earlier."

"Which could be dangerous with a crowd of nobility in my establishment."

"Have you *seen* the Dukes of Thorndon and Ravenwood? No one's going to consider them targets."

"And Lady Henrietta?"

"I was thinking I wouldn't tell her about it until it's all over."

Jax raised his eyebrows. "Are you sure that's a good idea?"

"I don't want her to risk coming to London. Act first and ask forgiveness later. She'll be overjoyed when her wine wins the contest and is heralded throughout London."

"What if she reads your notice in the paper?"

"I made her promise to stay at Rosehill, and she has to stay anyway because it's almost time to harvest the grapes."

"I don't know." Jax shook his head. "I don't like it. It's too risky."

"You're the one who told me to stop living my life in fear. I'm not going to slink around jumping at my own shadow. If Coakley wants his revenge, let him come for me. I'm not afraid."

Jax laid a hand on his shoulder. "All right. I'll do it. Now tell me about the game."

Ash laid out the plan. He'd refined the details with his duke allies. Jax listened intently. When Ash was finished, he nodded thoughtfully. "I like it. But we'll fix it, right? Make sure that her wine wins?"

"We're not going to fix anything. We'll run it straight as an arrow."

"You think her wines are that good?"

"They're bloody fantastic. Remember that case I had sent over after my wedding?"

"What, those French bubbles?"

"That was wine she made. She's damned talented, Jax. All she wants is a few lines about her wine from Mr. Ross in the latest edition of his book. He didn't even give her wine a chance."

Jax burst out laughing.

"What? What's so hilarious?"

"Can you hear yourself? Hetty this, and Hetty that. You've fallen in love with her."

"I haven't. I admire her. I want to help."

"Uh-huh."

"Now, don't go accusing me of going soft just because I want to help her achieve her goals."

"What about your Thoroughbreds?"

"I haven't thought that far ahead." Ash had no idea how any of this was going to end. He only knew that he'd hated seeing Hetty sad about Mr. Ross dismissing her wine, and he was going to do something about it.

Chapter Twenty-Five

$\mathcal{A}$SH HAD BEEN gone several days. Hetty had thrown herself into harvest preparations, and estate management, but all of it seemed so . . . tame.

It used to give her a great sense of satisfaction and accomplishment to tick off the items on her daily to-be-done list. Sometimes, she'd even list something she'd already finished, just to have the satisfaction of crossing it off.

Now, thoughts of Ash, of their time together, crowded everything else, taking her mind and her heart away from the task at hand.

For example, she should be in her study right now, going over the accounts, but instead she was mooning about in her chamber, curled up with Lucy on her bed.

On the day after he left, Lucy had dragged one of his shirts into Hetty's room and laid it atop the bed, making a little Ash-scented nest for herself. The shirt still smelled of him. The custom scent that Della had mixed, and the warm male scent that Hetty remembered too well. She hadn't allowed the maids to remove the shirt, on the pretext that Lucy wanted it for sleeping.

"You miss him, don't you, sweetheart?" Hetty whispered into Lucy's fur.

Lucy's blue eyes were placid, but Hetty knew she missed Ash.

Hetty had a secret. She'd stolen his old scuffed boots. She'd pushed them under her bed, where no one could see them.

Battered, well-worn leather that had been used hard.

He loved those boots. If the boots were still here, then he'd be back for them.

Try as she might to banish maudlin thoughts like that, Hetty couldn't stop thinking of him. The memories stomped around, teased her, strewed their clothes and boots around her mind.

They wouldn't let her go.

"Where do you suppose your father is right now?" she asked Lucy. "He's probably not thinking about us. And therefore, we shan't think of him. We have many other things to think about, don't we, Princess Lucy?"

Lucy purred her agreement. Hetty flopped Lucy onto her back and rubbed her belly. Bacchus would rather die than submit to such an indignity. He only allowed Hetty to scratch behind his ears every once in a while, holding still and tolerating her touch for about thirty seconds before bolting away again through the fields.

Speaking of fields . . . Hetty dragged herself off the bed and pulled her hair back into a knot.

It was time to join Renault in the vineyards for their daily testing of the grapes.

"It won't be long now, milady," Renault said, tasting a grape. "If the weather continues fine, I'd say two or three days."

It was the first week of September, and the weather was sunny and clear. Some years, they picked the grapes as early as the third week of August. Or sometimes they waited until mid-September. It all depended on the color of the grapes and the stems, the taste, and the juiciness.

"I agree. Though I don't want to wait too much longer. Better to pick early, I think."

"Lady Henrietta!" came a faint, hoarse call from the house.

Hetty shaded her eyes. "Is that Dobbins?"

"Yes, milady. And he's running."

"Running? Dobbins never runs. I'd better go and meet him halfway."

"Milady," Dobbins panted as Hetty reached him.

"What is it? Something about father?" Her heart clenched. Please, God. Not another shipwreck.

Dobbins paused, doubling over slightly, his breathing coming in swift gusts. He handed her a page cut from a newspaper. "I noticed this in the London paper."

Hetty lifted the page.

Mr. Ashbrook Prince, heir to the Duke of Granville, challenges Monsieur Jules Chabert and Mr. Clive Ross to a blind tasting of English sparkling white wine and French champagne, to be hosted by Their Graces, the Dukes of

Thorndon, Ravenwood, and Westbury, at 20 Ryder Street, St. James's, this Saturday at eight o'clock in the evening.

There was more, but Hetty's eyesight started to blur. "What on earth has he done?"

"It's a gauntlet, your ladyship," said Dobbins. "He's challenged those conceited, pompous know-nothings on your behalf."

"Dobbins." Hetty was shocked. Dobbins never had an unkind word to say about anyone.

"It only serves them right," Dobbins muttered. "They insulted your wine."

"Is anything the matter?" asked Renault, joining them.

Hetty handed him the paper and jabbed at the announcement. "Read this."

Renault read it. "He's a bold one, that Mr. Prince."

"This could be wonderful for Rosehill wine," Dobbins said. "If we win."

"Or it could be very, very bad," said Hetty. "How could he organize something like this without consulting me first? It's a ridiculous idea."

"He's doing it for you, milady," Renault said.

"Hosting it at The Devil's Staircase? He can't go behind my back and decide the fate of my wine!"

"It's to be hosted by several dukes. Surely that will lend the occasion some respectability," Dobbins pointed out.

"I don't care if it's hosted by three members of the royal family! Chabert and Ross will never lower themselves enough to accept the challenge, so what's the point?"

Dobbins handed her another clipping.

Monsieur Jules Chabert, of the House of Chabert, and Mr. Clive Ross, author of A World of Wines, *gladly accept Mr. Ashbrook Prince's challenge of a blind tasting to be hosted by Their Graces . . .*

She stopped reading. "Oh, good gracious."

"And this one." Dobbins handed her another clipping. "From the society pages."

Everyone who is anyone will be attending the wine tasting challenge tomorrow evening, presided over by not one or two, but three dukes.

"Saturday." Hetty's mind whirled. "But that's today! I must go and put a stop to this madness."

This was folly so big, and so bold, it could only have been conceived of by her husband.

"You promised Mr. Prince that you wouldn't leave Rosehill Park," Dobbins reminded her.

"If he thinks I'm going to sit idly by and allow a bunch of men to step in and manage my affairs without consulting me, he'll have quite a rude awakening."

Lady Spitfire was back.

And she'd load her pistol this time.

HETTY FOUND ASH eating a solitary meal in the dining room at Granville House. He jumped up when she entered the room.

"Hetty! You promised me that you would stay in Surrey."

"That was before you decided to play fast and loose with my affairs, dear husband."

The sight of him brought back all the longing, the immediate rush of desire, and she had to remain firm and disciplined.

His face fell. "You saw the notices in the paper."

"I wouldn't have if Dobbins hadn't flagged them for me. Ash, how could you?"

"I was hoping you wouldn't find out until your wine had won the tasting and I could bring you the triumphant news."

"You thought you'd just take the helm of my life, did you? Husband knows best?"

"Why don't you sit down and let's talk about this. I found an old bottle of red from Rosehill in the cellar. I've no idea what grapes were used to make it, but it's actually quite decent. And then I opened a bottle of the white as well. Sit down and eat with me."

Hetty remained standing. "I don't understand why you had to involve all of those dukes."

"Well, you did promise to introduce me to them, and since that hadn't happened yet, I thought I'd enlist their services on my own. The tasting is a brilliant idea, everyone agrees. No matter who wins, it's brought great notoriety to Rosehill wines. The whole *ton* is abuzz."

"You've made a spectacle of me and my wine."

"I didn't say it was your wine, Hetty. You'll reveal yourself when the time is right."

"Rosehill wine, or my wine, it's one and the same. It's my goal, Ash. The dream I've been working toward for seven long years. You wrested the control away that I've fought so hard to win and maintain."

"Please, sit down and have some wine."

"You have to call it off."

"I'm afraid it's too late for that. Sometimes you have to take a gamble, Hetty."

"We can't make a game out of this."

"All the world loves a wager. I had the Duke of Westbury place a bet on the outcome at White's. It's the very best way to generate notoriety for your wine."

"The wrong kind."

"Trust me, any notoriety is good. If you can place the name of your wine on people's lips across London, you've won half the battle."

"And I've made two very powerful enemies."

"I know men like Chabert and Ross. They will continue on as they always do, in their insular insider world, until an outsider calls their bluff. They must be challenged, and publicly, or they'll never take your wine seriously. At least you have a chance this way."

"You can't just decide to take matters into your own hands, Ash. This marriage is meant to be a business arrangement, and we are meant to be equal partners."

"I'm sorry, Hetty. I should have consulted you, but there wasn't time. Chabert is leaving London tomorrow and I had to act swiftly. I didn't want you to know because it's not safe for you in London."

"I'm tired of you dictating what I can and can't do based on some nebulous threat that you won't even fully explain to me."

"It's a real threat. I want you to return to Rosehill right away. Don't you have a grape harvest to supervise?"

"I'm not leaving until you call off the wine tasting."

"Are you frightened that your wine won't win?"

"I think I have a good chance."

"So do I. That's why I had the idea. Think about it—your wine beating out the French. It would be an international sensation."

"Or an international incident with real diplomatic consequences. I don't think you understand quite how protective the French are of their wine dynasties."

"You're half-French. Surely they won't object to being beaten by one of their own."

"They will if the wine was grown on British soil. This is a potential disaster, whether I win or lose. It's too big of a gamble." She sighed. "I know you were trying to help me, Ash. But you went about it in such an arrogant, bullheaded manner."

"And you like to manage your own affairs."

"Can you understand why I'm angry?"

"Of course. Can I show you something, Hetty?" His voice was sincere, his gaze direct. "Come with me." He held out his hand.

She wavered, still angry at him, but disarmed and nearly overwhelmed by the wave of longing she always felt in his presence.

If he took her to a bedroom, all would be lost.

She placed her hand in his. He took a lit candelabra from a sconce on the wall and led her down the hallway and into the ballroom.

The cavernous room was empty and dark. Their footfalls echoed on the parquet floor as he walked to the balcony. He released her hand, and opened the door.

"Here's where it happened," he said, his gray eyes soft in the candlelight as he drew her onto the balcony.

"Where what happened?"

"Here's where I tasted your wine, and your lips, for the very first time."

She remembered it well.

He set the candelabra on the balcony floor, the flames flickering in the breeze.

"You told me that all you wanted was a seat at the table for English sparkling wine. You were so filled with conviction. And then you said you could do impulsive things. You could be wild. And then you kissed me."

She'd said that. She'd done that. The memory tickled her mind with effervescent sweetness.

His face went still. "I'm asking you to do something impulsive. To take a gamble on your wine. I know I went about it in the wrong way, but I truly believe it will help you achieve your goals."

He was asking her to throw away her rules and regulations and live life on the edge, as he lived it. The angles of his face were strong and unyielding, etched from stone. His eyes glittered with silver.

"What would your mother have advised you to do, Hetty?"

She didn't hesitate. "My mother would have told

me to walk into The Devil's Staircase like a queen, confident in the quality of our wine, and give Mr. Ross hell."

Ash grinned. "And so . . . ?" He tilted her chin up so she couldn't avoid his eyes.

She met his gaze. "And so . . ." She rose onto her toes and lifted her lips to his. "We have a wine tasting to win tonight."

And then she kissed him, as she'd been dying to do from the moment she'd stepped foot in the house.

He was arrogant and domineering, and he thought he knew what was best for her.

He also believed in her wine and her dreams.

He believed in her.

Chapter Twenty-Six

❧ 🌹 ❧

THE DEVIL'S STAIRCASE had been transformed for the evening.

Gone was the gaudy scarlet velvet and gold leaf, replaced with good solid furniture and tasteful oil paintings on the walls. All the gaming tables had been removed, replaced by rows of seats facing a makeshift stage with a long table occupying the center.

On closer inspection, Hetty reflected, the oil paintings were, perhaps, not entirely tasteful, being all nudes.

The noble hosts were arrayed like granite pillars on the stage. Westbury and Ravenwood to the right of the long table, and Thorndon on the left.

The table was laid with a pristine white cloth, and there were crystal wine goblets standing in a row. A clerk from a prominent London solicitor's office was at the ready with quill and ink, waiting to record the scores assigned to the wines by the judges. A clerk who looked exceedingly familiar . . . *Isobel*. Sweet lord. She was here, but in disguise as her brother.

She winked at Hetty.

This was her most daring feat yet. She truly looked the part. She wore a short, dark blond wig and had thickened her eyebrows with the aid of cosmetics. Her collar was high and stiff, her posture masculine, and her boots had a high sheen. She looked every inch the young, eager law clerk, the severe lines of her face lending themselves to the illusion.

But Hetty knew the brave, feminine heart that beat beneath her disguise.

Hetty's heart was thudding and her stomach was tied in knots.

"Your friends are here," Ash said.

Hetty noticed Viola, Beatrice, and Della sitting in the audience with Mina, Duchess of Thorndon, and India, Duchess of Ravenwood. They smiled and waved.

Hetty recognized several newspapermen from the gossip sheets in the front row. She felt their gazes like the heat from a blazing fire on her face. She lifted her chin and sailed past them to the seat Ash led her to. Whispers followed them.

"Chabert and Ross are in the back room, waiting with the judges," Ash explained as they took their seats. "Chabert won't be a judge, since he created one of the wines being tasted, but Ross will be."

For one stomach-dropping moment, Hetty wanted to rush the stage, wave her arms about wildly, and tell everyone to go home.

But then Ash encased her hand in his large, strong fingers. The die was cast. There was no turning back now.

This is for you, Mother.

Monsieur Chabert and the judges filed into the room and took their seats. Before he sat down in the front row, not far from her, Chabert approached and bowed over her hand. "Lady Henrietta, we meet again."

"Monsieur Chabert," Hetty said. "It's my honor."

"May the best wine win," he said in French.

The room was buzzing with conversation, and the bets were flying fast and furious.

"Twenty quid on the Frog," Hetty heard someone shout.

"Fifty on The Devil's Own Scoundrel!"

Pretty barmaids, clothed in nearly demure gold silk gowns, were doing a brisk business in wine, whisky, and gin, poured by the huge red-headed barman in the strangely misshapen green cap she'd noticed on her previous visit.

Mr. Smith circulated around the room, elegantly dressed and suave, chatting with the guests.

"I've posted guards at the doors, and Jax has personally vetted every guest," Ash explained. "We'll be safe here."

The Duke of Ravenwood clapped his hands. "Ladies and gentlemen, we are assembled here to witness a blind tasting of English and French wines, to be judged by several distinguished personages. Allow me to introduce to you His Excellency, the Swedish envoy to London, Baron Olaf Hans Gustaf Algernon Nilsson."

The audience applauded politely.

"He will be joined by Mr. Clive Ross, wine expert and author of *A World of Wines*." More applause. "And Mr. Pierre Lavigne, French champagne maker."

"Ash," Hetty whispered, "how on earth did you arrange all of this so swiftly?"

"Apparently Ravenwood called in some favors in the diplomatic circles."

"We have two representatives from vineyards here this evening," Ravenwood continued. "Monsieur Jules Chabert of the House of Chabert, who produces the top-quality French champagne being tasted, and Lady Henrietta Prince, of Rosehill Park in Surrey, representing her father, the Duke of Granville, whose vineyards were started by the fourth duke and continue to this day."

Hetty began to sweat. Even though she knew her wine had an excellent chance, she couldn't help being nervous about the outcome. She never would have chosen such a public spectacle to introduce her wines to society.

"There will be four wines tasted this evening," Ravenwood continued. "Three of those wines are French champagnes, of varying qualities, and one is the sparkling wine from Rosehill Park. The wines will be concealed in velvet coverings to mask the shape of the bottles and any labels attached. Each judge will rank each wine, and the results will be tallied by the clerk, with the results delivered directly to me while you watch. Now, let the tasting begin!"

The first wine, opened and wrapped in purple velvet, was brought forward by . . . Dobbins?

"You're full of surprises," Hetty whispered to Ash.

"Jax said that he appeared at the gaming house an hour ago and volunteered his services. Said he wouldn't trust the pouring of Rosehill sparkling wine to anyone else."

Dobbins poured the wines solemnly, with the utmost dignity, taking care not to spill even one drop.

The judges swished the wines around, sniffing the bouquet, and murmuring to themselves.

"Your Excellency, gentlemen, this is wine number one," said Ravenwood. "Please assign it a value on a scale from one to ten, one being the lowest. Remember, you will have three other wines to taste. When you have arrived at a score, please indicate so, and the clerk will come and record your vote privately."

"You can't hold your breath the entire time," Ash whispered in her ear. "And your fingernails are marking my palm."

Hetty shook her shoulders and tried to relax.

After each wine was tasted, it was set aside, in the order it had been served. Everyone in the room was witness to the tasting. Everyone saw the wines were placed in their respective receptacles labeled from one to four.

After the four wines had been tasted, and the scores assigned and recorded, Ravenwood rose again. "Your Excellency, will you stand watch as the clerk tallies the scores?"

The Swedish envoy stood over Isobel's shoulder as she recorded the results.

When all was finished, Isobel handed the paper to the envoy.

"Do we have the results, Your Excellency?" Ravenwood asked.

"We do, Your Grace." He handed the paper to
Ravenwood.

The assembled crowd leaned forward, Hetty with
them. The moment of truth had arrived.

Ravenwood read the results silently and then
pointed at a bottle. "This wine was ranked fourth out
of four. Please reveal it for the spectators." Dobbins
removed the velvet wrap and the crowd gasped.

"The fourth bottle is the inexpensive-quality French
champagne," Ravenwood intoned. He pointed at
another bottle. "This wine ranked third."

Dobbins removed the wrap.

Hetty nearly cried aloud. The third place was the
medium-quality French champagne, which only left
her wine, and Chabert's.

She squeezed Ash's fingers. His eyes were shining.
Chabert looked worried.

Mr. Ross's already florid cheeks had gone nearly
purple.

Hetty's wine had placed either second or first.
Which was it?

"Remove the wraps from the remaining two wines
please," Ravenwood said.

Dobbins removed the velvet wraps with a flourish.

"Second place goes to the champagne from the
House of Chabert in France. And first place goes
to the sparkling white wine from Rosehill Park in
Surrey, England!"

Hetty and Ash embraced. She could scarcely believe it. She kissed him on the lips before she remem-

bered that she wasn't supposed to do things like that in public, but no one saw her, everyone was talking at once.

"This is an outrage!" Mr. Ross cried.

"Impossible!" Monsieur Chabert sputtered. "There must be some mistake. We were tricked."

Shouts and clapping erupted from the crowd as wagers were called in. "Bully for British wine!"

The Duke of Thorndon clapped his hands loudly. "Order, please. The tasting has concluded, and the vineyards at Rosehill have been declared the winner. And now, representing those vineyards, I call to the stage Lady Henrietta Prince."

A lump rose in Hetty's throat. "I can't go to the stage," she whispered urgently to Ash. "I haven't prepared any remarks. I don't have a plan."

"You'll think of something," Ash said, with pride stamped on his face.

Hetty rose from her seat and walked toward the stage. Thorndon and Ravenwood helped her up. She looked out over the audience. There were her ladies, giving her encouraging smiles and waves. There was Monsieur Chabert with a sour expression, as if he'd stepped in *merde*. And there was Ash, so incredibly handsome, so strong and stalwart, and yet the light in his eyes was soft, tender, and meant only for her.

She still felt his firm hand clasp, imparting strength and courage.

"Ahem." Her voice wobbled. Her knees shook. "Assembled gentlemen, ladies, honored guests and esteemed visitors." She nodded to His Excellency and to Monsieur Chabert. "I thank you for the great honor of your presence this evening. It was not my intention to cause an international incident between England and France"—scattered titters from the audience—"nor to disparage French champagne in any way. On the contrary, my mother was cousin to you, Monsieur Chabert, and she raised me with a reverence, and a deep respect, for French champagne. It was my mother's dream to revitalize the vineyards at Rosehill Park and restore them to their former glory. And it was her dying wish that I should continue managing the vineyards and producing sparkling wine. My vigneron, Mr. Renault, and I certainly don't purport to have created wine that is in any way superior to the great champagne houses of France. All we ask, all I ask, is that English wine be given a chance to prove its worth. We should no longer be a laughingstock. We have earned a seat at the world's table."

People seemed to be listening and nodding as she spoke. A few "hear hears" sounded throughout the room. Her courage strengthened.

"And, might I add, that while my father lends his blessing, and his lands, to the endeavor, the wine tasted tonight was not only created by English hands, but by female ones."

"Huzzah!" her ladies shouted, as one.

Thankfully, Isobel remembered, just in time, not to join in the cheer. But she did catch Hetty's eye and give her another wink.

ASH'S CHEST SWELLED with pride, and he felt about ten foot tall as he listened to Hetty claim ownership of the wine. Her speech probably hadn't softened their hearts. Wounded pride wasn't easily set aside. But the people who needed to hear her speech had heard it.

"She's a remarkable lady, your wife," said Jax, when Ash found him after Hetty left the stage and was swallowed by a group of her friends, hugging her and cheering.

"Isn't she?" Ash said. She was gorgeous and intelligent. She could accomplish anything.

He leaned back against the bar, watching her. No one could take their eyes off her, least of all him.

"I never thought it would happen to you, my friend," Jax said. "But I knew the moment Lady Spitfire walked through those doors that she'd take nothing less than your heart."

Ash didn't even have the will to contradict his friend this time.

He was going to make Hetty his tonight.

She stared at him from under her lashes, and his entire body rippled with a desire so urgent and powerful it was all he could do to restrain himself from rushing to her and bundling her into the carriage and back to Granville House.

"Still no more threats?" Ash asked.

"Nothing. Maybe we scared him away chasing after him in Seven Dials."

"That wouldn't stop him, if it's truly him."

"So maybe it was all just a sick joke, and when we showed up with pistols, the perpetrator got cold feet."

"I hope you're right. I didn't want Hetty to be here

in London. She's going back to Rosehill first thing tomorrow morning."

"Here's your winnings, Ash." Gus shoved a pile of banknotes across the bar. "Should I send half to the usual place?"

Ash nodded.

"Wish I'd been as confident as you in the lady's wine. I lost twenty quid," Gus grumbled.

"Are you going to introduce me to the dukes?" Jax asked. "I wouldn't mind gaining their patronage for the gaming house."

HETTY WATCHED ASH lead Mr. Smith over to the Duke of Ravenwood. She'd moved closer, to speak with Ash, and overheard the barkeep ask if he should send his winnings to the usual place.

What could that mean?

As soon as she'd said goodbye to her friends, Hetty approached the barkeep. "Gus, is it?"

"Yes, milady. Would you like some wine?"

"I'd like some answers. What did you mean about sending half of Mr. Prince's winnings to the usual place?"

"I can't tell you. He doesn't like anyone to know."

"You can tell me, Gus."

He glanced around. "I'll tell you, but only because I don't want you to think that he's keeping a mistress on the side. Any winnings he makes, he sends half of them to a boarding house for child laborers. The ones that were too weak or too injured to continue on at the bottling factory. He funds their education."

"Thank you for telling me, Gus."

"I take the money there myself, won't trust no one else to do it. Those little fellows, it's very sad. Some of them crippled from the hard work they had to do. I was a laborer at a factory myself until Ash hired me and trained me to be a barman, gave me employment when the entire world had given up on me."

The gentle giant dashed a tear from his eyes. "Don't mind me, milady."

Hetty smiled warmly. "Thank you, Gus."

He touched his fingers to his green cap and hastened away to help other customers.

"There you are, Hetty," said Ash, walking toward her. "It's time to leave. I want to see you safely back at Granville House with a guard posted by the door."

She gave him a teasing look. "I think I'd rather stay here tonight. In the Violet Room."

"I don't know what you're talking about."

"Don't play coy with me, Ash. I read that love note from your former mistress. She described the upstairs rooms in intimate detail. I want to see the devil's decadent lair. The one with mirrors on the ceiling and silk cords hanging from the bedposts."

"Ah. *That* room. You don't need to see it. Let's go back to the townhouse."

"I want to see that room. There are things I'd like to have done to me. And things I'd like to do to you." She whispered a few of them in his ear.

"Lady Henrietta Prince, you're flush with victory, and you've become thoroughly wicked. Here's the problem. You're my wife. And I'm quite certain that no married couple has ever made use of that room."

"Don't you understand what I'm telling you, Ash? You win. I've been corrupted."

"It's not going to happen."

"Care to place a wager on it?" She pulled a deck of cards from her reticule. "If I replicate the card trick you showed me, then you take me upstairs."

She fanned the cards out in a semi-circle on the table, the way he'd showed her. "Select a card, Ash. Any card."

He chose a card and tilted the edge up. The Queen of Hearts.

She performed the maneuver behind her back, the movement thrusting her breasts forward enticingly. She was slightly too slow, but she had the makings of an excellent card manipulator.

He was so busy staring at her bosom that he hardly even noticed when she brought the deck back around and produced his card.

"Here's the card you picked. The Queen of Hearts," she said, her eyes flashing triumphantly. "Now take me upstairs."

They'd be safe here with Jax and Gus guarding the doors, he told himself.

The beauty standing before him had stolen his heart, though he could never admit it to anyone.

He could deny her nothing.

Chapter Twenty-Seven

❧ 🌹 ❧

"THIS IS A wicked room," Hetty said, taking in the details. Everything was just as his mistress had described, the violet silk on the walls, and the purple velvet curtains. The only light came from rose-tinted lamps. A very large bed with a quilted headrest, piled high with velvet cushions, dominated the center of the room.

The paintings hung on these walls made the ones downstairs seem timid and tame. An enormous gilt-framed mirror was mounted on the plaster ceiling, directly over the bed. There were amethyst-colored wine goblets on a table, and a bottle of wine chilling in a bucket of ice.

"I'm not satisfied with merely looking, Ash. This room was designed for one purpose, and one purpose only, and I intend to make full use of it."

She walked bravely into the room, swept along by the lingering pride and elation of the evening's events.

Ash stayed in the doorway.

"Well?" She cocked her hip and gave him her most seductive look. "Are you going to scandalize me?"

He briefly closed his eyes. "Hetty, you know I want nothing more than to scandalize you in every position ever invented, and some I'll invent in the heat of the moment, but not here."

She traced the line of a gold silk tasseled loop hanging from the bedpost. "I wonder what these are for?"

"You know very well what they're for, minx, having read my private correspondence."

Her second attempt at seduction didn't appear to be going very well.

"I know your secret, Ash."

He went still, and the teasing light left his eyes. "What secret is that?" he asked warily.

"That boarding house you're funding is for former child laborers. You're actually good, and noble."

"I'm not, Hetty. Really, I'm not. I have dark and shameful secrets, I'm The Devil's Own Scoundrel, and you shouldn't believe anything to the contrary."

"Why didn't you set the gossips right? Let them know that the children aren't your by-blows but vulnerable young laborers who would have died if you hadn't rescued them."

"It's not my way."

"You don't like to show any weakness. Caring for those children isn't weakness, Ash, it's strength."

"Still trying to reform me in your mind, I see."

"You believed in me tonight, you urged me to follow my dreams, and I believe that you've changed. That you're not the sum of the things you did in your past. That together, you and I make up something wholly new. Something unprecedented for both of us."

"You think you're in safe, gentlemanly hands?" he asked roughly.

"I do."

"You think I'm a jolly good fellow, giving my money to charity in selfless acts."

She faltered. "Well . . . yes. I'm beginning to think that your heart is in the right place."

"Wrong. My heart isn't anyplace at all. It's hollow. Empty. You can dress me as a gentleman and I can fraternize with dukes, but nothing can change who I really am. There's no going back, no transforming my past into something clean and honorable. I'm bad, through and through."

"Because of what you did to Coakley?"

"That and more. I don't want you to think that I'm on your leash. I live for danger. I'm not like you and your friends in your grand houses behind locked iron gates, reading books by the fireplace. Lulled into placidity and stupor by a warm hearth and a pair of soft slippers. It's a prison, Hetty. It's not for me and it never will be."

"You're wild, are you?"

"And free from the ties that bind."

Something almost wild came over *her* then. He was trying to push her away, when all she wanted was to hold him close and strip away the protections he'd built around his heart.

He'd infiltrated her defenses.

She would launch a counterattack.

"You're such a big, bad brute." She kicked off her slippers. "You don't want the safe life with the duke's daughter in her grand house." She undid the clasps of her diamond necklace and bracelets and threw them onto a table. "You're untamed and free." She wrenched hairpins from her coiffure until the heavy coils of her hair fell around her shoulders. She shook her head back and forth, and curls tumbled around her face. "We're not in that house tonight, Ash. This is your world, not mine. And here's what I want."

Her breathing heavy and ragged, she slipped her pink silk gown down one shoulder until the curves of her breasts were exposed. "I want you, Ash."

"Hetty." Her name fell from his lips on a low moan. "What are you doing to me?"

He kicked the door closed and locked it.

A decadent thrill sang through her body.

He shed his coat in a heap on the floor. His cravat was next, his fingers fumbling with the knot. One of his waistcoat buttons popped off as he ripped it open.

She freed the hem of his shirt from his trousers and slid it up his torso, marveling at every inch of hard, muscular flesh revealed.

The naked goddesses in the paintings on the walls looked on approvingly. Oh, the things they'd seen.

He dropped to his knees before her, hugging her tightly. His hands moved to cup her buttocks as he left rows of soft kisses along her belly. He was moving dangerously close to . . .

Hetty's knees buckled, and he lifted her into his arms and carried her to the bed.

He unfastened her gown and removed it, along with her petticoats and chemise.

He tied her wrists to the bedposts with the silken cords. The knots weren't too tight—she could have escaped with some maneuvering—but she had no desire to escape.

Not now. Not ever.

With her arms tied overhead, she was vulnerable to him. She couldn't cover herself, couldn't even move her hair over her breasts.

He smiled wolfishly. "Look at yourself, Hetty. See how beautiful you are."

She looked up into the mirror and a small gasp escaped her lips.

She was a goddess as surely as any of the wanton nymphs undulating across the walls.

Her limbs firm and supple. Her hair tangled and wild.

Eyes bright and cheeks flushed.

She'd been told she was beautiful. Now she *felt* beautiful.

Attractive and wanton. Sprawled for his pleasure with her arms stretched overhead, nipples rosy and pointing to the heavens.

He kissed her lips, savoring her with his tongue and with soft nips of his teeth on her lower lip. The caress of his hands over her breasts made her body fizz and her mind whirl.

With every kiss, the heat and longing built inside her.

Each kiss had a beginning, a nectar-sweet middle, and a lingering aftertaste.

He left her, but only briefly, only long enough to uncork a bottle of sparkling wine and bring it back to the bed. He poured a thin stream of foaming, fizzing wine over her breasts and lapped it up, teasing her nipples to firm peaks.

More wine poured in her navel, over her belly. His tongue in her navel, swirling and pressing.

He licked and lapped, drinking the wine, tasting her, increasing the rhythm of the pulse that beat between her legs.

He set the wine bottle aside and knelt over her, reverently, and parted her thighs. "Keep looking in the mirror. Don't stop watching."

She kept her eyes open, watching overhead in the mirror as he moved down her body and his head moved between her legs. She saw the moment when his head dipped, and his tongue found her innermost heart.

She couldn't move her arms. She twisted and turned, but he held her trapped.

He lifted his head, his lips glistening, eyes dark and swirling with danger. "You're mine, Hetty, mine to do with as I wish."

She had to submit to his tongue and his hands under her buttocks lifting her as if she were a vessel of water and he was thirsty.

"You're not a goddess," he whispered. "You're flesh and blood, and you taste like honey and champagne. I could drink you all night."

Under his expert touch, pleasure was all that existed, all she'd ever wanted.

Pleasure knocked and she answered, opening her heart and her body to the sensation. She didn't have to strain or push for this release. It ran gently beside her, waiting until she was ready, and then it melded with her body in gentle, lapping pulses.

He moved back up her body. "Had enough?" he asked, but there was a wicked, daring gleam in his eyes.

"Not nearly. It's a good view in the mirror, but it could be better."

He peeled his clothing off slowly, teasing her.

When he lowered himself over her again, she had a very nice view of his taut buttocks, rounded and firm, moving over her.

"Show it to me," she ordered. "I can't see it."

He shifted onto one hip and gripped his thick, hard sex with his fist, watching their reflections in the mirror.

"I want to become acquainted with it," she whispered. "And I will, if you untie me."

She was free in a trice.

He lay back on the bed.

She was suddenly unsure of what she should do. She wanted to give him as much pleasure as he'd just given her.

She wanted to touch him. Test the girth in her hand.

"Do it, Hetty," he growled. "Do whatever you're picturing doing."

She slid her hand down his torso and found the shape of him, the width of him. She ringed him with her hand.

"Gods." He stretched his legs out. "Yes. Just like that."

She moved her hand up and down the length of him, mimicking the motion she'd seen him use.

"I would like to know the rules, please," she said.

"The rules . . . ?" He gasped.

"The rules for fondling a phallus, what are they?"

"The rule is: there are no rules. You can do whatever you want, within reason."

"I saw how you touched yourself. You really gripped tightly." She squeezed tighter and moved faster.

"Ungh," he said incoherently, still watching the scene in the mirror.

"I want to do . . . what your mistress described in her note." Hetty moved over him, placing her thighs on either side of his hips. Now she couldn't see their reflections.

All she saw was thick, hard, red-helmed maleness. She flipped her hair over one shoulder and lowered her lips.

She gave him a kiss. She knew what she'd read. It had sounded unbelievable, but now that she'd seen and felt what he'd done to her, she thought she understood.

She took the plunge, opening her mouth as wide as possible and lowering her lips around him.

"Christ above, Hetty," he groaned.

"Am I hurting you?" she asked, lifting her head.

"In a very good way."

She resumed her efforts, trying to fit as much of

him into her mouth as possible. It wasn't easy, and it wasn't very comfortable, but judging from the low moans he made, and the look of ecstatic concentration on his face when she paused for breath, she was doing it right.

Chapter Twenty-Eight

❧ 🌹 ❧

*A*SH HAD THOUGHT about those full lips of hers closing around his cock too often to count, but he'd never actually considered that his fantasies might become a reality.

He watched in the mirror as his wife, his gorgeous, refined wife, did this extremely dirty thing to him, her head of lustrous hair bobbing up and down, her lush lips closing around the head of his cock and moving back up with a lewd sucking sound.

If she didn't stop soon, he'd spill like a randy youth.

He stilled her with his hands on her cheeks. "Hetty, it's so good, but I won't last long."

"Oh." She licked her lips, and he had to fight for control. "Oh, I see."

He lay back, cock swollen and throbbing.

"Ash? I . . ." She bit her lower lip, and his heart gave a pang as though her teeth had pierced him there. "I'm like last year's vintage. I wasn't ready to be tasted yet. And now I'm ready. I want to know what you and I taste like together. I want you inside me."

Those words: a clarion call.

A boxing match judge sounding the count on your opponent, lifting your fist into the air.

A royal flush fanned out on the table. Aces high.

All of the triumphant moments of Ash's life all added up together could never touch the rush of overwhelming gratification her words produced, the nearly dizzying sensation.

I want you inside me.

"Are you certain, Hetty?"

"More than certain."

Instead of reversing their positions and rising above her, he lifted her body higher, keeping her on top. "You'll have more control this way. You can stop if it hurts. Or keep going if it feels good. It's all up to you."

She lowered herself onto him, her knees on either side, his hands holding her thighs, not too tightly, just enough for her to know that he possessed her, he claimed her.

HETTY WAS IN control, and she loved it. Loved sliding down a few inches and watching his head fall back and the moans rise in his throat.

"Woman. You're torturing me. Please."

"Are you begging for my touch, Ash?"

"You win, Hetty. You won a long time ago. I'm not ashamed to beg."

She won all of it. All of him. His body, hard and hot beneath her, ready to enter her completely. She was ready to accept him. To take him.

His body. And his heart. His kind, good heart.

He hid it under so many layers of rough and tough.

But she knew what manner of heart he had. What kind of man he was. The kind of man who knew where to search for a lost child, who'd been a lost child himself.

The kind of man who gave away his profits to charity. And planned to advocate for labor law reform.

A man who'd bet on her wine. On her.

He clung to her thighs with his hands, his knuckles white, the cords in his neck prominent.

"What do you want, Ash?"

"I want you to slide all the way down. Take me inside of you to the hilt, until we're joined. Until we twist and heave together."

"Like this?" She took a deep breath and pushed down, slowly, angling until she found the right way, the way that only stung a little, and stretched her deliciously.

She closed her eyes and braced her hands on his chest.

I want you, she told him silently as she slid all the way down, sheathing him in her body.

I love you, she thought as he rose to meet her, filling her completely.

He was inside her, pushing up, and she began to rock then, matching his movements, surging her hips to meet his. It was still uncomfortable, but there was a growing sensation inside her, a thought that perhaps something good would happen . . .

She rocked forward, then back, experimentally.

He cupped her breasts and teased her nipples until they were swollen and sensitive.

What felt good? That?

No, that was too much. That was . . . *oh*.

His breath rasped in his chest. His voice was ragged. "Hetty. That feels incredible." He took a fistful of her hair and bent her head forward. He kissed her, his tongue reaching up and diving into her as he slid inside her. She was filled, her mouth, her sex.

"I knew it would be like this. Like nothing I've ever felt before," Ash said. "I knew it would be different with you, Hetty."

Her heart was full. About to be uncorked. She must say what was in her heart.

"I . . ." She was going to say it. She must say it.

I love you. I love you, Ash. She bit her lip to keep from blurting it out.

They rode and moved and sweated together, pleasure building in an erotic dream. She threw her head back and stared up into the mirror at the sensual portrait they made. Her breasts swayed with every one of his thrusts.

"Hetty," he groaned. "I'm going to come. Will you . . . ?"

"I think if I . . . change the angle slightly." There. That was the right way. Every time he moved inside her, her sensitive core brushed against the hard heat of him.

She rode faster and he gripped her waist, screwing his eyes closed, the lines of his face rigid.

Her crisis caught her unawares, exploding like fireworks in her mind in flashes of red and pulsing orange. She slumped against his chest, boneless, riding the wave of pleasure.

He moaned, low, and thrust deeper, faster, holding her hips in an iron grip. She rested her head against his chest.

"Hetty," he moaned, his back arching from the bed as he reached his release. He held her against his chest. She heard his heart pounding. He stroked a finger down the small of her back, just as he had while they'd been waltzing the first night she met him.

A hint of greater pleasures to come.

She flopped back onto the cushions feeling as though she'd been taken apart and put back together again into something new.

She'd almost told him how she felt. She'd almost said those perilous words aloud.

The enormity of what she'd almost done rushed at her like an adversary searching for a weakness to exploit.

It was unacceptable. Love wasn't part of the plan. She'd been warned against it, and she'd prepared the rules and regulations to protect herself against it.

She hopped down from the bed, donned her shift and pulled her gown over her head, and began pacing up and down the length of the room.

Why was she flummoxed?

Because of Ash. His silvery eyes, and the long, hard lines of him.

Because she loved him.

Because he'd awakened a side of her that she'd buried deep and tamped down ruthlessly.

A longing for closeness. A desire for love.

"Hetty," he murmured sleepily. "What's wrong? Come back to bed. You'll catch a chill."

She'd caught something much worse than a chill. Love. Foolish, reckless love.

"I've come to a conclusion, Ash. If you stack all of the evidence up, it's clear to see. I don't know how I allowed it to happen."

He raised his head off the pillow. "What are you going on about? What evidence?"

"The kiss on the balcony, invading your rooms, how I couldn't stop thinking about you in that blasted towel, the way you sleep curled up with Lucy."

"What about Lucy?"

"You call her Lucifer and you curse at her, but you secretly love her. You do. Don't deny it. I've seen it. And it makes my heart melt. And that's wholly unacceptable."

"You're right. Hetty, I confess." His head flopped back on the pillows. "I love Lucy, that little furry she-devil. Now, will you come back to bed?"

"I will not." She resumed her pacing. "And it's not just Lucy. It's the way you talked to Davy Clapham about being bullied. And the new laws you want to create. And then you urged me to gamble on my future and we won. And then, to top it all off, I discover that you've been giving your profits to child laborers. Here's the thing, Ash. You haven't upheld your end of the bargain."

"Hetty, I have not one clue what you're on about."

"You were supposed to be dastardly, cold, heartless. You were supposed to only care about your own interests. You were supposed to be a fortune-hunter and a scoundrel."

"I'm . . . sorry?"

"You should be."

"Will you come back to bed so we can have a nice conversation with you in my arms?"

"I will not. It's dangerous in that bed. There's entirely too much naked Ash in that bed. It's too much for my heart."

"Then I shall have to leave this bed, entirely naked, and throw you over my shoulder and place you back under the nice warm covers."

"Against all advice, against my better judgment, contrary to all of my rules and regulations and with a blind disregard for my future happiness, I've allowed it to happen to me."

He sat up, the bedclothes sliding off his shoulders and down his powerfully muscled chest.

Mustn't be distracted. Something very important to say.

He rubbed his eyes. "What's happened?"

"The very worst thing that could happen to an independent-minded lady." Hetty stopped pacing and faced him. "I've fallen in love with a scoundrel. With you, Ash."

Chapter Twenty-Nine

ASH WAS FULLY awake now, the pleasant after-effects of bliss fading to nothingness. "You can't love me."

"I can't seem to stop. Now that I've acknowledged it, the feeling keeps bubbling up inside me."

"I don't know how to love you in return, Hetty. I can't fall in love."

"Because you think you're too damaged." She sat on the edge of the bed. "I know you had a difficult childhood and you never had enough love. I know that left scars on both your body and your mind. I think you're more than your past, Ash."

"I killed a man."

"Tell me why you shot him, Ash."

"You know the old gold-plated pocket watch I wear?"

"I wanted you to replace it, but you refused."

"It's a symbol for me. John Coakley lured me away from the factory with that battered old watch. It looked like untold riches to me. It looked like a stairway to heaven. What it turned out to be was just another prison."

"He was the leader of the gang of pickpockets you joined?"

"We were beaten at the factory, overworked, exhausted, starved. But what Coakley did to us was even worse. He gained our trust. Made us believe he was on our side. And then he turned on us. Became greedy and sadistic. He took a sick joy in stripping us of the day's earnings, forcing us into ever more dangerous situations, never satisfied with our haul. Jax and I finally escaped and fled England, traveling to Spain, where we made our living as gamblers using the tricks Coakley had taught us. We thought we were safe from him. Until he found us. And then I killed him."

"You must have had your reasons," she said crisply, the same words she'd used when he took her to visit the factory.

A curious mixture of laughter and anguish welled in his chest. "He was going to kill Jax. He had a pistol. I had no choice but to try to stop him. I grabbed his arm, twisted his aim away from Jax. Coakley was shouting that he would kill both of us for stealing from him. I overpowered him, turned the pistol toward him. I shot him."

"Then it was self-defense."

"It doesn't matter what it was. I've carried the guilt with me of what I did, the weight and horror of that moment frozen in time. I did what I had to do, to save Jax, to save myself. But I can never be exonerated. There's nothing that can wash me clean."

"If he's alive, then you didn't kill him."

"If he's alive, he'll try to kill me. Or he could try

to harm you, Hetty. You shouldn't be here. I never should have allowed you to stay. We should leave right now."

"Do you know something, Ash? I thought my chance at love was past. I was wrong. And you were wrong. You think you don't need caring, or love, or warmth. But you crave those things, I know you do. I've seen it in your eyes, felt it in your touch. The stories you tell me about your past only confirm it."

For a moment he glimpsed what it might be like to lay down that heavy guilt, that burden, but it had been his companion for too long.

The shame. The helplessness. The horror of what he'd done. Blood seeping into cobblestones. Coakley's blank stare.

"Don't you think I can forgive you for an act of desperation that was done to save your life, and the life of your friend?" she asked.

"That's not all." He would tell her the one thing that would be certain to dim the light in her eyes. "I don't know for certain that I'm the heir to your father's dukedom."

"But the birthmark . . ."

"I hired Mrs. Goddard."

"Hired her?"

"Her son owed our house a large gambling debt. I forgave his debt in exchange for her testimony."

Her face went white as a sheet. "You knowingly deceived me and my father. You preyed on my father in a moment of weakness. He was desperate to marry Madam Bianchi."

"I'm not denying anything. I gave you my motivation when I showed you the factory that he used to own."

Her head dropped into her hands. "I can't believe this is happening. I married you. And it's all a lie."

"I thought it was a victimless crime, that everyone emerged a winner. Your father didn't have to sire an heir, you kept your estate, and I became a duke with all of the power and prestige that goes along with that. It's plausible that I could be the heir, Hetty. I do have that memory of my mother singing to me. The dates align."

"And the signet ring?"

"You were right. I purchased it at a pawnbroker. It's what gave me the initial idea for the game."

"The game," she said bitterly. "Is that what you call ruining my life?"

He bowed his head.

She rose from the side of the bed, walking to the wardrobe and retrieving her cloak. She stuffed her jewelry into a velvet reticule. "I shouldn't have come to London tonight."

He started speaking. Stopped. She didn't want his comfort.

He had nothing to give her. Nothing but more pain. He'd lied to her from the very beginning.

"He's always running a game, princess," said a rough voice. A window slid open and a man vaulted into the room, landing beside the bed and rising to reveal a crooked smile that glinted with gold, and a hand that held a pistol aimed directly at Ash's heart.

Coakley.

Chapter Thirty

❦ 🌹 ❦

COAKLEY WAS HERE in the room with them. The sickening shock of it crashed through Ash's body, convulsing him for a brief, terrifying moment.

Coakley had a pistol trained on him. Ash was still unclothed. At least Hetty was dressed. She must escape unscathed.

He vowed that she would come to no harm, if it was his last act on earth to save her.

"Good evening, Coakley," he said evenly. "Why don't you lower that pistol, let the lady go, and we can talk man to man."

"Not a chance. She'll only run for help."

Keep him talking. Maybe someone heard the thud he made landing on the floor. Jax could burst in at any second. Coakley would turn toward the door, and Ash would leap out of bed and tackle him.

He tensed his muscles, ready for his opportunity.

"You left me bleeding in an alleyway," Coakley spat. "Lucky for me, I was found and brought to a hospital. You and your mongrel friend left me for dead."

"You were attacking Jax. I had no choice but to defend him, and myself."

"That's your story. And mine is that my two best pupils, my protégés, my little friends, decided to rob me and leave me for dead."

"Why did you wait so long to return to England?"

"My recovery was slow. And then there was no point in coming back. I was running more lucrative games in Spain. I only decided to come back when I heard that you were being declared heir to a dukedom. That's when I decided that enough was enough." His laughter grated over Ash's nerves. "You don't get to be a duke, Ash, my boy. Here's what you get: a sad, scandalous ending. You'll be a disgrace. You'll have a thief's grave."

"Afraid not, Coakley. I'll have a big stone crypt at Rosehill Park."

"I've been biding my time, waiting for the perfect moment to strike, and this will do nicely. Thank you for playing into my hand so neatly. I've had time to work out the best way to have my revenge. I've written a letter in Lady Henrietta's hand and already mailed it to the *Times*."

She gasped.

Stay silent, Ash pleaded. *Maybe he'll forget you're there.*

"I'm an excellent forger, princess. Would you like to know what I wrote?" Coakley asked.

"I certainly would," she replied sharply. "If it's purportedly written by me."

"Such a plummy accent she has, eh? And such a beauty. You've done well for yourself, Ash. It's a pity it all has to end like this."

Coakley never wavered or looked at Hetty long enough for Ash to make his move. He was too wary for that. He knew all the tricks.

He was the one who'd taught them to Ash.

"Here's what I wrote, princess," said Coakley. "I said that you shot your husband through the heart after you learned that he wasn't the real heir. That he'd paid off a witness by forgiving a gambling debt."

Ash sucked in his breath. How did he know so much?

"No one will believe that I wrote something like that," Hetty said. "Everyone knows we're very much in love."

"Everyone also knows that your little club of viperous bluestockings all have pistols and are rabid man-haters. It won't be long before everyone believes that you're capable of such a deed."

Ash edged closer to the side of the bed. He wasn't going to listen to much more of this. He'd take a bullet if it meant incapacitating Coakley enough for Hetty to escape.

"As for you, Ash, you've obviously forgotten the very first rule that I taught you." Coakley laughed mirthlessly. "You fell in love with a mark. You always were too weak to be truly hard-hearted."

"You're wrong. I don't love her."

"Oh, so you wouldn't care if I did this?" Coakley swung the pistol toward Hetty.

Ash threw off the covers and was out of bed in an instant.

"Hold right there," Coakley said threateningly. "Or I'll shoot her."

Ash stopped.

He'd lied. He did love Hetty. Blindingly. Completely. If they survived this nightmare, he'd tell her so, every day until he died.

Coakley turned the pistol back to Ash, his gaze deadly. "Here's what's going to happen in this room tonight. First, I'm going to shoot you through the heart. Next, I'll take the lady and leave back out the window and down the ladder I had positioned against the building. I'll take her somewhere for a week, as if she's hiding out, while the world reads about her crime of passion in the scandal sheets. Then I'll deliver her to the constabulary. She's a duke's daughter. I don't think she'll hang. Not for killing a known thief and gambler, who nearly got away with the unforgivable crime of impersonating a nobleman."

Hetty lunged for her reticule and pulled out her pistol. "I don't think so, Coakley."

It happened so swiftly that Ash didn't have time to react. She was so brave.

And so foolish.

Coakley swung his pistol in between Ash and Hetty. "Shall I make it a murder-suicide, milady? You've just provided me with an even better murder weapon."

Hetty cocked her pistol and stared down the barrel. "I know how to use this, Coakley."

Coakley swiveled his firearm toward Hetty, and this time Ash was ready. He lunged forward in a burst of concentrated speed and power. He had to reach Coakley before he shot Hetty.

A shot sounded. Ash grappled with Coakley, flinging him to the ground. He couldn't see Hetty. Was she on the ground? Had she been hit?

The sound of voices. Jax and Gus. Rattling the doorknob. The sound of a boot slamming against the door. The door cracking off its hinges. Ash held on to Coakley with all his strength, pinning his arms and keeping him immobile.

"It's Coakley," Jax shouted.

The three of them made quick work of wrestling Coakley into submission.

Ash staggered to his feet. Hetty lay on the floor, unmoving. He raced to her side, or he tried to run, but he felt woozy, and slow, as if he were running through molasses.

"Hetty!" He dropped to his knees. "Hetty, are you all right?"

She lifted her head. "Ash? What happened?"

"You," Jax said to Coakley with venom in his voice. "I knew it was you. I've had my spies at the docks, and someone saw your ugly face."

"I've been biding my time, waiting for the right opportunity," Coakley said. "You'll have to kill me again. I won't go quietly."

Ash cradled Hetty in his arms. "Everything's going to be all right. Are you injured?"

She ran her hands over her limbs. "I seem to be in one piece."

"That was foolish, but unspeakably brave." He hugged her. "I could have lost you. I'm so sorry, Hetty."

Did he have the right to hold her now? She wasn't

rebuffing him, but then, she'd had a shock. She'd remember all the reasons she hated him soon enough.

Though Coakley was alive. And that meant Ash wasn't a murderer. At least there was that.

"We've got you now, Coakley," Jax said. "Attempted murder of a duke's heir. You're going to hang for this."

"You never should have come back," Ash said, though his mouth was having trouble forming words for some reason.

"I already posted the letter," Coakley said defiantly.

"Then we'll intercept it," said Hetty. "My maid's cousin works at the *Times*."

Coakley finally looked worried, the mad light fading from his eyes. "I don't want to hang," he said, his voice breaking.

"You should have thought of that before you climbed through the window," said Ash.

Jax and Gus forced Coakley to a standing position, and escorted him from the room.

Ash staggered on unsteady legs, his head swimming. He grabbed his trousers but couldn't seem to make his legs fit into the openings. Hetty placed an arm around his waist and he finally managed to struggle into his trousers. His left arm didn't seem to be following orders. He had to concentrate intensely to pull his shirt over his head.

Hetty touched his arm. "Let's go home, Ash."

"Yes." But where was home? Did that mean she still wanted him at Rosehill Park? His vision blurred and his left arm ached.

She lifted her hand from his arm and her fingers dripped with blood.

"Hetty, you're bleeding!"

"No, Ash. It's you."

He looked down. His sleeve was soaked with blood. So that explained the sluggish feeling in his arm. He'd been so focused on Hetty, he hadn't even noticed he'd been shot.

"It's only a scratch," he said. "I'll be all right."

"It's more than a scratch, Ash. My God," she said, her voice rising as he swayed on his feet, nearly toppling her over.

"Hetty, I think . . . I think I'm going to . . ."

The world went dark.

Chapter Thirty-One

❧ 🌹 ❧

HETTY SAT IN a chair at Ash's bedside at Granville House. It was exactly the same as when her mother had been ill with a fever. The same sweat on Ash's brow, the pallor of his face and the moaning and babbling. She remembered the babbling.

Her mother had experienced incoherent fever dreams; visions of elephants stampeding through the room, or blood running down the walls.

She kept hold of his hand, as she'd held her mother's hand. "Don't leave me, Ash," she whispered.

"I thought you said the wound was shallow," she accused the doctor when he returned that evening. He was the same elderly family physician who'd treated her mother. And she'd died.

Hetty wouldn't think of that right now. She wouldn't allow it to happen to Ash. She'd keep him alive by force of will.

"It is shallow, the bullet went through the muscle of his forearm. He's lucky it didn't sink into his side. He has an infection, and that's what's causing the fever. Make him comfortable, keep on with the cold compresses, and wait and pray. That's all we can do."

The day stretched on and became night. She slept in the chair and woke there, cramped and sick with worry.

She'd sent Dobbins to hire extra men to help Renault oversee the harvest. All reports were excellent.

She felt worn out, as though she'd gone through the winepress and all the color had leached out of her when Ash had collapsed, bleeding, on the floor at her feet.

His face was so pale, his lips parched. She tilted his head back and dripped water down his throat from a sponge.

She'd married a good and noble man. One who would meet her halfway, who wasn't afraid to lock horns with her, who would never run away instead of dealing with the painful things in life; a man who was her match in intelligence, in skills, and in ambition. He was often infuriating, but, she supposed, so was she.

"You're going to live," she said firmly. "You're going to live to plague me yet. You're The Devil's Own Scoundrel," she scolded him. "You're strong enough to defeat a silly old fever. How could you let a little infection bring you low? Fight, Ash. Damn it, I need you to fight! You can't die. I love you."

ASH WAS HAVING a good dream. Hetty was there holding his hand. Even after he'd confessed everything to her. She was still there, wiping the sweat from his brow. She said she loved him. And that made no sense.

He'd lied to her. Tricked her.

Her scent stayed with him throughout the night, vanilla and lemon flowers.

But when he woke up, she was gone.

He was so thirsty. He sat up in bed. Where was he? Granville House, by the look of it. His arm ached, and it hurt to take a breath. His ribs must be bruised.

Everything came flooding back. Coakley coming through the window. A bold bluestocking with a pistol.

Where was she? He climbed out of bed and found some of his clothing in the wardrobe. He wanted to go outside, to breathe some real air. He'd been shut in too long.

"Where do you think you're going?" Hetty blazed into the room. "Get back in bed this instant."

"While normally I love it when beautiful women tell me to get back in bed, today I must decline. I'll go back to 20 Ryder Street. I don't belong here. You know the truth now."

"What a load of bollocks."

"Look around you, Hetty. This grand house in Mayfair. You were right about me all along. I deserve the inventive names you called me when you stormed into my hell and gave the devil his due."

"That may be." She tossed her head. "But you're going back to bed. You're not well enough to leave yet."

He allowed her to take his arm and lead him back to bed, only to feel her touch, to be close to her. He lay back on the pillows, and she perched on the bed beside him.

"I thought you'd be harvesting grapes."

"Renault was perfectly capable of overseeing the harvest."

"I kept you from Rosehill."

"I'll be there soon enough to ensure all is well with the fermentation process. I wasn't going to leave you on the ground in a pool of blood, now, was I?"

"I thought you hated me after what I told you. I'm most probably not the—"

"Hush. Those words must never be spoken in this house. It will be our secret. I almost lost you, Ash." She smoothed a lock of hair away from his eyes.

He clasped her hand and brought it to his heart. "Thank you for taking such good care of me, but as soon as I'm fully recovered, I'll leave. You know this can never work."

"Ash Prince. As soon as you're fully recovered, we're going home."

Something akin to hope bloomed in his chest.

"Here's what I realized while you were in the grip of the fever for three days." She left his side and began pacing up and down the room.

He loved it when she paced. He liked watching the way her hips swayed so forcefully.

"I realized that I'd been afraid of loving anyone because I lost my mother so young. I thought that love was too much of a risk, since the person you cared about could die. Could leave you all alone. I was frightened, Ash. I hid myself away at Rosehill and I wasn't truly living my life. I created all of these rules for myself, boundaries I couldn't stray from, to create a safe space where nothing bad could happen to me again."

"I created this tangled mess, Hetty. My life is chaos, and I dragged you down into it."

"I'm not going to dispute that you're a force for chaos. All one need do is view any chamber you occupy to know that."

"We're opposites."

"Don't go spouting that nonsense about different worlds again."

"It's not nonsense. You're a nobleman's daughter, born to privilege and wealth. I fought my way up from the gutter using my fists and my intellect."

This was all wrong. When Coakley had jumped through that window, Ash's life had flashed before his eyes. He wasn't worthy of Hetty. And she was a symbol of oppression. But he'd vowed to tell her that he loved her and he was making a hash of it.

"Hetty, come here."

"Are we going to have another fight? I'm tired of fighting, Ash. Didn't you hear what I told you? I won't lose you like I lost my mother. We're tied together now, by marriage and by affection, at least on my part. And I was hoping that . . ." she bit her lip.

Ash didn't care if he still felt woozy. If she wasn't coming to him, he'd damn well find the strength to cross the room. He rose, only a little unsteadily, and stalked, or attempted to stalk, toward her.

"Ash, you're not supposed to—"

He gathered her into his arms, clasping her against his heart. "Your campaign to make me love Rosehill was a success. But I fell in love with more than the estate. I fell in love with you, Hetty. You and Rosehill are one and the same. You're those grapes, ripening on the vine. You're the soil, rich with life. And you're the Temple of Bacchus, a sensual, hedonistic goddess who intoxicates me. Someone I want to worship, to light candles to, to fall on my knees before. Hetty, you've not only reformed me, but I've also been transformed. I'm something completely new, and it scares me. I don't know how to be this new man. Vulnerable. Aching for you."

"I'm not a goddess on a pedestal. I'm just a woman with a head full of fairy tales who dreams of moonlit kisses."

"Can you live a lie?"

"I can live a truth. And this is it: I love you, Ash. And you're truly noble. Nobility isn't some blood-born right. Your ambition to change the laws governing child labor is more noble than all the dukes in the realm put together."

"Don't get carried away."

"We can rebuild the fortune together and put it to good and noble use. We'll find a way to make both of our dreams come true."

He gazed into her eyes. "You truly don't care that our marriage is based on a lie?"

"I know that my love for you holds risk, but it also holds action. I choose to give you this love, Ash, whether you accept it or not. I give it, gift it, freely, because I know you to be worthy of owning my heart."

He closed his eyes, the joy of it ringing through his mind. He tested his left arm, rotating it one way and then the other. He was strong enough.

He scooped her up and lifted her into his arms.

"Ash, stop. Your arm!"

He ignored her protests and carried her to the bed. "What are you wearing beneath that cloak, Hetty?" he growled.

"Ash. You're still recovering."

"It might help."

"You're impossible."

"I'm a worthy adversary."

"You're worthy. Full stop."

He paused, searching her face. "Can we have a do-over, Hetty? Start anew? I'd like to try to win your heart again. In fact, I'll try to win your heart every single day for the rest of our lives. And I'll never lie to you again, I promise you that."

"Ash," she sighed dreamily. "You stole my heart the first time we waltzed. I didn't want to fall for you. But you definitely knew what you were doing."

"And sometimes it's best to let the expert take the lead."

He kissed her like a man who'd stared death in the face and lived to tell the tale. His kiss was a vow. A prayer for their future.

"I love you, Hetty," he murmured against her lips, the joy and wonder of it flooding his heart.

Chapter Thirty-Two

❧ 🌹 ❧

"*I*T'S GOOD TO be home, Hetty," Ash said the next day in his chamber at Rosehill Park.

Lucy hopped up onto the bed.

Ash cradled her in his arms, burying his face in her fur to hide the fact that he was perilously close to tears.

She squawked in protest.

"Now see here, you adorable ball of fluff. You're not half-bad. Even when you dig your claws into my arm." He kissed the top of her head and released her. She raced a safe distance away and sat atop a chair, regarding him reproachfully.

"I think she likes it better when I call her Lucifer and threaten to release her into Hyde Park," he remarked.

"She's only playing hard to win. She's secretly pleased by the affection."

Ash pulled Hetty down on top of him on his huge bed. She fit against him so well. He cupped her bum, loving the feel of her curves overflowing his hands. "It's good to be home, but what have you done to my rooms?"

"A little tidying up."

"A little?" He flipped her over, pinning both of her arms above her head with one of his hands. "You've reorganized the bookshelves. And where are my old comfortable leather boots? They're nowhere to be found. I was quite envious of Ford Wright's well-worn boots."

"I stole your boots," she confessed.

"Naughty girl." He grabbed her and flipped her across his lap, giving her bum a playful smack. He smoothed his hand over her plump arse. "I ought to give you a spanking." He smacked her again. "What did you do with my comfortable boots, minx?"

She brushed her hair away from his eyes and gave him a mutinous glare, but there was light dancing in her smile. "Wouldn't you like to know."

He lifted his hand.

"Let me go!" she squeaked.

"You're in no position to make demands," he said with mock roughness. "What did you do with them, throw them in the rubbish bin?"

"I . . . I kept them under my bed."

"What?" He released her and she rolled off him, propping herself up on one elbow.

"I know it was silly of me. I told myself that you loved those boots, and you'd come back to Rosehill to search for them."

"When I departed Rosehill I left more than my boots with you, Hetty." He kissed her lips. "I left my heart."

She sighed as his hands roamed to her breasts.

He had a hand beneath her skirts when the knock sounded on the door.

"Damn," he muttered. "Don't answer that."

"Yes?" she chirped, scrambling off the bed and tidying her hair.

"A caller for you, milady, Mr. Prince," Dobbins said, staring at a fixed point on the wall to give them more time to rearrange their clothing. "Mrs. Goddard."

"Why's she here, do you suppose?" Hetty asked.

"We'd better find out." Ash leaned closer to whisper in her ear. "Though we'll start right where we left off when we return."

They walked downstairs and greeted Mrs. Goddard.

"I heard that you were ill, Mr. Prince, and I came to inquire about your health," the widow said, perusing him from head to foot with that assessing look of hers.

"I'm quite recovered."

"I'm glad to hear it. And now, I should like to taste that sparkling wine of yours that everyone is going on about. I hear it's sold out across London."

"Whatever do you mean?" Hetty asked. "I haven't been selling it, only giving it to my friends to serve at parties."

"Haven't you been reading the papers?" Mrs. Goddard asked. "Bottles of your wine are fetching record-setting prices at auction. London has been swept by a patriotic fever for English sparkling wine. They can't get enough of it. You'd better start selling them some or they might come and storm your gates."

"This is wonderful news. Do you hear that, Ash? My wine is fetching record prices."

"I'm glad to be the bearer of good tidings," said Mrs. Goddard.

"You shall have two of my finest bottles," Hetty said warmly.

"Lady Henrietta knows, Mrs. Goddard," Ash said.

"What does she know, Mr. Prince?"

"She knows that you helped me prove my claim in exchange for the forgiveness of your son's gambling debts. She knows that I extorted you into lying."

Mrs. Goddard sniffed. "I, lie? Such an idea. I would never lie."

"But you did lie," Hetty said mildly. "It's all right. But you must never tell another soul about it."

"I didn't lie. I told the truth."

Ash and Hetty stared at one another.

"What are you saying, Mrs. Goddard?" Hetty asked.

"I'm saying, my dear lady, that I truly am Mr. Prince's godmother. I was present at his birth. And the babe really did have that unfortunate purple birthmark."

Ash's mind reeled. "Why didn't you tell me that when I visited you?"

"Why should I have told you? Then you wouldn't have had any incentive to forgive my reckless son's gambling debts."

"I'm truly the heir?" Ash asked, his mind buzzing with the shock of it.

"You are, my boy. And I must say that I'm glad about it. It would have been a very sad thing if the title went extinct."

"You knew my . . . mother?" Dolores Vela had really been his mother. He knew his origins at last.

"Dolores was a good young woman, very cheerful and tidy. She loved your father fiercely. She didn't deserve such a sordid end."

Hetty took Ash's hand. "We'll have to hear more stories about her, Mrs. Goddard. Any memories you have. Will you honor us by coming to visit from time to time?"

"Certainly." Mrs. Goddard frowned. "What on earth are those two cats doing in the gardens? Why, it looks like they're . . . my word! And right in front of the windows."

Hetty ran to the window and opened it. "Bacchus, leave poor Lucy alone, you wicked scoundrel!"

"POOR LUCY," HETTY said, after Mrs. Goddard had taken her leave with a whole case of her finest sparkling wine. "She's been despoiled."

"I'll despoil you, minx," Ash growled. "Now, where were we? Ah, yes. I had my hands just here." He cupped her bum and squeezed, pulling her against his stiff arousal.

"Ash," Hetty squeaked. "Not in the parlor!"

"I'm the legitimate heir to this dukedom. I'll kiss my wife wherever I damn well please."

She lifted her lips to his, and he kissed her with the door open, for anyone to walk by and see.

"Let's go to bed," she said.

At the stair landing, he lifted her into his arms. He opened the door to his chamber with one hand, while she clung to his neck.

He kicked the door closed and pressed her against it, kissing her until she was breathless and giddy with desire.

"Please, Ash."

"Please what?"

"I want you to take me." They'd never stop their little games for dominance, but Hetty didn't mind if she was the one to beg this time.

Garments fell into untidy heaps on the floor. Books were swept off the bed. Jeweled hairpins went flying. Waistcoat buttons hung by threads.

Limbs tangled in the bedclothes as they devoured each other.

"Is this what you want?" Ash entered her with luscious slow strokes, prolonging their pleasure after the sweaty, hasty, chaotic rush to the bed.

"Yes, my love." It thrilled her to watch the play of the muscles in his shoulders, the way he groaned softly as he entered her. She was wet for him, wet with wanting.

Wet like dewdrops on grape leaves, shimmering in the morning sun. Existing to give sustenance. To create beauty.

Later, when they were spent and satisfied, Hetty nestled into his arms and laid her head against his swiftly beating heart.

"How did this happen?" she asked.

"I rescued you from the wall and took you for a spin around a ballroom."

"I think I rescued you from a life devoid of love. And devoid of quiet evenings reading books by the fire. I'm looking forward to many of those, you know."

He kissed her on the nose. "We rescued each other."

"One waltz with a scoundrel and look where I ended up."

"In my arms. Where you belong."

"What are we going to do with all of these orders for wine? We won't be able to bottle it fast enough."

"I've been meaning to tell you about an idea I had," said Ash. "What if we opened a new bottling factory? We'd run it on ethical principles and pay a more-than-fair wage to our employees. No children, which goes without saying. We'd model progressive labor policies for others to emulate."

She raised his hand and kissed his scarred knuckles. "It's a very good idea. But what of your Thoroughbreds?"

"There's only the one at the moment. He may wish to mate, but he doesn't have to have the pressure of siring an impressive bloodline. Not if your wine keeps fetching record prices."

She kissed him. "Then we can plant more vineyards?"

"I didn't say that."

"You'll come around. All I need to do is . . ." She whispered something naughty in his ear.

He nodded. "Yes. That would do it. Plant as many vineyards as you like."

She laughed.

"I can't wait to taste the new vintage, Hetty."

"You might be disappointed with the first tasting from the barrels. It will be quite tart and flat. The fizz doesn't happen until the second fermentation in the bottles."

"It's going to be your best wine yet."

"It was made with our love."

And that love would be tested over time, and it would mature as it aged. It would be fed by the sweetness of trust. And nurtured by laughter and quiet nights spent reading by the fire.

And pleasure. The pleasure when their bodies joined together.

The pleasure she felt right now, cradled in his strong, solid arms.

Effervescent and heady.

She couldn't wait to taste her future with Ash.

Epilogue

❧ 🌹 ❧

A little less than one year later . . .

"READ IT TO me again," Hetty said.

"Again?" Ash laughed. "That will be the third time."

"I'll never tire of hearing it." Especially read to her in his deep, gruff voice, so tender and proud.

They lay on a blanket in the vineyards, bees humming nearby and the earth singing a song to her about roots growing strong, and vines curling toward the sun.

She dug her fingers into the sun-warmed soil, and she felt alive. And there was new life growing inside her.

She hadn't told Ash yet.

"Very well." He cleared his throat. "An excerpt from the Fourth Edition of *A World of Wines* by Clive Ross.

"*Good wines require time to mature. So, too, authors must sometimes take time for their words to ripen into maturity. In a previous edition of this title, I described the efforts of the fourth Duke of Granville on his vineyards at Rosehill Park, his estate in Surrey. I concluded that while his efforts were valiant, the rocky English soil and dismal weather were ill-suited to growing grapes and producing wine of any excellence, and therefore, his toils had been in vain.*

"It has recently come to my attention that a white sparkling wine made from the Miller grape and produced at Rosehill Park by the duke's great-great-granddaughter has shown distinct potential. It shall be noted that the grapes were grown from seeds and cuttings procured from the illustrious champagne House of Chabert, in France. Perhaps it is because of this illustrious connection, or perhaps the soil in the southern region of England truly does show promise for winegrowing. Whatever the case may be, this author can confirm . . ."

Hetty joined in for the last few sentences. She knew them by heart.

". . . that the white sparkling wine from Rosehill is light on the palate, and creaming on the tongue, with flavors of honey, jasmine, and oak. We look forward to the coming year's vintage from this noble English estate."

"I still can't believe he wrote something nice about us. Whatever changed his mind? He was humiliated at the blind tasting."

Ash's smile was secretive. "Your wine changed his mind."

"What did you do?"

"I may have sent him a case."

"And?" Hetty prompted.

"And nothing. Your wines speak for themselves. I was wondering when we can taste this fabled new vintage. It's been almost a year since we bottled it."

And what a wonderful year it had been. Not

without its share of heartache and arguments. They were both stubborn as mules, and adjusting to life together hadn't always been smooth. But their love had grown strong and sturdy as their lives and their bodies intertwined.

They'd purchased the bottling factory where Ash had labored as a child, and they were in the process of transforming it into a safer and more ethical kind of workplace.

Young Davy Clapham was excelling at his lessons at Ash's boarding house, and always took the time to write to them to apprise them of his high marks. Ash had purchased another boarding house, and more children had begun their schooling.

The duke and his new duchess were still taking Hetty and Ash's honeymoon, somewhere on the Continent. They received letters from them occasionally, filled mostly with descriptions of meals. If her father's new bride was to be believed, the duke was drinking less whisky, and was healthier and happier for it.

The sunlight was beginning to fade. Birds were singing songs about gathering sticks for their nests and tucking their babies in tightly.

Hetty clasped Ash's hand. "Let's taste the new wine."

They walked through the vineyards as peach- and lavender-tinged clouds drifted over their heads, and entered the barn where the wine was kept cool.

A furry gray head peeped over one of the wine barrels. Another brown-striped kitten was exploring the basin of the winepress.

Bacchus and Lucy had been busy. It was the second litter of kittens this year. Hetty was beginning to think they'd have to separate the two of them.

Lucy was a very good mother, grooming her babies and holding them by the scruffs of their necks to move them where she wanted them to go.

Bacchus was usually nowhere to be found. Typical scoundrel.

"Beatrice has spoken for this fluffy gray one with the white spots on its belly," Hetty said. "And Della will take the black-and-white-striped one."

She caught one of the kittens as it streaked past her feet. "But I don't think I can bear to part with this little hellion." She nuzzled the kitten's head and handed her to Ash. "Just look at her. She's got Lucy's eyes and Bacchus's tiger-stripes. She's the perfect blend of both of them."

The kitten curled up, purring loudly and kneading Ash's palm with her tiny claws.

"Ash," Hetty said, "what if Bacchus isn't the only proud father at Rosehill?"

"Do you mean . . . ?" He glanced at her belly.

"Yes." She laughed. "That's exactly what I mean."

He set the kitten carefully onto the floor, and she scampered away to join her brother in an exploration of dark corners.

Ash twined his arms around her, and she relaxed into his warm embrace.

"I never thought I could be this happy, Hetty. I thought that love would tear me apart, and it has." He pressed his cheek to hers. "I've been ripped apart and remade as a better man, one who will never stop loving you. Never."

He dropped to his knees and placed his head on her belly. "And I'll love you, little one," he whispered. "You'll have your mother's fine dark eyes, I hope. You'll be loved. And wanted. I give you my promise."

When they tasted the new wine that had been aging for a year, it was still very tart, but there was a fullness in the middle of the palate, a wideness that held the promise of enchantment.

"It will take more time for the softer characteristics to develop. It's a good beginning."

His kiss was both tender and passionate. It spread through her like sunshine, warming her to the core.

"A very good beginning," he agreed, bending to taste her lips again.

Author's Note

I BASED THE VINEYARDS at Rosehill Park on the actual vineyards at Painshill Park estate in Cobham, Surrey. The estate and vineyards were developed by Charles Hamilton, ninth son of the sixth Earl of Abercorn in the 1700's. I had to be satisfied with virtual tours and historical documents, though someday I intend to visit in person to see the newly restored Temple of Bacchus and taste the sparkling wine! I was also privileged to be given a personal tour of the family owned and operated Devotus vineyards in Martinborough, New Zealand, while I was writing this book. Don McConachy and Valerie Worsdale are passionate advocates for the use of traditional, natural and sustainable organic methods in their winemaking—and the resulting Pinot Noirs are nothing short of sublime.